D0579095

Starstruck

BOOKS BY LAUREN CONRAD

L.A. Candy

Sweet Little Lies
AN L.A. CANDY NOVEL

Sugar and Spice
AN L.A. CANDY NOVEL

The Fame Game

LAUREN CONRAD
Style

LAUREN CONRAD
Beauty

LAUREN CONRAD

Starstruck

HARPER

An Imprint of HarperCollinsPublishers

Starstruck

Copyright © 2012 by Lauren Conrad

All rights reserved. Printed in the United States of America.

No part of this book may be used or reproduced in any manner whatsoever without written permission except in the case of brief quotations embodied in critical articles and reviews. For information address HarperCollins Children's Books, a division of HarperCollins Publishers, 10 East 53rd Street, New York, NY 10022.

www.epicreads.com

Library of Congress catalog card number: 2012945602
ISBN 978-0-06-207980-0 (trade bdg.)
ISBN 978-0-06-221885-8 (int. ed.)

Typography by Andrea Vandergrift
12 13 14 15 16   CG/RRDH   10 9 8 7 6 5 4 3 2 1
❖
First Edition

*To Farrin Jacobs, for working unbelievably hard
and making the writing process so fun.
Thank you for not just being an amazing editor
but a wonderful friend.*

Dear Madison,

You probably don't remember it, but a few months ago I wrote you a letter. I told you that I was your biggest fan. And I really was! My screen saver was a picture of you from the <u>Fame Game</u> premiere. My ringtone was the theme from <u>Madison's Makeovers</u>. I loved you.

Well, I'm writing now to tell you that I don't love you anymore. At all. Everything I said in that letter—about how you were true to yourself, how you worked so hard for what you got—I take it all back. Because everything that you said was a lie.

You had it all, Madison. Money, looks, fame. But I guess that wasn't enough. Stealing is wrong. Didn't your parents teach you anything?

Sincerely disappointed,
Becca B.

PS: I unfollowed you on Twitter.

1

COURTROOM COUTURE

Madison Parker stood in the echoing marble foyer of the Beverly Hills Courthouse, her back pressed against the wall and her purse clutched tightly in her freshly manicured fingers. People in ill-fitting suits and outdated shoes hurried past without a second glance at Madison's uncharacteristically pale face. (Seriously, was there a law against natural fabrics and current-season pumps around here?)

Madison's own outfit was carefully thought out. She'd taken a page from Lindsay's book (after all, who had more experience when it came to courtroom couture?) and opted for white, although Madison wore a bra with her ensemble. Her dress hit right below the knee, and she accessorized with a modest heel and pearls. She had a quilted Chanel that would have looked perfect, but instead she'd chosen a simple black bag. "No labels," her lawyer had instructed her. She'd been charged with theft, and flaunting an expensive wardrobe wasn't going to help her case.

She sighed. For the last ten minutes she'd been waiting

for Andy Marcus, Esq., to emerge from wherever he'd disappeared to in the moments after her hearing. He was probably off congratulating himself, as if it had been his performance that had convinced the judge not to give Madison jail time for grand theft. Madison knew the truth, of course: When she took the stand, with her big blue eyes full of tears and her voice full of remorse, she saw the judge soften. In seconds, she had him wrapped around her finger. (She often had that effect on men.)

She'd practiced what she was going to say for days. She'd even hired an acting coach—the same one she'd used to help her prepare for her guest-starring role on an episode of *Family Guy*. She had to be prepared, because every word was a lie.

I got caught up in the moment, Your Honor. All the excitement and the glamour and the celebrity went to my head. I'm a small-town girl, sir. I never could have imagined all this would happen to me. I just—I don't know—when the Fame Game *premiere was happening, I wasn't myself. There was so much pressure and insanity. It was wonderful, but it was also really confusing. I was exhausted and I wasn't taking care of myself. Like I said, I just sort of forgot who I was. I saw this beautiful diamond necklace, and I felt like I needed it in order to be as special as everyone thought I was. Even though I know that I didn't. I'm so sorry, Your Honor. I take full responsibility for my actions, and I deeply apologize to you and to my fans and to the wonderful people at Luxe. . . .*

This line of defense was inspired by the recent antics

of action star Austin Beck, who, after being caught climbing a flagpole in a pair of women's underwear, claimed "reactive psychosis" from stress and dehydration. (Surely his weakness for psychedelic drugs had nothing to do with his stunt.)

But defending herself in a court of law hadn't been easy for Madison. While she was experienced in exaggerations and manipulations, she was not actually a good liar. On top of that, she was unaccustomed to taking blame for anything, even if she deserved it. She'd spent the last five years of her life looking out for number one, and number one had always been Miss Madison Parker. The words "I was wrong" tasted like poison in her mouth.

But when her estranged father, Charlie Wardell, showed up in L.A., rumpled and sweet and ashamed of the way he'd abandoned her, Madison discovered a selfless side that no one thought existed. She rented him a house. She welcomed him into her life. She forgave him for leaving all those years ago. And when he vanished into thin air the morning after the *Fame Game* premiere, along with the diamond necklace she'd borrowed from Luxe Paris, she took the fall.

Of course she'd thought about telling the truth and letting him suffer the consequences. But he'd already done time for theft. She couldn't bear the thought of him being locked up again, making license plates for twenty-seven cents an hour or whatever it was they did in there. Not when he'd finally come to find her—to be a part of her life.

No matter what anyone else said, Madison knew that Charlie hadn't reappeared with the intention of taking advantage of her. She'd offered him money dozens of times, and he had always refused it. "I don't want to take anything from you," he'd say. "All I want is to spend time with my daughter."

She'd been right to believe him—at first. But then something changed. Who knew exactly what had happened? Only Charlie did, and he wasn't around to explain. Maybe one of his bad debts had come due, or maybe he experienced his own moments of reactive psychosis. All Madison knew was that her father had stolen the necklace and split town. *Just tell them you lost the necklace. They're insured. Nobody loses. I love you always—Charlie,* his note had said.

Nobody loses? If only it was that simple! But it wasn't, because Charlie had been caught on videotape pocketing a pair of Luxe diamond earrings to match the loaner necklace.

(Questions of morality aside, how could he be so bad at stealing? Really, it boggled the mind.)

In the hours after she discovered that he was gone, a deep familial loyalty rose up in Madison. And today, she had pled guilty to cover for him. And for that act of generosity, she got a long lecture from the judge about honesty and personal responsibility, along with three hundred hours of community service. She had to pay back Luxe, too, although they'd given her a little break on what she owed because of the free press they were getting. So generous of them! (They had agreed to "lose" the security tape of Charlie and the earrings, so Madison knew she should be grateful, but she just couldn't muster up the feeling.)

"Oh! There you are," said her lawyer, appearing at her side and looking pleased with himself. "I lost you for a minute."

Madison took a small step away from him. Andy Marcus wore too much hair product and even more cologne. "You're the one who disappeared," she pointed out. "I've been standing here in the middle of . . . well, where I can only assume people are sent for crimes against fashion. I'm surprised everyone isn't walking around here with black bars across their faces."

Andy laughed. "Down but not out!" he said. "There's the Madison Parker the world knows and loves."

"Whatever," she said, noting his own poor choice in suiting. "We should probably walk out together, right?"

Madison knew what was on the other side of the courthouse doors: a sea of photographers, TV cameras, spectators. A crowd of people waiting to see her. A few of them were her fans, of course. Most of them were not, though, and they waited impatiently, holding signs painted with mocking slogans, itching to unleash what she knew she had coming. While Madison was thrilled to have avoided jail time, there were plenty of people who felt differently. They wanted her to pay for what she'd done.

She thought of Lacey Hopkins, the young actress

who'd been in Madison's shoes more than a few times herself, thanks to a fondness for prescription drugs and petty shoplifting. Would Madison's career suffer the way Lacey's did? She told herself that it wouldn't. It couldn't. She'd do her community service and be a model citizen from now on.

Andy Marcus's phone rang. "It's your publicist," the lawyer said, glancing at the screen. "She's calling because you need to make a statement. Or I can do it, if you want me to. I like to think that talking to the press is one of my personal strengths."

Madison snatched the phone from his hand and answered it. "Why are you calling the lawyer instead of your own client?" she demanded.

Sasha didn't miss a beat. "Oh, hello, Madison," she said smoothly. "I wasn't sure how you'd be feeling, so I thought it would be best to call Andy."

"I'm great, thank you," Madison said. "Best day of my life."

"I've been so worried about you."

"I'm sure you have," Madison replied. She liked her publicist fine, but she understood that Sasha was actually more worried about herself. It was always a hassle for publicists when their clients got in trouble; they had to field calls from every gossip blogger and magazine out there. It was a headache. And whoever said that all press is good press hadn't posed for a poorly lit mug shot recently.

"Well, I have great news," Sasha said.

"Really?" Madison felt her heart lift a little.

"Yes. I just got off the phone with Veronica Bliss, and she has agreed to run a huge spread on you. An exclusive. A sit-down with Madison Parker, with a photo shoot and everything. Isn't that incredible?"

"So Veronica wants me to tell her *Gossip* readers all about my troubles," Madison said, her voice flat. This wasn't the kind of good news she'd been hoping for. Out of the corner of her eye, she saw Andy give her the thumbs-up. God, he was such an idiot.

"Yes. It's your chance to tell your side of the story, Madison. Your chance to regain some of the sympathy you've . . . well, temporarily lost."

Madison smiled grimly. At any other time in her life, she would have cut off a limb to get a two-page spread in *Gossip*. But today? Today was a different story. Today she couldn't tell anyone what really happened: not Trevor Lord, her boss; not Kate Hayes, who seemed like she'd be a sympathetic ear; and certainly not the entire circulation base of *Gossip* magazine. Besides her sister no one knew the truth, and Sophie wasn't going to let that one slip. She was more than enjoying Madison's fall. Funny how things worked out. "No thanks," she said. "I don't want to talk about it. Besides, given my history with Veronica, I hardly think it would be a positive story."

"Are you sure?" Andy mouthed.

Madison waved his question away. "Let's just make a statement," she told Sasha. "Something about how I

9

support the judge's decision and I'm looking forward to starting my community service immediately and putting this all behind me, blah blah blah. You can make it sound good, right?"

"That's what you pay me for," Sasha said.

"Well, then you've earned it today. Here, Andy can give you the details." Madison shoved the phone back into her lawyer's hand. He looked at it in surprise for a second, as if he'd never seen it before. Then he held it to his ear. "Sasha," he said.

Madison watched him for another moment and then turned to go. She didn't need to wait for him. She had a life and an image to rebuild . . . again.

She strode toward the exit, still holding her bag in its death grip, and paused for a moment before the huge oak door. A large, red-faced security guard appeared beside her.

"I'm going to escort you to your car, Miss Parker," he said. "There are . . . a few photographers outside." He was six foot three and well over two hundred pounds, but he looked a little uneasy as he eyed the door. This didn't help to calm Madison's nerves.

Own it, she told herself. *Own it. The perp walk is the new catwalk, after all.*

She gave the door a defiant shove, and the bright September sunlight that came pouring in nearly blinded her. Or was it the burst of what felt like a thousand flashbulbs? Madison couldn't be sure. All she knew was that she'd never been more thankful for her superdark sunglasses.

She walked down the steps, keeping close behind the security guard as he created a small path ahead of her. People were screaming her name. A woman in a jade-green suit pushed through the crowd toward her. "Madison Parker," she said, holding out a microphone. "How do you feel about the outcome of today's hearing?"

Another reporter appeared to her right. "Miss Parker, has Lacey Hopkins offered you any words of wisdom on dressing for court appearances?"

"Hey, Mad," someone yelled, "what's it like to be a convict?" (It was the TMZ guy. She didn't even have to look to know.)

The shouts from the crowd grew more deafening. Meanwhile the camera shutters kept clicking and the flash-bulbs popped like fireworks around her. It was exactly the sort of chaos that she usually loved. Usually craved. (Once a reporter had asked her where her favorite place to be was. "That's easy," she'd purred. "Right in the center of all the attention.")

But now, in this moment, she wanted to be anywhere but here.

"Hey, Parker, nice shoes. Did you steal those, too?"

"Madison, are you going to rehab like your sister?"

"Madison, Madison, stealing is a sin—"

Madison tossed her blond hair and held her head high. She took slow, defiant steps to the waiting car. She imagined that the shouts were coming from her fans, the ones who used to scream and beg for photos and autographs as she walked down the red carpet.

The PopTV camera crew had staked out a place right near her car. On Trevor's orders, Bret, the camera guy, moved toward her. She could practically feel the camera focusing in on her face, searching for any hint of emotion.

Of course PopTV wanted to broadcast her humiliation, the same as everyone else did. But at least their version would be sympathetic. If Madison had to exit a courthouse on TV, she might as well have the shot color-corrected in postproduction, slowed down for dramatic effect, and set to the tune of Kelly Clarkson's most recent hit.

She reached up and took off her sunglasses. Let them see exactly how strong she was.

A girl—a freckled, redheaded teenager—came running toward her. "I still love you," she called. "I still do!" And before Madison's driver stepped in front of the girl and cut her off, she tossed a single red tulip at Madison's feet.

Madison gazed at it for a moment, lying there on the pavement, and then looked up. *Down but not out.* And then the unblinking eye of the PopTV camera caught a tiny but resolute smile flickering around the edges of her perfect red lips.

2

MOVING ON

Kate stretched out her legs on the chaise longue by the Park Towers pool and wriggled her toes, admiring the blue polish she'd picked out at Brentwood Nail Garden.

"I always thought blue would make a person look like they had poor circulation," Natalie said. "Or frostbite. But you actually pull it off."

Kate grinned at her former roommate. "Wow, thanks. You really know how to pay a girl a compliment."

Natalie shrugged and popped a grape into her mouth. "What can I say," she said, chewing. "I was raised by wolves."

"At least they were wolves with a sense of fashion," Kate said, noting Natalie's colorful ensemble, which consisted of a leopard-spotted crop sweater paired with a royal-blue chiffon dress, a wristful of gold bangles, and a pair of navy Oxford-style flats. (Kate had, with some effort, convinced Natalie to ditch her opaque black tights; the girl needed a little vitamin D.)

"I found this sweater at a church rummage sale," Natalie said. "Awesome, right?"

"It looks designer," Kate agreed.

"It's very Marc Jacobs," Natalie said. (As a student at the Fashion Institute of Design & Merchandising, she knew the names of every designer.) "But it cost five bucks." Then she poked Kate with an unmanicured toe. "Speaking of designer, are you getting free clothes now that you're a superstar?"

Kate laughed. "I wouldn't say superstar. But I have been getting some things sent to me." She thought about the box that ShopAddict, an L.A.-based PR firm that repped some of the hottest designers, had messengered to her apartment and which she hadn't even had time to open yet. It sat next to a Rebecca Minkoff handbag, several dresses from Alice + Olivia, and a pile of shoe boxes from Kate Spade. And they were all for her. To keep. Simply because they hoped she'd be photographed or filmed wearing them.

"Good-bye, Coffee Bean and Tea Leaf apron; hello, fashion plate!" Natalie said. "I'm so incredibly jealous that I don't even know if I can be friends with you anymore."

"Oh, please," Kate said. "For one thing, you have a huge wardrobe of amazing clothes. And for another, I haven't worked at Coffee Bean in ages." She took a sip of Evian and reapplied a bit of sunblock to her nose. All this L.A. sunshine was threatening to bring out her freckles. "You'll probably always be better dressed than me. I have the fashion sense of a teenage boy."

"Just promise to give me whatever you don't like," Natalie said. "I'm begging you."

"Sure," Kate agreed. "Come to think of it, I did get this jumpsuit that might be right up your alley. . . ."

Natalie clapped her hands in excitement. "Only the truly fashion-forward are bold enough to rock the jump-suit. Gimme, gimme, gimme."

"It's all yours," Kate said.

"Brilliant. So tell me everything else," Natalie said. "I saw you on D-lish.com yesterday. There was a picture of you walking down Rodeo Drive."

Kate's stomach still did tiny somersaults when she heard things like this. *Really?* she couldn't help thinking. *A paparazzo followed me? (And did he get a decent photo?)* "Oh, that's funny," she said, as if she weren't dying to Google the picture immediately. She had spent three hours in front of the mirror the other day, practicing smiles and poses after seeing a few extremely unflattering photos of herself on Popsugar.com.

Natalie nodded. "Yep. You were drinking a Starbucks and wearing those cute new brown platforms. Can I just say, it is so weird to have a famous friend!"

Kate laughed. It was weird, weird, weird to be so sud-denly well known. It seemed like only yesterday she'd been a Midwestern nobody, working two jobs and living in a run-down Los Feliz two-bedroom, fantasizing about making it in the music industry. And now here she was after three episodes of *The Fame Game* had aired, lounging beside a beautiful pool, freshly manicured, pedicured, and waxed, and looking at her picture splashed across the pages of *Life & Style*.

The Fame Game's producers had warned her that her life was going to change overnight, but it had never seemed real. Even though PopTV cameras had followed her around for weeks and she'd done a photo shoot and talked to reporters . . . the fact that she was actually going to be on TV and millions of people would watch her seemed unbelievable. And in a way, it still didn't seem real. The attention was all around her, but it hadn't completely sunk in that this was her life now. She didn't even feel that different. Not yet, anyway.

And there were even better perks of fame than good pedis and free clothes. Her single, which Trevor had chosen to be the theme song for *The Fame Game*, had been in the top ten on iTunes for two whole weeks. She'd gotten calls from three different record labels, all of them expressing interest in her music. (They also wanted to know if she had any shows coming up. Ugh.) Trevor said she wasn't ready for all that, though; in the world of *The Fame Game*, her getting a recording contract was more of a second-season story line. Meanwhile, Courtney Love—whose barely comprehensible tweet about Kate's YouTube video had first brought Kate into the spotlight—seemed to be watching over her like some crazy fairy godmother (*O gawd, gurl iss makin it! hitthe top sister, and sned me a postcard!!!!* she'd recently tweeted). If Kate ever met the former lead singer of Hole, she was going to give her a big, fat kiss.

Kate reached down to brush a dragonfly away from her ankle. Yes, she was really, really lucky. There was no doubt about it.

But it wasn't as if life was all sunshine and roses. For one, she had—against her castmates' advice—read some of the comments about her on the internet. People were brutal. *Who is this random chick who thinks she can sing?* asked NeNe67. Bru43ski wrote, *Why would they cast this girl? She is sooooo boring.* Kate, horrified, had stopped right there. Lesson learned. Quickly.

Then there was Luke Kelly, the drop-dead gorgeous Australian actor she'd fallen for at the beginning of the summer. Even though Kate knew she'd been right to break up with him—if a guy wouldn't own up to dating you, you had to give him the boot, right?—the decision still hurt. She'd thought they had something. Something real.

For a while, Luke had seemed to feel that way, too. But then his attention turned to something fake: his manufactured-for-the-cameras relationship with Carmen Curtis. As costars of *The End of Love,* Luke and Carmen were the new Hollywood It couple. Kate saw pictures of them everywhere she turned. She couldn't even buy her overpriced salad at Whole Foods without them smiling at her from the cover of a magazine.

Then, to add insult to injury, she'd learned that Luke and Carmen had hooked up—for real—in the spring. Nothing had come of it, and it was before she'd met either of them, but still. If it didn't mean anything, why had they both kept it a secret from her?

Kate thought she'd found a true friend in Carmen, but now she felt like an idiot. Carmen had been texting her—at first acting like there was nothing wrong, and then wanting to talk—but Kate wasn't interested in anything she had to say off-camera.

"Life is different, all right," Kate said, rolling over onto her stomach and letting the sun warm her back. "It's mostly great, though." She felt like she was reminding herself of it as much as she was telling Natalie.

"Oh, hey, you guys," chirped a voice. "What's up?"

Kate turned back over and saw her costar Gaby Garcia approaching them, wearing a pair of six-inch strappy sandals and clutching one of her trademark spirulina smoothies.

"What is that?" Natalie asked. "It looks like you put Oscar the Grouch into a blender."

Kate laughed, but Gaby only looked confused. "Gaby," Kate said, "you remember Natalie. She was my roommate before I moved here. Natalie, you remember Gaby, my fellow *Fame Gamer*."

"Hi," Gaby said. She sat down on a chaise longue and sighed. Her brow twitched almost imperceptibly, which was—thanks to all the Botox injected into her forehead—her best version of a frown.

"What's the matter?" Kate asked. "You look upset . . . I think."

Gaby took a sip of her smoothie and sighed again. "It's Madison," she said. "I'm worried about her." She slipped off her high heels and contemplatively rubbed at her toes. "I mean—wow. Like, I'm really worried? I just . . . like . . ."

Kate waited for Gaby to finish her sentence, but then realized that nothing more was forthcoming. "It's pretty crazy," Kate said.

Gaby turned her brown eyes to Kate. She bit her over-plumped lip. "I tried to talk to her about what happened with the necklace, but she totally shut me down. And I tried to ask her about my diamond earrings, too. I mean, those were totally on my dresser until her dad came over. And then he leaves, and suddenly they're gone. I was all, *Like that's really a coincidence!* But then after the whole necklace thing, I'm thinking maybe Madison took them. I mean, it was obviously one of them, right? And of course she didn't want to talk about that, either."

Gaby stopped and took a deep breath. It was a long monologue for her.

Kate nodded. "Yeah, well, I'm sure it's a hard thing to talk about."

She had tried to talk to Madison, too. In the first days after the *Fame Game* premiere, when it seemed like their whole world was exploding in flashbulbs, Madison had been practically invisible. She'd been a no-show at the morning-after brunch, and she'd spent ten minutes at the informal cocktail party for cast and crew before making a French exit out the back. And no one had seen her since.

Kate had figured she was just taking a break from things, lying low in Charlie's bungalow, and ringing up quite the LAbite.com bill. But then things had gotten weird: Suddenly Madison was nowhere and everywhere at the same time. Her photo was on every celebrity website and on the cover of every gossip magazine. And they all accused her of the same thing: theft.

It was so unlike Madison to avoid attention—they'd all thought something was up. Sophia had said Madison was upset because their dad had to leave town unexpectedly. Kate could tell how much Madison adored Charlie, so that explanation made sense. But Kate, for one, certainly hadn't expected the headlines: STARLET STEALS STONES; MADISON MAKES OFF WITH MILLIONS. Kate's reaction had been shock, quickly followed by confusion. Really? Madison had stolen and sold her loaner necklace? *Really?* One could argue that Madison was a lot of things: cruel, sly, manipulative, and selfish. But an honest-to-goodness thief? It didn't sound right. The girl had a collection of Birkins that rivaled Victoria Beckham's. Why would she steal a diamond necklace when she had a wardrobe worth double that in value?

Gaby set her drink down on the concrete. "Between Madison and her father . . . well, you know what they say: The apple doesn't fall far from the pie."

"I think the saying is 'the apple doesn't fall far from the tree,'" Natalie suggested.

"Whatever," Gaby said. "Same thing."

"I find it all really hard to believe," Kate said. "I don't

get why she'd steal a necklace and then sell it. Did she actually think she wouldn't get caught?"

"Who knows with that girl," Natalie said. "She lied, slept, and cheated her way to the top in the first place. Is this really so out of character for her?"

Kate looked up at the big windows of Madison's and Gaby's apartment. She could see the passing clouds reflected on their shiny surface. Madison hadn't been living there for a while now, but she still thought of it as Madison's and Gaby's place. Maybe she hadn't known Madison as well as she thought she had. It wasn't like they were good friends or anything, but she'd started to like her. She'd thought everything was cool with them. So the more Madison avoided her, the more Kate began to think she really was guilty. Maybe it didn't make sense that Madison would have stolen the necklace, but it made even less sense that she would say she'd stolen it when she hadn't.

Kate leaned back and rearranged the Egyptian-cotton towel she was using for a pillow. She didn't want to think about Madison anymore. Obviously the girl didn't want to talk, and maybe she never would. "Mad'll be fine," Kate said. "It will do her some good to see things from the bottom for a change."

Gaby shot her a look of surprise. "Ouch," she said.

Kate shrugged. She knew that didn't sound like something that the nice girl from Columbus, Ohio—the one who couldn't bear to pack her old teddy bear in a moving box because she was afraid she'd hurt its feelings—would

21

say. (Instead she'd carried Paddington to her new apartment in her purse, with his legs sticking out like some furry kidnapping victim.) But she had reached out to Madison and got a whole lot of nothing in return. So, moving on.

On second thought, maybe fame *had* made Kate feel different. But just a tiny bit—and anyway, she didn't have much of a choice. In this business, it was kill or be killed. A girl needed to develop a thick skin or she wouldn't get anywhere.

"I miss her," Gaby said softly.

Kate reached out and patted her knee. "She'll be back, Gaby," she said. "Madison Parker will always be back."

3

NICE GETS YOU NOWHERE IN HOLLYWOOD

"Roll that rack over to the wall, will you? And the other one can go by the doorway. You don't need to get to your dining room anytime soon, do you, Carmen?" But Alexis Ritter, lead costume designer for *The End of Love*, which Carmen was due to start filming in a matter of days, didn't wait for Carmen to answer. "Well, whatever," she said. "Shouldn't eat during a fitting anyway."

Alexis clapped her hands briskly, startling her poor assistant, who nearly tripped over a pair of thigh-high leather boots decorated with fringes, buckles, and spurs. Carmen eyed them with trepidation. Was she going to have to wear those?

"Just put the rack right there," Alexis said. "For God's sakes, there! Come on. We've got a lot to do and not very much time to do it in."

Carmen couldn't believe the number of tunics, dresses, gowns, leggings, scarves, and capes being wheeled into her house. (Her dad was out of town, so her mom had agreed to let the PopTV cameras film for a few hours. Carmen was glad her parents didn't see eye to eye on this whole *Fame Game* thing.) The costume budget for *The End of Love* alone must be three times what it cost to make *The Long and Winding Road*, the arty, indie movie that had been her first big-screen experience.

Alexis glanced at Carmen, giving her figure a once-over. "So this is you," Alexis said. "Your size, which you plan on staying for the entire movie. No juice cleanses or carb binges, do you hear? It's important that your weight doesn't fluctuate, because there's a lot of boning and corsets involved here, and they need to fit perfectly." She ran her fingers through the white streak in her ebony hair.

"Uh, no, I mean, yes. I'm staying this size," Carmen said, glad that the PopTV crew, which had set up in the far corner of the room, had not begun filming yet. "No crash diets in my immediate future," she joked.

Alexis nodded, unamused. "Good. I want to get you into the ball gown from the opening scene first, because that has some complicated stitching going on. Boning, laces, whatnot. A sort of futuristic corset, with a busk front, so that your costar can tear it open in that first moment of passion. . . ."

Carmen blushed slightly. A moment of passion with Luke Kelly, in front of who knew how many cameras, while wearing one of these insane garments. It was going to be . . . interesting. But she didn't doubt that she was up to the challenge.

24

Then Alexis made a series of angry-sounding phone calls as Carmen stood around, shifting her weight from foot to foot and feeling like a trespasser in her own space. Eventually Carmen plucked her own phone from its place on the mantel and tried, for what felt like the millionth time, to get Kate to text her back.

It had been over two weeks since the *Fame Game* premiere, and Kate and Carmen had barely spoken. It was starting to bum Carmen out. She didn't know how she was supposed to act around Kate. Were they still friends? She'd thought everything was going to be okay, but then came the night of the premiere. Kate had been friendly when they were all on the red carpet, but by the end of the evening she was acting as if she couldn't stand the sight of Carmen.

At first Carmen was totally confused, but then Fawn had come rushing up. "I can't believe you didn't tell Kate about your hookup with Luke," she'd said breathlessly.

Carmen paled. "What?"

Fawn had put her arm around Carmen's shoulders. "I assumed you'd told her already, so I just sort of mentioned it in passing. You know, about how cool it was of her not to mind you guys fake-dating, when you practically almost did date. . . . Oops!"

Carmen had wanted to ask Fawn what the hell she was thinking, but she wasn't surprised. Fawn loved gossip of any kind and wasn't always careful with it. She didn't mean any harm, though, and Carmen knew that.

Remembering that night, Carmen shuddered. What

a terrible way for Kate to find out. No wonder she was angry.

But what did it mean for them now? Was their conflict a problem for Trevor's planned story line, or was this the exact sort of drama he wanted for his show? There hadn't been a fight, exactly—but obviously there was a lot unsaid between the two of them.

Assuming her text would go unanswered like the rest, Carmen decided that she might as well ask Laurel for a bit of advice. The producer was drinking a giant mug of coffee—as usual—and staring at her BlackBerry. Carmen remembered her doing the exact same thing back at Palisades Charter High School, when Laurel was a senior and already interning at PopTV. "Hey," she said, smiling as Carmen approached. "You ready to get into character?"

"Into the costumes, anyway," Carmen said. "But that's a lot of clothing. Am I supposed to try on all of that?"

"Probably not," Laurel said. "But don't ask me. Ask Alexis."

"I'm scared of her," Carmen whispered. "She has that whole Cruella de Vil thing going on."

Laurel looked at Alexis thoughtfully. "Yes, I see it," she said. "Definitely. Trevor will love that."

"She's probably going to make me wear a cape made out of puppy fur."

"Or kittens, maybe. But seriously, you don't get nominated for three Oscars for costume design without being tough," Laurel said. "You know just as well as anyone, nice gets you nowhere in Hollywood." Her phone buzzed, and she glanced down at the screen. She frowned, tapped a few keys, and then met Carmen's eyes again. "Dana's always telling me I need to be more of a bitch if I'm ever going to be promoted."

"Can I talk to you about something?" Carmen blurted.

"God, yes, why am I babbling about myself?" asked Laurel, putting her BlackBerry down and turning the full brightness of her attention to Carmen. "My job is to listen to you."

Carmen smiled wryly. She knew that Laurel's job was to listen to her so that she could report it back to Trevor. But whatever—those were the rules of the game. What she needed right now was a sympathetic ear, even if that ear was attached to Trevor's current protégée. Carmen took a deep breath and began to tell Laurel about the situation with Luke Kelly. But almost before she got to the end of her first sentence, Laurel put a hand on her arm.

"I know," she said softly. "Kate told me that they were dating. That it was her on the back of that motorcycle in the *Gossip* magazine photo. Not you."

Carmen looked at her in surprise. "She did?"

Laurel nodded.

"Well, the thing is, there's more to the story. I hooked up with Luke," she said.

Laurel's eyebrows lifted in surprise.

Carmen hurried on. "It was way before they were dating. We had a little too much wine one night at a party and we made out and it was no big deal. But Kate found out, and now she's not talking to me."

"Aha," Laurel said. "I knew something else was going on between you two."

"Kate wasn't even a twinkle in Trevor's eye back then!" Carmen went on. "How can she blame me for something that happened before she even existed?"

Laurel laughed. "She did in fact exist, Carmen. You just didn't know her. And I have to say, I understand Kate's side of things. You didn't tell her, and you were her friend. She probably feels betrayed. Not by the kiss, but by the fact that you kept it a secret from her. Keeping a secret can turn something into a much bigger deal than it ever should have been."

"Hello, Dr. Phil," Carmen said drily. "I didn't see you come in."

Laurel smiled. "Hey, I'm a reality-TV producer. Knowing people is part of the job. Trevor knows more about interpersonal psychology than your average PhD."

Carmen had to agree with that. Trevor did always seem to be one step ahead of them, didn't he?

Laurel sipped her coffee, then set the cup on the windowsill near the little bonsai tree that had been a gift from Carmen's best friend, Drew. "Kate wasn't born into this world the way you were," she said. "She doesn't understand all the rules. She doesn't know that illusion is sometimes more important than truth."

"You're getting really metaphysical on me," Carmen

said. "It's too early in the morning for that."

Laurel laughed. "It's eleven a.m. That's not early. But anyway, I think you should apologize to Kate. Sincerely. I'm telling you this as a friend. Trevor is very interested in what's up with you two. Your developing friendship was giving the show its heart—he'd mapped out the rest of the season with you two as besties. So, if you can't fix it, I'm sure that Trevor will try to orchestrate some knock-down, drag-out fight, preferably on camera."

"In a pool filled with Jell-O," Carmen said. Laurel snorted, and Carmen put her head in her hands. "It's so complicated," she said.

"Look," Laurel said. "You need to get this thing taken care of quickly. If Trevor gets wind of a love triangle, then he's going to want to run with it. And it's probably not going to paint you in the best light. Kate is the one wronged here, and she's the resident nice girl."

Carmen was about to ask Laurel if Kate was the nice girl, what did that make her . . . when she heard Alexis call, "Where is my actress? My Julia?"

"Whoops, gotta go," Carmen said, rushing off. "Thanks for the pep talk."

Laurel smiled. "Good luck," she said.

Once Carmen and Alexis had filmed their hellos for the PopTV cameras as if they hadn't just spent an hour in the same room while it was being set up, the costume designer proceeded to stuff Carmen inside a gown made from a strange material that Carmen had never seen before.

(The dress reminded her of a golden, tight-fitting Hefty bag, with threads of silver running through it.) Carmen was still thinking about what Laurel said. Maybe it wasn't enough to just text Kate things like HEY GIRL, WHAT HAPPENED TO U? and SHOULD WE TALK? If she wanted to mend what was broken, she was going to have to try harder and make an honest attempt at apology (even if, in her heart of hearts, she still didn't think she'd done anything wrong).

Carmen gazed unseeingly at the abstract painting on the wall as Alexis manhandled her, tightening laces and stays. She should probably try to be more open and honest in general, she thought.

Yes, openness and honesty. She would make this resolution now, months before the new year. Be more honest. Eat more vegetables. Read more books and fewer blogs. There. Now she could sleep in extra late on New Year's Day.

Of course, there had to be limits to her honesty. For instance, she didn't have any plans to stop fake-dating Luke yet. For one thing, their "relationship" was keeping their names in the tabloids, and for another, she liked hanging out with him.

"Ow," she yelped, as Alexis stabbed her in the ribs with a pin.

"Sorry," Alexis said insincerely. "I've got to get this belt tighter."

"Tighter?" Carmen said breathlessly, as Alexis gave

another tug on the dress's shining gold laces. "I feel like a sausage."

"Ha! The golden wiener," said a voice, and Carmen looked up to see Fawn standing in the foyer and smiling behind an oversized pair of Chanel sunglasses.

"Thanks a lot," Carmen said.

Fawn shrugged. "Just telling it like it is. You know that brutal honesty is one of my best qualities."

Carmen laughed, which was difficult because Alexis was currently squeezing her inside the dress. "Yes, and shamelessness. I mean, do those Daisy Dukes even cover your butt?"

Fawn, grinning, ignored this; she was looking at the PopTV cameras. "Didn't know you had your fitting today," she said. "I just stopped by to say hi."

But Fawn knew perfectly well that Carmen was filming her fitting today; they'd talked about it on their hike the day before. And obviously someone had miked her on her way in. Funny how Fawn had developed a habit of casually dropping by whenever cameras were rolling. Not that Carmen minded. It was fun to have her actual friend be a part of her fake reality every once in a while.

Fawn waltzed into the room, flung her glasses on the couch, and put her feet up on the tiny part of the coffee table that wasn't covered with costume accessories. "So I have a little information that might be of interest to you," she said, "concerning one of your friends."

Carmen thought first of Kate. Had Fawn heard from

her? Then Alexis gave her a sharp poke in the ribs. "Put your shoulders back," she snapped. "You're not going to slouch like that on camera, are you? You're a princess. Also, who is this person and why is she here?"

Carmen stood up straighter. She should probably be imagining herself as Julia Capsen, post-apocalyptic princess, even as she was being fitted. But she was dying to know what Fawn had to tell her. "Spill it," she said to Fawn. To Alexis, she said, "She's my friend. It's fine."

Alexis sniffed. "That means nothing to me. Daisy Dukes here can have five minutes and then I need silence."

"So," Carmen said, turning to Fawn, "tell me."

Fawn couldn't hide her smirk. "That bottle-blond bitch has been convicted of stealing that diamond necklace, and she has to pay back the store. Plus—this is the good part—she has to do like a million years of community service at Lost Paws."

Carmen wasn't sure she heard Fawn right. "Los Paz?" she asked. "The Mexican restaurant on La Brea?"

Fawn let out a delighted cackle. "No, dummy, Lost Paws. It's an animal shelter. I just read it on TMZ."

"Well, that sounds all right," Carmen said. "I'd rather walk a stray dog than chop cilantro. I hate cilantro."

"Oh no," Fawn said, shaking her head. "My friend Jeff went there once, and he calls it Lost Cause. You won't find any rescue bichons frises there. No cute little teacup poodles, unless they're missing an eye and have a thing for eating your underwear. They take dogs that bite, cats that

32

pee on your pillow . . . It's like San Quentin for pets." Fawn could hardly contain her glee. "It's soooo good, right?"

"Wow," Carmen said, as Alexis grappled her out of the golden dress and tossed a pair of leggings at her. "I mean, it's not like I'm her biggest fan, but poor Madison."

"Poor Madison nothing," Fawn said. "That girl got off easy. She may have to spend the next couple months accessorizing around a pooper-scooper, but she committed a crime—a serious one—and she isn't getting any time."

Carmen looked pointedly at her friend as she struggled to pull the leggings over her calves. What was all this material they were using—had space engineers woven the fabric? "May I remind you that you might have gotten something similar, had not a certain person stepped in and taken the blame?"

Fawn's eyes widened and she turned briefly toward the PopTV camera before stopping herself. "Oh, please. That tank top was worth less than two hundred bucks. I would have gotten a slap on the wrist."

Oops, Carmen thought, remembering the camera. *Well, no going back now.* "But you didn't have to get that slap," she pointed out. "I got it instead." If Trevor decided to use this footage, then the world would know that Carmen wasn't a shoplifter after all. Maybe her dad would finally stop being mad at her for taking the blame for Fawn.

"Suck in your stomach," Alexis hissed, and Carmen immediately complied.

Fawn sighed. She was clearly annoyed that Carmen

had brought the matter up on camera, but was trying not to show it. "I know, and you're an absolute angel. Do you have any Zone bars around here? I'm starving."

Carmen couldn't help but laugh again, which prompted Alexis to frown deeply at her. Fawn was so . . . Fawn. She was self-centered and gossipy, but she was also funny and smart. And she was a good actress, too. When they first met in that acting class in WeHo, it was Fawn who'd been the best student. As Carmen listened to her friend rooting around in the cupboards and drawers, she wished, under her breath, that Fawn would get a break one of these days. Her voice-over work was paying the bills, but Fawn wanted to be seen. Maybe if she made it past Trevor's edit, someone would notice her.

"These Cheerios expired last year," Fawn called. "Also, I don't get this fat-free half-and-half crap. It's half what, and half what else? Just drink the coffee black, for God's sakes."

Alexis looked up at Carmen from the floor, where she was adjusting the cuff of the leggings. "If you don't get her out of here in the next minute, I am going to throw her out the window."

Looking into Alexis's fiery black eyes, Carmen could almost believe this.

"Hey, Fawn," she called. "I sort of have to deal with this now. Want to meet later?"

"Always," Fawn said, coming into the room with a handful of Zone bars. "You don't mind if I take these, do you?"

"No," Carmen said. "I don't. If I want to wear these costumes without passing out, I'm going to need to eat air for the next few weeks. Air and lettuce."

"Don't lose more than three pounds," Alexis said sternly. "Or I'm going to have to do this all over again."

Having this costume fitting had seemed so glamorous until Carmen was actually in the middle of it. In reality, it was about as pleasant as a trip to the dentist.

"I won't," she whispered.

"That's what I want to hear," Alexis said. Then she smiled, and it was like being smiled at by a spider.

"Later," Fawn called. She let herself out, but then poked her head back inside. "Oh, and those leggings you're in now? I swear I saw it on that guy over on Robertson who wears Rollerblades and carries a boom box on his shoulder."

Carmen raised her hand as if to wave good-bye to Fawn, but instead she gave her the finger.

"Kisses!" Fawn called, and then she was gone.

Carmen shook her head in amusement. It was appropriate that she worked in entertainment, because she certainly knew a lot of characters.

4

A LOT LIKE JAIL

Madison sat in the parking lot of Lost Paws, sipping the cooling dregs of her nonfat latte and gazing grimly at the dirty white building in which she would be spending three hundred court-ordered hours. Its paint was stained and peeling; steel bars covered its small windows. On the other side of its chain-link fence was a mini-mart (Slushees only fifty-nine cents!) and a dingy-looking Laundromat. It was a Southern California no-man's-land—a place of barren streets and merciless sun.

Her phone buzzed on the seat next to her. ICED COF-FEES BY THE POOL LATER—YOU IN?

The text was from Kate. Madison appreciated how she reached out now and then—her concern seemed genuine (unlike, say, Sasha's). But Madison would not be joining Kate in the sun this afternoon. For one thing, she had to walk dogs all day, or whatever one did at a shelter. And for another, Madison didn't want to encourage a real friend-ship with Kate. She might be tempted to confide in her then, which was an obvious no-no. Madison couldn't afford to look back; she had to keep looking forward.

But the view forward was so depressing! Seagulls picked at little hills of trash while airplanes, descending into LAX, rumbled and roared overhead. She glanced down at her Rag & Bone skinnies, her Miu Miu top, and last year's black Chanel flats. She thought she'd dressed down, but no: She didn't even have the clothes in her closet to dress this far down.

Madison figured that working with the animals wouldn't be too bad—even in a dump like this—but she wished it didn't have to be filmed. Because every second Trevor showed Madison being punished was another second that the *Fame Game* viewers got to judge her. Or label her a criminal. (Or see her in an old pair of shoes!)

She'd asked Trevor if he could skip filming the whole community-service business, and he had laughed.

"Madison Parker asking not to be filmed?" he said, leaning back in his Aeron chair. "I never thought I'd see the day."

"Don't pretend I'm being unreasonable," she'd argued. "This isn't exactly the image I've worked toward."

"Then you shouldn't have pocketed a diamond necklace." He scanned her face for a reaction, but she gave him none. "Listen, do you want to be on the show or not?" Trevor had asked. But it wasn't really a question, because he already knew the answer. "This show is about your life in L.A. And right now, Madison, this is your life."

Of course he was right. What else was there to say? She'd gotten up to go. But Trevor had stopped her at the door. "Oh, and Madison?" he called. "Move back into your apartment. That's about enough hiding out at your dad's place."

She gritted her teeth. He knew everything. "No problem," she said, making her voice breezy. "I've really missed tripping over camera cords all the time. Bret never puts everything away. You know that, right? I'm going to start selling your equipment on eBay."

Trevor shrugged. "Well, apparently you could use the cash. . . ."

She'd said nothing to that; she'd just clenched her fists and left.

Trevor hadn't known it, but he was already getting what he wanted: She'd been planning on moving back into Park Towers. Not because she missed Gaby and her horrible boyfriend, Jay. No, Madison simply couldn't afford the rent on the bungalow anymore—not with the Luxe payments.

Madison gave herself one last check in the rearview mirror before gracefully stepping out of her car. She made her way toward the crew van so they could slip a mike on her before documenting day one of her humiliation. The sound guy didn't say anything as he peeled the backing from a strip of tape and quickly secured it to the inside of the neckline of her top. Come to think of it, none of the crew had had much to say to her since her incident with Luxe jewelers.

Laurel gave her a cool glance. "Can you get back in the car and pull out of your parking spot?" she asked.

Madison nodded silently. She knew what they wanted: one long shot of her driving in, stepping out of the car, looking up at the Lost Paws sign, and then walking in. Trevor would be milking this day for everything he could. And Madison had no choice but to let him.

She wasn't inside the building for more than thirty seconds when a bubbly, silver-haired woman whose name tag read Glory said, "You'll be wanting these today." She thrust a pair of thick plastic gloves at Madison's chest and smiled.

Madison took the gloves from her slowly, with narrowed eyes, wondering what sort of job required them. Glory winked at her. How did she manage to be so cheerful here in this small, dirty employee-break room, where even the smell of bleach and burned coffee couldn't cover the rank tang of animal urine?

The other new volunteers—who had apparently all arrived early, bright-eyed, and bushy-tailed—included a seventy-something woman, as tanned and wrinkled as a golden raisin; a pair of twins around Madison's age, with lank, dark hair and goth eye makeup; and a middle-aged man with forearms the size of Christmas hams. No one, in other words, that Madison was eager to get to know.

But the guy who stood quietly in the corner was a different story. He had light brown hair, sea-green eyes, and a body like a Greek deity's. If she'd known that volunteers could look like that, she would've been giving back to the community all along. Who was he? Madison wanted to know. And why was he off to the side, so carefully avoiding the cameras?

Glory moved to the front of the room; all eyes followed her. "Lost Paws relies on its volunteers to keep its doors open," she told them. "And while not all of you are volunteers," she added, looking in Madison's direction, "I hope you will all have a great experience during your time with us."

Madison rolled her eyes up to the ceiling, which was stained acoustic tile. "Can't wait," she muttered.

Glory either didn't hear her, or else she chose to ignore Madison's lack of enthusiasm. "We accept challenging pets," she went on. "Lost Paws is the place that people come when they have no other options. When you meet some of these animals, you're going to have to remind yourself: It might be ugly or it might be mean—or, honestly, it might be both—but every animal in here deserves to be taken care of and loved. Remembering that makes a big difference. These animals are in some of the most difficult circumstances of their lives. They're in cages. They're frightened. Even though we do our best to try to take care of them, we are a shelter. We are not a home." She looked at all of them, her vivacity suddenly muted. "Our job is to make this feel as much like a home as possible."

Madison suppressed another eye roll. Was this lady for

real or was this speech for the cameras?

"Sounds good to me," said the guy with the giant fore-arms. "I dig it."

Madison decided instantly that she hated him.

"So let's go around the room and introduce ourselves, all right?" she said.

Forearms said his name was Stan. The twins were Hazel and Ivy, and the raisin said that her name was Sharon. Madison felt she needed no introduction, but she offered her name anyway. It was clear that neither Stan nor Sharon had heard of her before (well, she never claimed to be a hit with the Geritol crowd), but Hazel and Ivy gazed at her with what seemed like awe.

Madison offered them a small, haughty smile, which neither of them returned. She assumed that they were star-struck. Maybe, if she was feeling generous, she'd give them an autograph later.

"So we're going to divide and conquer now," Glory said, before the gorgeous guy had had a chance to say his name. "Let's get you your assignments."

Madison looked down at her industrial-strength gloves and wondered why she was the only person who had been given a pair. They looked like the kind of thing you'd wear if you were going to clean up hazardous waste.

Glory's voice was brisk and efficient. "Stan, I'm going to give you to the Great Danes. They need a walk—and a strong person to do it. Sharon, you're going to work with me in intake, greeting people and getting them started on their paperwork. Hazel and Ivy, you'll be in the Family Room, which is where we work on animal socialization. All right, shall we?"

"Excuse me," Madison said briskly. "What about us?" She indicated the hot guy in the corner.

Glory shook her head. "Wait here. I'll take you to your duties after I introduce Stan to the Great Danes, Billy and Spike."

She turned and left, with the other volunteers following her. As Hazel (or was it Ivy?) passed by her, Madison readied herself to smile again. She had to be nice to her fans, even under these unfortunate circumstances. But the girl stared out from beneath her greasy bangs and said, "Scarlett should have challenged you to a cage match, you backstabbing bitch."

Madison flinched. That wasn't what she'd expected. But she sat up straighter and smiled. "Sure," she said sweetly. "And I would have kicked her skinny, angsty college ass." Then she turned away and stared at the ancient coffeemaker and the dusty vending machine until Glory returned.

When she did, Madison held out the gloves. "These must be for Stan, right? The guy with the arms? Because they're giant."

Glory smiled pertly. "Nope. They're for you. Try them on."

Reluctantly Madison did as she was told. What was she going to have to do? The gloves were much too big and they smelled like a petroleum by-product. She flexed her fingers. "I feel like my hands are paws."

"Then maybe it'll give you some empathy for the animals," Glory said.

"I have plenty of empathy," Madison retorted.

"Oh, I'm sure you do, dear." But bubbly Glory sounded pretty darn sarcastic.

Madison decided not to pick a fight. She could convince these people of her compassion some other time. Or . . . not. Whatever. "Anyway," she said. "Show me which cute little puppy you want me to walk."

Over in the corner, that gorgeous guy made a noise in his throat. Was it a cough? A laugh? Madison couldn't be sure.

"Uh, right," Glory said. "Come with me."

The cameras followed them down a narrow hallway lined with laundry hampers and mop buckets. Wild barking was coming from somewhere, and from somewhere else, a terrible, high keening that sounded almost human.

"Here we go," Glory said brightly. She opened a heavy metal door and gestured for Madison to walk in.

The room was windowless; it held stacks of metal cages. The air was thick with excremental stench, and Madison nearly stumbled from the olfactory assault.

"But there aren't any animals in here," she said, her voice tight. She didn't want to open her lips very much because she was afraid of letting the horrible smell into her mouth.

"Nope!" Glory said. "But there will be. And that's why I need you to clean these cages." She pulled a bucket and a giant bottle of bleach down from a shelf. "The water in that faucet is cold," she said, pointing to the small industrial sink. "If you want hot, you'll have to hoof it back to the break room." She gave Madison what was clearly an insincere smile. "All set, then?"

Madison was so shocked that she didn't even know what to say. And by the time she thought of something—*Wait, what? Are you kidding me? Get me a kitten to pet, stat!*—Glory was gone.

She stood silently in the dank, smelly room, surrounded by metal bars and shining locks. She looked in panic at Bret, the cameraman, and noticed he had a bandana wrapped over his face to mask the smell. It felt, she realized suddenly, a lot like jail. But jail, no doubt, was nicer.

"I'm not doing this," she yelled to the empty room. "I am so not doing this!"

It was all she could do not to turn to Bret and mouth "What the fuck?" There was no way in hell she was going to clean all these cages. She remained motionless in the center of the room for a minute, and then she stormed back into the hallway. The camera quickly followed behind her. She found Glory by the front desk, showing one of the twins how to work the computer.

"No way," Madison said. "You can't make me do that."

Glory looked up, her eyes glittering. "Oh, but yes, my dear, I can. This is your court-ordered community service.

You can either clean those cages, or you can go back to the judge and see what other punishments he can find for you. I hear they need people at the morgue. . . ."

Madison shuddered.

"Anyway," Glory said. "I don't make the job assignments. Ryan does."

"Who's Ryan?" Madison demanded.

"You'll meet him later," Glory said. "Now go clean."

The next three hours were pure hell. Madison nearly passed out twice from the stench of the dirty cages. She broke a nail, and the soapy water destroyed her Chanel flats. (She made a note to wear her Jimmy Choo hunter boots the next time around.) And no one came to check on her, to see if she was hungry or if she needed help or if she could use a break. She threw a mini fit around lunchtime, but only the PopTV camera paid any attention.

By the fourth hour, Madison was cursing to herself. "I think we're done here," said Bret. "The smell is kind of getting to me. And they said it'll probably take you the rest of the day to finish." He looked thrilled to be leaving, and no wonder.

So now Madison was utterly alone. Until she turned around and saw the hot guy she'd spotted earlier, leaning in the doorway.

"Oh, hey," she said, giving her hair a toss and trying to muster as much sex appeal as possible (which was not much, considering her state of disarray). Maybe Trevor had hired this guy to spice up her community-service story line. "Did you come to rescue me?" She smiled.

The guy shook his head as he took a step into the room. He did not look charmed by Madison's smile; in fact, he was looking at her the way she'd look at gum stuck to the bottom of her Louboutin. "I'm Ryan," he said. "And no, I didn't."

Well, that was enough to wipe the smile off her face. He wasn't another volunteer at all. "So I have you to thank for this fantastic job," she said, suddenly finding Ryan a lot less attractive.

"Fun, isn't it?" he asked, offering a small smile. Dimples appeared in his tan cheeks.

Five hours ago, Madison might have fantasized about reaching out and touching one of those dimples. Or thought about running light kisses along his collarbone, or slipping her hand inside his shirt and feeling the warmth of his smooth skin. Instead she suddenly wanted to hit him with her purse. The big one with lots of hardware.

"I'm in charge of the volunteers," Ryan said. "And you too, of course. I'll be signing your attendance sheets and reporting on your progress to the judge."

"Well, I hope you'll tell him that I did a stellar job today," Madison said bitterly. "And that I ruined a pair of six-hundred-dollar shoes in the process."

"I'm pretty sure no one cares about that but you," he said. He walked over to the cages and ran a finger along the now-gleaming bars. "Not bad," he said. "Better than I expected."

Madison ignored this. "How come you weren't on camera?" she blurted.

"I didn't sign a release," said Ryan. His voice was brusque. "I don't like cameras."

"Huh. I thought that was practically a prerequisite to living in L.A."

Ryan gazed at her. His green eyes were cool. "Not everyone's a fame whore," he said. And then he turned and left.

Madison reached down, took off her ruined shoe, and threw it after him. She missed, though, which was probably a good thing. No need to add assault to her charges, too.

5

THE SIMPLE THINGS

Kate eyed her cocktail with a mixture of curiosity and suspicion. It looked delicious, but then the bartender had referred to it as a Nutty Bloody Scotsman, which had given her pause. It had whiskey and blood-orange juice or something, which sounded fine enough—but why nutty? Why bloody? Whatever happened to nice drink names, like the Tequila Sunrise or the Pink Lady?

She stirred the pinkish liquid with her cocktail stick and gazed around the dimly lit room. So far she and Gaby and Carmen and Madison were the only ones in it, unless you counted the bar staff and the PopTV camera crew. But the Library Bar at the Roosevelt was so tiny that it almost felt crowded.

Gaby had just filmed a spot here for her new job as the host of some late-late-late-night party-and-lifestyle show, and Trevor took the opportunity to get two scenes out of one location by gathering the whole cast here after Gaby's shoot and turning it into a girls' night out. It was the first time they had filmed all together since the premiere, and Kate was nervous. (That was how she'd ended up with the Scotsman: "Surprise me!" she'd told the bartender.) Things were tense with Carmen and awkward with Madison, and being able to have a satisfying conversation with Gaby was never guaranteed.

She snuck a glance at the exit. What if she just pretended like she didn't feel well? Would Laurel let her leave? It was doubtful. Plus she hadn't faked illness since third grade, when her mom stopped falling for it.

So Kate reached for her drink and bravely took a sip. She turned to Gaby, who was sitting next to her. "Not bad!" she said brightly. "Actually, it's pretty good. What's yours?"

"I got a Bad Habit," Gaby said. "I don't know what's in it, though."

"A Bad Habit? That's appropriate," Madison noted. "If only your glass had a picture of a tattooed guy on it."

Gaby sniffed. "I don't only date guys with tattoos," she said. "It's just—what's that word?" She looked pensive for a moment. "A coincidence. It's just a coincidence."

Carmen laughed and tried to meet Kate's eyes, but Kate looked away—not out of anger so much as confusion. Now that a little time had passed and practically everything in her life felt different, exactly how mad at Carmen was she? Kate had been ignoring her texts and messages because she wasn't sure how to answer that question. A moment later, her BlackBerry buzzed. The text was from

Laurel. TRY NOT TO LOOK LIKE UR BEING TORTURED.

Right! This was fun, wasn't it? Girls' night out!

Kate thought of the first time she'd gone out with her castmates, when filming had only just begun. That was the night she met Sophia, who was now officially part of the *Fame Game* lineup, although in a supporting role (which Kate knew annoyed her). It was also the night she'd met Luke Kelly.

Almost imperceptibly she shook her head: Best not to go down memory lane. Best to focus on what had changed for the better rather than for the worse. For instance, her wardrobe. Granted, she still needed helpful texts from Laurel (DRESS CUTE: MAYBE NEW NUDE DRESS & GIVENCHY BOOTIES?), but still. The old Kate wouldn't have even known what Givenchy booties were. It was a miracle Luke had spent more than a minute with her.

Gaaah, stop thinking about Luke, Kate told herself. But the fact that she couldn't was what made things still weird for her with Carmen. Carmen probably saw Luke every day, either at work or on a fake date. Of course, after Kate learned that the two had history, their attraction seemed a little less fake.

She fixed a bright smile on her face. Her job was to make conversation and have enough fun to fill four minutes of airtime, max—how hard could that be?

She took a deep breath and dove in. "So, Madison, I saw your picture in *Life & Style* the other day," she said. But then she bit her lip in dismay. She was such an idiot:

How could she have forgotten that the editors had Photoshopped Madison into a prison jumpsuit? Kate coughed loudly and tried to recover. "Your hair looked amazing," she gushed. "Aren't you the spokesperson for Joolie heat-styling spray?"

Madison nodded slightly as she crossed one slim, tan leg over the other. "I have a lot of endorsements," she said. "Unlike some people." Her eyes darted toward Carmen.

Carmen smiled slyly at this. "And maybe, thanks to your work at the shelter, you'll get even more. Like, for a pet product or something," she said.

Madison scoffed. "Weren't you the face of that zit cream a couple of years back, Carmen? Of course, that wasn't so much an endorsement as it was a testimonial, because no one had any idea who you were without your mom by your side."

Kate saw Carmen's cheeks flush. She'd had no idea that Carmen had done commercial work; she always seemed so . . . indie.

"TV ads pay great," Carmen said, her voice sharper. "If you do enough of them, you can afford to buy your own diamonds."

Madison inhaled and stiffened. Kate waited for her to say something, but she didn't. She just turned away and took a sip of her pink-tinged drink.

Awkward, Kate thought. Suddenly the already-small room felt claustrophobic.

The exchange had quickly put a damper on whatever

goodwill the girls had managed to build up, and now no one was saying anything. Well, if tense silence was any interest to Trevor Lord, he'd have plenty of it, Kate thought. Maybe he'd have Carmen do a voice-over. *We were all supposed to go out and have fun, but Kate and I weren't talking, and Madison certainly wasn't in a party frame of mind. . . . At least we had Gaby to lighten the mood.*

If the whole thing weren't suddenly so uncomfortable, Kate would have smiled to herself. Who knew what this night would look like when it appeared on the nation's television sets? All she knew was that right now it was pretty unpleasant.

Kate didn't understand, really, why it had to be like this. Sure, Madison had been sort of snubbing her. But she obviously had a lot on her mind. It wasn't like Kate ignoring Carmen's texts—Kate knew she hadn't done anything to upset Madison. And Carmen was probably exhausted from filming, which was why she was being sort of bitchy. But what, really, was Kate's own problem? What did she have to complain about? She had a hit TV show and a hit song: She ought to feel a little better! Why in the world couldn't she just relax and enjoy herself? Tell a joke or a funny story?

She cleared her throat and started to say something, but then stopped. The fact was, she had her own anxieties to worry about, besides making pleasant small talk. For one thing, Trevor had told her that she was going to have to play some real shows one of these days. "Open mics aren't for people with top-selling singles," he'd pointed out. "We're getting you an actual gig." Thinking about that made her feel sick.

And for another thing, this whole interpersonal stuff was tricky. It seemed like all of her castmates had secrets and touchy spots. Skeletons of various sizes rattling around in their walk-in closets. With Natalie, everything had been so easy. They trusted each other implicitly. But with these girls, Kate felt like she never knew what they were really thinking.

"So, have you gone on any hot dates with Luke lately?" Gaby asked Carmen.

Speaking of skeletons and secrets! Kate rolled her eyes (but subtly, and not so the cameras could see it). She was getting pretty good at guessing how these scenes would go.

Carmen shifted uncomfortably in her seat, while Kate had to pretend like she wasn't anxious to hear Carmen's response.

Then she felt a hand on her shoulder, and she smelled a pungent essential oil that was perhaps best described as a combination of lilac, cinnamon, and . . . mud? Kate didn't even have to look up to know that Madison's sister had arrived. But she did look up, and she saw golden-haired Sophia beaming at all of them, silver bracelets clinking noisily on her arms and peacock-feather earrings brushing against her toned shoulders.

"Namaste, *chicas*," Sophia said warmly. "What are we talking about?"

"We weren't really talking about anything," Carmen said quickly. "Have a seat."

"Don't mind if I do," Sophia said. She made a beeline for the spot Carmen already occupied—at Laurel's instructions, perhaps?—which meant that Carmen had to scoot over so that she was sitting inches from Kate.

"Hi," Carmen said quietly.

Kate didn't answer for a moment, and she then said, with a bit of an edge to her voice, "Hi yourself." She wasn't going to offer anything more.

It seemed to Kate as if she could feel the camera's devilish red eye boring into the side of her skull. So far, this evening out had been about the longest night of her life (and they had only been at the Roosevelt for twenty-three minutes).

Sophia leaned forward, removed her sandals, and flexed her bare toes. "So you are not going to believe who came into Kula Yoga this afternoon," she said.

"Are you seriously taking off your shoes?" Madison asked, sounding horrified. "What are you? An animal? We're in public!"

Sophia ignored her sister and took a delicate sip of what Kate hoped was seltzer. "Rob Schappell! You should see the abs on him. He's got, like, a twelve-pack."

"I thought you were too enlightened to notice that sort of thing," Madison said.

"Oh, sis, you'd have to be a nun not to notice. Honestly, it disrupted everybody's practice." She giggled.

"Not that I'm complaining."

She fingered a large crystal that hung on a chain around her neck. She looked, Kate thought, lovely and healthy and impossibly statuesque—maybe there really was something to this yoga business. Kate herself had no experience with it. Yoga hadn't been big in Columbus; it was more of a Zumba kind of town.

"What's so interesting about yoga, I'm finding," Sophia said, "is that the simple things are the most challenging. Breathing correctly, for one. You think, how hard is it to breathe? We do it all the time! But the fact is, it's extremely difficult to do it right. And Savasana—corpse pose?"

"I always fall asleep in Savasana," Carmen offered.

Maybe, Kate thought, Carmen was trying to make up for being mean to Madison by being nice to her sister. Though considering Madison's and Sophia's rocky past, it wasn't clear whether that'd be an effective strategy. But maybe that was the point? She sighed. Once again, interpersonal stuff: tricky.

"Well, it's so important that in addition to quieting the physical body, you must also pacify the sense organs," Sophia said.

Whatever that means, thought Kate.

Madison rolled her eyes. "I never imagined I'd have such an evangelist for a sister," she said drily.

Sophia turned to her. "You really should try it. It would help you process some of your rage."

Madison burst out laughing. She laughed so long and

so loudly that Kate began to wonder if she was faking it. "You're killing me," Madison finally gasped.

Sophia raised a knowing eyebrow but said nothing.

"Can we go back to the part about the twelve-pack abs?" Gaby asked.

"If he's single, I already called dibs," Sophia said. She nudged her sister playfully in the ribs. "Though I might lend him to Maddy. There are other ways to work out rage besides yoga. . . ."

At this, Madison's laugh was definitely sincere.

What do you know? The sisters actually seem to be getting along better lately, Kate thought, watching them with a tiny glimmer of envy. (Jess, her own sister, was great, but she was just so damn sporty—all she wanted to talk about was her free-throw percentage and how many crunches she'd done.)

Kate had never realized how much Madison and Sophia looked alike, too—like twins, but with radically different senses of style. Madison had poured herself into a scarlet bandage dress, while the maxidress that hung loosely off Sophia's shoulders resembled a tie-dyed tent. If Mattel ever made a Hippie Barbie, they should look to Sophia for inspiration.

"I've got a celebrity story for you, too," Kate offered. Because she really should give the camera something, and she didn't want to talk to Carmen. And because she needed to at least look like she was having fun.

"Oh, goody," said Gaby, rubbing her hands together.

"Please tell me it's about that British guy who just starred in *Infinite Action*. He is so hot! I mean, not that it matters to me—I'm totally in love with Jay."

"Of course you are," Kate said. "How could you not be?" It was hard for her to say this with a straight face. Jay spent his days playing video games and his nights drinking cases of MGD. He was a cretin. It was impossible to understand what Gaby saw in him, except for maybe his washboard abs. "Anyway," Kate said brightly. She quickly took another sip of her drink and then proceeded to tell them about how, when working at Stecco the other night, she had had the "privilege" (according to her boss) of waiting on Gemma Kline and Carson Masters, who had flown in from London for some megastar charity event. "So Gemma—who, when she says she doesn't do Botox, is lying—said to me, 'I have numerous allergies. When I'm exposed to certain inflammatory foods, my adrenal cortex goes haywire.' And I'm picturing some cartoon robot, you know, where steam starts coming out of its ears and then it explodes? So I'm like, 'Great, that's fine, we can deal with that. What can't you have?' And she lifts up a pale, bony hand and starts ticking off fingers. 'Dairy, wheat, gluten of any kind, soy, yeast, nuts, garlic, and anything that's acidic. Tomatoes, for instance. Or lemons and other citrus.' And I'm like, 'Um, okay, what *can* you eat?' And Carson—who also totally Botoxes—sort of rolls his eyes and says, 'Lettuce. Lettuce and steamed fish.' So that's what Gemma gets. Fish poached in vegetable broth and a pile of wilted spinach. It tastes awful, you can just tell, and she gets charged seventy-five dollars for it because it's a special order. I know I'm not from this town, but why would you go to a fancy L.A. restaurant if you can't eat anything they serve?"

Madison smiled gently, as if this were a very stupid question. "To see and be seen," she said. "Think of all the girls on juice cleanses who still show up for lunches on Melrose. They just push their salad from one side of the plate to the other. But they're there, Kate, and so are the paparazzi."

"Point taken," Kate said. "But she could just go get coffee somewhere if she wants to be seen. Or, like, walk anywhere along Robertson."

"You act like wasting seventy-five dollars matters to her," Madison reminded Kate. "When in fact it means as much to her as a grain of sand does to the Sahara."

"Right. I forget that kind of thing because I'm not rich and famous."

"Well, you might be one of these days," Madison said. And then she winked at Kate. "Almost as famous as me."

Kate laughed. Madison suddenly seemed like she was warming back up again. Maybe, thanks to that pink cocktail she was sipping, she'd magically hit a turning point in her personal emotional drama. Then maybe she'd stop with the whole weird and cagey act she'd been working for the last few weeks. Maybe there was hope for her and Kate to be friends.

Gaby piped up with some sort of inanity, and Kate was trying to decide whether it was worth paying attention to her or not when she noticed that Carmen's best friend, Drew Scott, had arrived.

He loomed in the doorway, dwarfing everything around him. He was wearing a pressed blue Oxford, but Kate could see a tattoo peeking out near his wrist, right above his vintage Casio watch. He caught her eye and winked.

"Ladies," he boomed, striding toward them with a giant grin on his face. "Is anyone here drunk enough to kiss me yet?"

Kate and Carmen both laughed as he plopped down right between them and put an arm around them both.

"Gaby is, I'm sure," Madison said under her breath.

Kate snickered. Drew certainly had the tattoos to be Gaby's type.

"What's with the button-down?" Carmen asked Drew, plucking at his sleeve. "French cuffs and everything. Have you gone square on us?"

"You look like Jesse James's accountant," Kate added. She was happy to see him and even happier that his arrival meant she no longer had to sit next to Carmen.

"Uh, I'm still waiting for the kisses." Drew laughed.

Kate saw Carmen smile, and then, as easy as anything, she leaned over and planted a giant one on his face, right near his mouth. Kate bit her lip. Drunk or sober, she was way too shy for something like that.

Drew turned to her. "Nothing from the left? Spurned by the singer-songwriter! In that case, I'll take matters into my own hands." And before Kate could say a word, he planted a sweet, warm kiss on her cheek.

Immediately she blushed and put a hand up to her face.

"Gotcha," Drew said, grinning and pleased with himself.

"Y-you," she sputtered. She swatted him on the arm, and he laughed.

"Sorry. Had to take a little liberty there. I just came from a work party. That Miller64 must have gone to my head."

"Wow," Carmen said. "You guys really live it up at Rock It! Records."

"You know it." Then just as quickly as he'd sat down, he was up again. "Who wants another drink?"

"Oh, I'm sure someone will come by to take your order," Carmen said.

Drew waved her off. "Ladies, I'm here to service—I mean, serve you."

Carmen rolled her eyes at him.

"You're sweet," Gaby said to him.

"It's true," Drew said. "I'm probably the sweetest guy ever." He held up a hand to stop Sophia's syrupy cooing. "But I'm manly, too. I'm, like, masculine and tough. But I'm really, really nice. Right, my Carm?"

Carmen—"his" Carmen, whatever that meant—smiled at him. "You're the best."

Drew held out his arms. "So now who wants to kiss me?"

Sophia and Madison were laughing, and both Gaby and Carmen were smiling up at Drew, and even Kate felt the glimmer of a grin tugging at the corners of her lips.

How quickly the atmosphere in the room had changed! And they had Drew to thank for it. He'd simply walked into the room, happy and confident, and had magically, goofily diffused the tension. There was no more silence. No more staring down at your own feet. Suddenly everyone was talking and giggling and acting as if they'd been besties forever.

Kate could really learn something from Drew, she thought. She needed to lighten up. Take things less seriously. Remember that life was fun. Fun! To not enjoy it was not only stupid, it was downright irresponsible.

When Drew returned from the bar, Kate reached forward and raised her glass. "To friends," she said. Because that's what she hoped they all were (even if they got mad at one another now and then). Or could be. Or could act like, for the next hour anyway. Besides, Trevor loved a good "cheers" moment; any toast always made the episode. Kate might as well beat Madison to it this time.

Everyone lifted their glasses and clinked them together. "Friends," they repeated. "Friends."

6

A MUTUAL FAVOR

Stepping out of what had been a long and scaldingly hot shower, Carmen Curtis pulled a plush bathrobe around her, cinched its waist, and slid her feet into fuzzy slippers. She gave her dark hair a quick towel-dry and then walked into the living room of her trailer.

Calling it a "living room" was generous—it was about a hundred feet square, aka about half the size of her bathroom at her parents' house—but Carmen was thrilled to have it. Her own movie trailer, with her name on the door and everything! It wasn't glamorous, but it was all hers. She didn't have to do anything but sit inside it to feel like she'd hit the big time already.

Or lie down inside it, she thought, flopping onto the cushioned bench under the window. She was utterly exhausted. Today's shoot had gone over by three hours, putting it at a thirteen-hour day, and her call time tomorrow was six a.m.

She was tempted to take a nap, but instead she reached

into the pile of magazines and newspapers that the PAs regularly replenished for her. Reading a trashy tabloid could be just as rejuvenating, right? Plus, she was curious to learn about the actress Samantha Mulder's in vitro triplets and Lacey Hopkins's latest scrape with the law. Heck, maybe there'd even be a mention of Madison Parker.

On the top of the stack was a copy of this week's *Gossip* magazine. Glancing at it quickly, Carmen was startled to see one of the cover lines: LITTLE CC NO MORE, it said, right above a photo of her (dressed to the nines, thank goodness) shopping in Beverly Hills. The accompanying article was four paragraphs, all of which heavily quoted an unnamed "friend of the actress." "Things are going really well for Carmen," this "friend" reported. "But she's stressed about all the pressure. She's starring in *The End of Love* opposite Luke Kelly, who, in addition to being her current crush, is a more experienced actor. So she goes for a little retail therapy!"

Carmen bit her lip. "Current crush"? "A more experienced actor"? Normally her publicist was the source for these little pieces. But this definitely didn't sound like something Sam would say. It was weird. She squinted at the picture. It wasn't her best, but it wasn't her worst, either. She could live with it.

Then she threw the magazine up in the air, rolled over onto her back, and kicked her legs in the air with glee. Live with it?! Hell! She was loving it! So what if the picture wasn't perfect? So what if the article wasn't completely accurate? Gossip magazines never got their facts right. As for the "friend," these rags tended to use that term rather loosely. It could have been anyone claiming to know her. But still: What a crazy and thrilling thing. She mattered to people—people she had never even met and probably never would! And it wasn't because of whose daughter she was anymore. It was because of her. It was so incredibly bizarre and so crazily amazing that she felt, for a minute, like she might jump out of her own skin.

Suddenly no longer tired, she got up and stood in the center of her living room. She was about to commence an impromptu oh-my-God-I'm-famous dance when a knock sounded on her door.

"Who is it?" she asked, startled and extremely glad she hadn't already begun said dance.

"It's your loooover," said a voice that she immediately recognized as Luke's. "Your lover . . . on-screen—and in real life." Then Carmen heard a laugh. "Can I come in?"

She sat down and composed herself, checking her robe to make sure she wasn't showing too much cleavage. "Yeah, it's open."

He stepped up into the trailer, even more handsome now that his face had been scrubbed clean of its makeup. "Did I hear cackling in here?" he asked.

Carmen widened her eyes and placed her hand so that it covered her picture in *Gossip*. "What? Me? No!" She smiled. "I'm just relaxing with some tea!" She nodded toward the mug of chamomile she'd made for herself and then forgotten about. "Do you want some?"

Luke looked at it and wrinkled his nose. "Is that herbal tea? Because, as a subject of the British crown, I must frown upon anything that is not Earl Grey or PG Tips." He laughed. "Also, forget tea—it's happy hour. Do you have any tequila?"

Carmen pointed him toward her mini refrigerator. "I don't know. Do I?"

Luke walked over and perused the fridge's shelves. He held up a tiny plastic bottle, like the kind they served on airplanes. "Patrón!" he said. But then he exhaled and put it back. "Actually, I'm too tired to drink it. If it wouldn't call my manhood and patriotism into question, I'd absolutely have some tea."

Carmen patted the seat beside her. "Sit," she said. "Relax." When he complied, she said, "I can keep it a secret if you want the tea."

He smiled and yawned. "You're a love."

That was what Carmen's grandma said to her, but with Luke's sexy accent it sounded totally different. Totally better.

His eyes fell to the cover of *Gossip* magazine, which she had forgotten to keep covered. "'Little CC no more,' huh?" he said, green eyes twinkling. "Check you out."

She yawned, too—it was contagious—and then giggled. "I'm sure the article, if you want to be generous and call it that, talks all about you, too."

Luke shrugged. "Probably," he allowed. "Seeing as

how I'm your loooover."

"Stop saying it like that." She laughed.

"Loooover," he whispered, grinning.

Carmen threw a pillow at him.

"I saw us on *D-Lish*," he said. "Not that I, uh, check that or anything."

"It's so weird," Carmen said. "Don't you think?"

Their pictures were all over: *Perez, Just Jared, Life & Style, Celeb!* According to Cassandra Curtis, who—incredibly—had a Twitter account that she actually checked regularly, "#LukeandCarmen" had trended high for the last eight days. Their fake relationship was making them a hot topic. Because what was more fun than a new Hollywood couple? Especially one playing lovers in the next Colum McEntire blockbuster?

But it was strange, too, because it was just more acting. Sam had even suggested that Carmen walk off set holding hands with Luke. The paparazzi had been camped outside every *End of Love* location lately, hoping to get photos of the two of them leaving. Carmen had always made an effort to avoid their lenses. After a day of acting in caked-on makeup, obscure hairstyles, and fitted costumes, the last thing she wanted was her photo taken.

Besides, she couldn't stand those creeps. It was one thing to show up to a red carpet—polished, brushed, powdered, and fitted—to pose for photographers with press badges. But the street photographers that waited outside celebrities' homes and hid in bushes across from elementary schools? They were a different breed. The idea of giving them exactly what they wanted didn't sit well with Carmen, but after some persuading she had reluctantly agreed.

"They're going to get their photos one way or another," Sam had pointed out. "Might as well make it on your terms."

Carmen had mentioned the idea to Luke earlier that morning, in a break between scenes, and at first he'd seemed unsure. He'd gazed out over the set, a wistful look on his face, and Carmen wondered if he was thinking about Kate. But then his manager had called with news about a script that Scott Rudin wanted Luke to read—some political thriller or something—and Luke had mentioned the cute-couple photo op.

His manager had been shocked at Luke's reluctance. "It isn't a coincidence that all these offers are rolling in after you two have come out as a couple," he'd said. "Your star is on the rise, and Carmen has a lot to do with it! You're a known quantity now. Go with this, Luke."

So Luke had agreed. And why wouldn't he? Since Kate had basically told him she never wanted to talk to him again, what did he have to lose? It wasn't as if he could piss her off much more than he already had.

But the more Carmen thought about it, the weirder she felt. Because Carmen probably *could* piss her off more. Based on their hesitant but not totally unfriendly interactions at the Library Bar, it seemed like there was a chance for Carmen to repair the damage that the faux-dating had done. Like—if Kate would ever call her back so Carmen could apologize.

On the other hand, what good would an apology do if Carmen kept flaunting her fake romance with Kate's ex? Following Sam's PDA instructions in order to get tabloid coverage would probably make her apology seem pretty bogus. Carmen thought back to her costume fitting and her resolution of being more honest. Maybe she and Luke should come clean—or feign a breakup. Which wasn't exactly being honest, but it was close enough.

She cleared her throat. "So I was actually thinking about this whole you-and-me business," she began.

Luke held up a hand. "Stop right there," he said. "I know you truly love me. But babe, this is just for the cameras. I'm sorry."

Lacking another pillow, Carmen threw one of her slippers at him. It landed squarely in the middle of his broad chest and fell into his lap. He laughed and put it back on her foot.

"Seriously, though," she said. "I do feel weird about it. Do you think we should keep it up?"

"It's like my manager said. It's crazy not to." He gestured to the magazine. "You can't buy publicity like this."

"But it's a lie. And it's sort of ruining my friendship with Kate."

He gazed down at his hands, silent for a long moment. "But we're not lying, Carmen. We're just not denying our relationship. We're not commenting. Let people fill in the blanks for themselves. Anyway, it's not your fault that Kate's mad." Luke reached out and patted her ankle. "It's mine. It was always mine."

"I don't like dishonesty," Carmen said. "And isn't holding hands for a bunch of paparazzi basically lying?"

"Well, not with words?" Luke said. "Look, I do feel weird about that. I get it. But this is simply good business. You and me, we both want the same thing, and we've both got a lot to prove, and if pretending there's more between us than friendship is going to help us out, then that's what we need to do. I ruined a great relationship with a girl I really liked—I can't back out now. This is helping the movie, too. And we want it to be huge. We need it to be."

"Of course, but—"

"And it's not like you haven't pretended to date someone before," Luke interrupted.

She frowned. "What are you talking about?"

Luke opened her refrigerator again and this time took out a Coke. "You let everyone think that you and Josh Hills were dating. That you had that romantic holiday weekend in Ojai."

"But that was different," Carmen protested. "It was a favor to Josh. He didn't want everyone finding out that the romantic weekend was really between him and his boyfriend, Juan."

Luke popped open the soda and shrugged. "Okay, whatever. So think of this as a favor to yourself. To your career. And to this movie."

"And to you?" she asked.

Luke poked her. "It's a mutual favor," he said. "Loooover."

"If you don't quit that, I'm going to kill you," Carmen said. Then she sighed and gazed into her tea. "But you're right, I guess."

"I'm always right," Luke smirked. "Now get your clothes on. We have a date with some paparazzi."

Carmen laughed. In a strange way, she could almost find the fake relationship comforting. In the past when she'd been actually dating someone, she could never be sure if the guys really liked her or were just using her for money, or connections, or both. (She'd made a rule for herself that she wasn't allowed to date any struggling musicians, after falling hard for one who'd turned out to be more interested in her father than her.) Whereas now she *knew* Luke was using her, just as she was using him. There was a simplicity to it. And a twisted honesty.

She got up and picked out a pair of skinny jeans from the tangle on the bedroom floor and located a pretty, ruffled top that was miraculously still on its hanger. She held them up in front of her as she stood before the mirror. It was important to have a decent outfit—casual but pretty; thoughtful but not studied—because she'd likely be looking at it in photographs for the next week. (She'd learned that lesson from Halle Berry, who had yet to live down the giant sweater-poncho she'd been photographed wearing back in March.)

"Did you get lost back there?" Luke called.

"I'll be out in a sec," Carmen said. She slipped into her clothes and then turned sideways in the mirror. Yes, the outfit would do. She applied a coat of lip gloss and brushed a little mascara onto her thick lashes. Her hair had dried into soft black waves.

She gave the mirror one last check. She looked . . . good enough. She was coming off a grueling shoot, though—no need to look like she was stepping off a runway.

She pulled her long raven hair around her shoulder and walked out to the living room. "How do I look?"

"Perfect." Luke smiled. "Ready, loooover?" he asked.

"Dead," she said, narrowing her eyes at him. "You're totally dead."

He laughed and jumped down the trailer steps. She followed him down more slowly—there would be no jumping in her Lanvin platforms—and found herself in a warm early fall evening. The sky was streaked with blue and lavender, and she could still smell the roses that they'd used during today's shoot, for the scene in which Carmen and Luke, aka Julia and Roman, get it on in a lush garden. (It had struck Carmen as more than a little funny—would people in a dark, post-apocalyptic future still cultivate roses? She sort of doubted it.)

She and Luke were quiet as they walked through the studio lot. It was a giant, walled compound on the edge of West Hollywood, housing soundstages, warehouses, parking lots, sets, and craft-and-prop shops. It was like its own city, Carmen thought, run by a government of studio executives and populated by everyone from A-list stars to Z-list PAs. But it was a ghost town tonight.

Meanwhile, on the other side of the walls, the real city was gearing up for the evening. New York might fancy itself the city that never sleeps, but it sure had competition with L.A. when it came to partying.

"Well," Luke said as they approached the studio gates, "ready for this?"

The paparazzi were lining the fence that blocked off the lot.

"Ready as I'll ever be," Carmen said. She took a deep breath. She felt Luke's hand wrap its way around hers.

They emerged onto the sidewalk and immediately dozens of flashbulbs went off, making thousands of bright sparks. "Carmen," someone yelled. "Carmen Curtis, give us a smile!"

Luke squeezed her fingers. "Looover," he whispered, grinning from ear to ear.

She dug her nails into his palm. Smiling, keeping her mouth shut, she hissed, "Seriously, I am going to murder you."

He laughed, thoroughly pleased with himself. He was like a little boy, Carmen thought; he was probably going to keep beating that dead horse of a joke forever.

She began to see spots from all the flashes. Who was going to buy all these pictures of her and Luke? It wasn't like there were an infinite number of celebrity magazines.

She tried not to squint. Instead of stopping, the flashes only seemed to increase in number. "What's going on?" she asked. "What's all the fuss? This is insane!"

"We're bloody famous," Luke whispered, "that's what."

But then Carmen began to hear another name being yelled.

She turned.

"Cassandra," yelled a male voice. "Cassandra, over here!"

And that was when Carmen saw her mother. Cassandra Curtis was walking toward them, stunning and exotic in a jade-green flowing dress and gold goddess sandals. Her arms were open to her daughter.

"Honey," she called above the clamor. "I know craft service is awful—I don't care what they say. Come with me. I've got a roast at home in the oven." She was smiling her warm, beautiful smile, and almost instantly Carmen felt herself pulled in by the mesmerizing force of her mother. Cassandra Curtis was like a magnet. A sun around which everyone agreed to orbit.

"Luke—" Carmen said.

"I'm going to go out for a steak," he said. "I think these guys have gotten what they needed. Almost." And then he leaned in and kissed her—lightly, gently—on the cheek. "See you tomorrow."

She smiled at him. He mouthed the word "looover" and vanished.

Still the flashes were exploding all around them.

Carmen turned back to her mother.

"Darling," Cassandra said. "Shall we?" She motioned to the waiting town car.

Carmen nodded. She was happy to see her; she really was. But as she heard the paparazzi calling "Cassandra, Cassandra!" she realized, with what she had to admit was a measure of annoyance, that she'd better not forget who the real star of the Curtis family was.

7

KNOW YOUR LINE

As a gift to himself, Trevor poured a packet of raw sugar into his maté latte. (His nutritionist had put sugar on the NO list.) But he felt he deserved it, because along with his hot drink, his new assistant, Michelle—or was it Melissa?—had just handed him the ratings for the first three weeks of *The Fame Game*, and the audience numbers were even bigger than he had expected. It had even beat out the new cop show starring some gorgeous blue-eyed English actor and Genevieve Waters, the buxom redhead who used to date the head of Hamptons Studios.

Not too shabby, Trevor thought, smirking. *Not too shabby at all.*

There was a knock on his door and his assistant poked her head in. "Matt LeBlanc wants to know if you're playing tennis weekend?" Michelle/Melissa said.

"Tell him I have the court at eleven," Trevor said. "And I need another sugar packet."

"I'll be right back, sir," Michelle/Melissa said, nodding pertly.

He liked how she called him "sir." He should learn her name. Or else he could just call her Melissa and wait to see if she corrected him. (Though maybe she wouldn't, even if he was wrong. Maybe she'd be too afraid to contradict her powerful, important boss—a thought that made him smile.)

He stood at the window and did a few knee bends as he sipped his drink. (His trainer had told him to take advantage of spare moments like this. "In every hour there are at least twelve minutes you could be working out," she always said. "Every moment you're not glued to your desk is a moment you could be increasing your fitness.")

Despite the *Fame Game*'s excellent ratings, Trevor had to acknowledge that not everything was perfect. For one thing, his purported star, Madison Parker, was suddenly unavailable for filming for thirty hours each week. It seemed to him like a pretty stiff sentence for stealing some silly necklace. Shoplifting was practically an extracurricular activity for young Hollywood.

Carmen, too, was turning out to be hard to pin down these days. He'd pushed for her to get the starring role in *The End of Love*, and now it was turning around to bite him in the ass. *Be careful what you wish for,* he thought, as he did ten reps of a deep squat.

And speaking of things biting him in the ass, Carmen was still playing along with the Luke Kelly business. Those two had quickly become a genuine power couple. When Trevor and Veronica Bliss had released the story about Luke Kelly secretly dating a *Fame Game* girl, he'd had no idea it would escalate to this level. He was looking for a quick buzz before the premiere, and suddenly he'd ended up with Carmen engaging in a very public relationship with a movie star who had no intention of stepping in front of PopTV cameras. Trevor had tried his best to convince Luke's representation that appearing on *The Fame Game* wouldn't tarnish Luke's acting career, but they weren't buying it. He'd gotten exactly one scene out of them—a meal at Stecco that would be airing in a couple weeks. He'd cut and rearranged it enough to make it feel romantic and hopeful, and his music supervisor had found a fantastic love song for it. Trevor had even planted a shot of Kate looking forlorn.

Trevor knew this meant he'd have to be a little creative. He already had his love triangle; he just needed to find a replacement for Luke. After all, in his show the men were interchangeable. A guy had clearly come between Kate and Carmen, and luckily for Trevor, they rarely referred to him by name.

But a half-baked, heavily edited love triangle wasn't going to carry the show all season; Trevor was going to have to rethink its focus somewhat. He had six strong episodes done, but now he had to figure out how the remaining six would play out.

Gaby could never be the central character. She was sweet, but she was vacant and hard to relate to. Kate Hayes had definite potential—she had the fresh-faced innocence, the whole pretty-girl-next-door thing that had made such a star of Jane Roberts. But while Kate was definitely sympathetic, she wasn't exactly charismatic. There was a chance she'd uncover some latent confidence, some hint of star power, in the upcoming shows he was booking for her, assuming she didn't pass out from anxiety first. The stage fright would be a part of her arc, of course. He'd been planning to work it in ever since he'd seen her play at the premiere. But she needed to deal with it. And he wasn't about to let her sign a label deal until she did. He'd mapped out her career trajectory and he couldn't have her skipping steps—it would all unfold in a way that worked for the show. But still, he needed someone with magnetism. He needed someone the camera loved—and who loved the camera right back in equal measure. What he really needed was Madison Parker.

He stopped doing squats when Michelle/Melissa slipped in with his other sugar packet. He sat down at his desk again, his pulse pleasingly elevated. Yes, he missed Madison's shameless camera-hogging. She'd been such a reliable source of drama for two-plus seasons, and now she just wasn't pulling her weight.

The footage from her first day at Lost Paws was perfect—he loved the hissy fit she'd pitched when faced with all those filthy cages—but he couldn't spin a dramatic and glamorous story out of a starlet's janitorial duties. Plenty of *Fame Game* viewers loved to hate Madison Parker, but they weren't going to stick around to watch her scoop poop for a whole season. Schadenfreude only took you so far before it got boring.

What he needed most right now was to get to the bottom of the Charlie Wardell story. Madison's father had been a big part of the first few episodes, and now he was suddenly gone. Trevor could hardly let him vanish without addressing it, which meant that Madison was going to have to talk about what happened to him. On film.

He got up again and paced the room. It didn't take a rocket scientist to figure out what had really happened. He didn't know the details (even Sophia hadn't cracked when he tried to pull the truth out of her), but it was obvious to him that Madison was covering for her father in some way. He didn't know why it wasn't obvious to everyone else. Then again, he had spent years painting Madison as a spoiled brat. So maybe it wasn't surprising that people believed it.

He jotted some notes onto a legal pad. Madison would say that Charlie had "gone away for a while." Her evasiveness would cause all sorts of speculation among PopTV viewers, which always worked to the show's advantage. And then, just maybe, he could figure out a way to suggest a connection between Charlie's disappearance and Madison's theft. Maybe he'd spin it so that she didn't seem like a greedy little starlet, but instead, a poor, abandoned daughter. Acting out in her grief and anger.

No one would ever come out and say there was a definite connection (because no one knew what had been going on in Madison's head), but through careful editing, he could certainly suggest it. . . .

He smiled. Yes, this could be something. He rubbed his hands together in satisfaction. If one of his stars was going to get arrested and charged with a crime, he was going to find a way to make it work for the show. Find a way to make a thief sympathetic.

The only problem was Madison herself. Would she do what he wanted? She had gone through a lot to take the fall for Charlie, and she clearly didn't want the truth to get out. He looked at the clock. Well, he'd have a chance to gauge her reaction in ten, nine, eight . . .

Madison opened the door on the count of two. She was immaculately dressed in a chic little navy number with a white collar. She looked, almost, as if she were headed to a courtroom again.

"Madison," he said, offering her his biggest smile, "you look like a million bucks." (*And she's probably spent close to that to look that way,* he thought.)

"Were you exercising in here?" she asked bluntly.

Trevor smiled. "What makes you ask that?"

She wrinkled her nose. "It smells like you were."

Trevor made a mental note to throw away the hippie natural deodorant his nutritionist had given him and go back to using Old Spice. "Anyway," he said. "Nice to see you. How have you been?"

"I think you can imagine," she said. "Instead of attending launch parties for Beyoncé's new perfume, I'm giving flea baths."

Trevor chuckled. "Yeah, that's kind of a bummer, isn't it? For all of us."

Madison raised a freshly plucked eyebrow. "I don't see how you're suffering."

Trevor picked up his Gripmaster hand exerciser and squeezed it. "Well, I can't build much of a story around you grooming dogs and cleaning cages, Madison. You look great in a pair of wellies, but custodial work isn't that exciting to watch." Plus, Ryan Tucker, the Lost Paws volunteer coordinator, had been downright obstructionist about filming.

"Yeah, well, it's not fun to do, either."

"It's too bad you had to go and steal that necklace, isn't it?" Trevor said coolly.

Madison didn't answer; she gazed out the window and pretended as if she hadn't heard.

Oh, Mad, he thought. *You think feigning deafness is going to work?* "I'll tell you what I want," he said, leaning forward and lowering his voice. "I want to show you talking about what really happened the morning after the premiere."

Madison crossed her arms and gazed at him, her blue eyes steely. "You know what happened. It's all over the news. I'm pretty sure you can read."

Trevor leaned back again and put his hands behind his head. "Madison, please. I'm not dumb, and more importantly, you're not dumb. What really happened? Where's your father?"

When Madison didn't answer, Trevor gazed up to the ceiling. "Let's see," he said. "He had a psychotic break and he's now at Beverly Hills Psychiatric, but you don't want the world to know about your family's history of mental illness so you're covering it up. Or maybe he wasn't really your father; he was just some actor you and Sophia found because you felt like your story line needed a little more meat. If so, kudos—that was awesome. You had us all going there. And here I was, thinking you can't act! Or maybe . . ." Trevor leaned forward, staring directly into Madison's eyes. "It's really Charlie who took the necklace, and you, for some completely bizarre and incomprehensible reason, are taking the blame for him. . . ."

"You can make up stories all you want," Madison said stiffly. "You already got me to humiliate myself on camera at Lost Paws. And if you were on top of your story arcs, you could keep doing it. I'm sure everyone would love to watch me get my comeuppance. But I'm not going to talk about it, all right?"

"I'm just trying to get to the bottom of it all," Trevor persisted. "I just want to know what happened. Where is Charlie, Madison? We can't just pretend he never existed."

Madison crossed her arms over her chest. "He decided he didn't like L.A. after all," she said finally.

Trevor knew that was far from the whole story, but at least for right now, the truth didn't actually matter. "Well, you're going to have to say that. On-camera. 'Daddy went away for a while.'"

Madison bit her lip. "Well, that's true enough."

Was that the sparkle of a tear he saw in the corner of her eye? Trevor almost felt sorry for her.

Almost.

"Good," he said. "You know your line, then. I'll set up a place for you to deliver it."

8

WHO SAID ANYTHING ABOUT LOVE?

"Lost in love, then lost without you / lost in the city where I first found you . . ." Kate sang. Her eyes were closed in deep concentration, but then, feeling suddenly self-conscious, she opened them. The small red light of the PopTV camera was blinking in her peripheral vision. She let the rest of the line trail off. Where was she going with this song? She felt just as lost as the girl she sang about. And she was saying the word "lost" too much. Maybe it was time she invested in a thesaurus.

Normally she would have leaned her guitar, Lucinda, against the couch and raided the pantry for Oreos, but with PopTV filming she didn't think that was such a good idea. For one thing, it would make her look like she had absolutely no work ethic; for another, she'd end up with cookies in her teeth. And as Laurel had informed her, producers preferred that the girls avoid eating on camera (which was funny, considering half their scenes were shot in restaurants).

Another one of Kate's favorite procrastination strategies included cleaning her apartment, which at the moment needed it desperately. (In fact, there were so many clothes on the floor of her room that the other day the cameramen had been instructed to film above the floors.) But who would want to watch her picking up her dirty socks?

She sighed and did a little finger-picking exercise that her first guitar teacher had shown her—plucking just the open strings, no chords at all. She could hear Laurel in the kitchen, pouring her ten thousandth cup of coffee. Starbucks French Roast had probably long ago replaced the blood in her veins.

Someday soon, millions of people would see her in this moment, sitting cross-legged on her couch in her faded jeans and the T-shirt her mom had gotten at a Bob Dylan concert in 1987. Her feet were bare and her strawberry-blond hair was a little messy, but at least she still had a decent pedicure.

The funny thing was that she wasn't really all that nervous. Composing was hard, sure, but playing in front of the PopTV camera was a lot easier than playing before a live audience. You couldn't edit out your mistakes in front of a live audience, and Kate always made mistakes. This was why she was pretty terrified whenever she thought about her upcoming show. She was opening for The Faze—a band she didn't even like—in a room that held hundreds of people.

"I can't do it," she'd said to Laurel earlier, as they

waited for the cameras to set up. "I'll die of stage fright."

Laurel looked unruffled. "Of course you can do it."

"Well—actually, maybe I don't want to," Kate had retorted.

"Excuse me?" Laurel asked, surprised.

"The Faze is a crappy band," she'd said. "You know who likes them? Fourteen-year-old girls who spend their days at the mall drinking Jamba Juice and buying cheap earrings at Claire's."

Laurel had stiffened then. "First of all, they've had two hit singles, which is more than you can say for yourself. And second of all, you're going to do it whether you want to or not," she said. "So you might as well figure out a way to enjoy it. Or if you can't enjoy it, at least find a way to make it through a whole song without hyperventilating." Then she'd stomped into Kate's kitchen to make herself some coffee, leaving Kate standing there like an idiot, feeling both hurt and offended.

Now, as she plucked idly at Lucinda's strings, Kate's BlackBerry buzzed. BACK TO SONG, OK? ALMOST DONE. ☺

Laurel was trying to make nice again. Like a smiley face would do the trick? Whatever. Kate didn't care. The Faze did suck.

On Laurel's orders, though, she went back to the basic chord structure she'd worked out: A E D Dsus D, with the capo on the second fret (otherwise she couldn't hit the low notes). She hummed for a while, just to get warmed up again. She knew the melody. It was the lyrics that were giving her the problem.

Every time she felt weird writing a song about breaking up with Luke, she reminded herself that Adele had written an entire album about breaking up with someone, and it had won about five hundred Grammys. Not that Kate was comparing herself to Adele—but it was okay to take a little inspiration from her, right? Out of a broken heart would come creative genius. In theory.

Before their little fight, she and Laurel had actually been discussing the Luke problem. Laurel was sympathetic, but she insisted that it was for the best that they'd broken up. What good was a love affair that couldn't be filmed? No good at all, if it was Trevor Lord you were asking. "He likes the love triangle thing with you and Carmen," Laurel had said, "but Luke won't be on camera in any significant way."

"There's no triangle," Kate had reminded her. "Luke and I broke up."

"I know. So now you need to fall for someone else."

Kate had laughed. "Like it's that simple?"

"It kind of is. Or it can be. I'll send over a DVD with some options next week."

"Wow," Kate said. "Producer and matchmaker. Is playing Cupid part of your job description?"

Laurel smiled. "Everything is part of my job description."

"I don't think love works that way."

Laurel had given her a strange look. "Who said anything about love?" she asked. "We just need an on-screen love interest."

Oh, right, Kate had thought. *Silly me.*

Her mind had flashed, for a moment, on Drew: He was fun to hang out with. Would he be willing to play her on-screen love interest? *No,* she thought. *Not in a million years.*

Well, she'd wait and see who Trevor came up with.

SONG, Laurel texted now.

Kate hummed the melody quietly and watched as Bret moved to get a different angle and nearly tripped over a pair of boots she'd left in the middle of the floor. Oops.

Maybe because her mind was stuck on breakups, she began, unconsciously, to play that Kelly Clarkson song, "Stronger."

"Doesn't mean I'm lonely when I'm alone . . ." and out of the corner of her eye she saw Laurel smile. Bret's foot tapped as he filmed.

All right, Kate thought, so it was just catchy tunes that they wanted. They didn't care if the songs were hers or not. Well, in that case she could play all night. She was like a one-woman karaoke machine.

She was actually starting to enjoy herself with a Rihanna cover when her front door burst open. And there stood Madison, statuesque in heels, sleek leather pants, and a silky nude-colored tunic.

"Sounds good," Madison said, smiling lightly. "Don't quit on my account."

Kate stopped halfway through the line anyway, surprised to see Madison in the foyer. Her castmate had been on the shooting schedule—Kate was supposed to ask her about community service, which was good because she genuinely wanted to hear about it—but she was starting to think that Madison would be a no-show.

"Thanks," Kate said. "Come in." She gestured to the couch across from her, which was littered with magazines and tank tops and the Lululemon yoga pants she liked to wear around the house. "Have a seat!"

Madison placed her giant Chanel bag on an end table, pushed aside Kate's clothes, and sank gracefully into the cushions. "Is that your new song you were playing?"

"Well, it's new to me," Kate said. "It's actually by Rihanna. Or by her people, anyway."

"Her people. Of course." Madison smiled. "We should all have more people."

"Right?"

"Totally." Madison gave her hair a flirtatious toss, perfectly aimed at the cameras.

Kate strummed a few more chords. Why in the world had she thought Madison wouldn't show up? Of course she would: She cared more about screen time than she did about avoiding Kate or any of the other *Fame Game* girls. She was drawn to a camera like a moth to a flame.

"Hey, do you know the words to Madonna's 'Like a Prayer'?" Kate asked. "I can only remember the first verse."

Laurel cleared her throat loudly. Both girls looked in her direction as she violently shook her head. Kate quickly realized that there was no way PopTV would be able to clear The Queen of Pop's hit.

Madison took the cue. "Sorry, I don't. And singing—well, let's just say it's one of the few things I'm not good at." She smiled, turning again slightly to ensure a good angle. She was clearly an expert in blocking.

Kate continued strumming lightly, because that's what her shooting schedule had said. *Kate plays guitar and writes song. Pref. one about love.* She was a good girl. An A student. She did what she was told to do. (Usually.)

Madison gave her another encouraging smile, and Kate realized that she was glad she was here. It had been getting kind of boring, not to mention uncomfortable, to be in a room full of people while pretending to be alone.

Kate played a bit more—her own melody this time—and then spoke. "We've missed you, you know," she said.

Madison nodded. "Well, I've been busy."

"Is everything going okay at the shelter?"

Madison thought about this for a moment. "I wouldn't exactly say that, no. It feels more like a maximum-security jail than an animal shelter."

"Oof," Kate said. "Doesn't sound fun."

"It's not supposed to be. But I'm so grateful that the judge gave me this opportunity to do something good. It's definitely helping me get my priorities back on track."

It sounded like she'd been rehearsing that reply for

a while. Kate assumed that Madison must be in serious image-rehabilitation mode, and wondered if she ought to try to draw Madison out more. She knew Laurel wanted them to have a real conversation. It had been so long since they'd talked; Kate didn't even know if Madison was back in her apartment with Gaby. She would have asked her, but since according to *Fame Game* reality, Madison had never moved out in the first place, it wasn't a question Kate could pose.

"Play me your song, why don't you," Madison urged. "The one you've been working on."

"Don't you want to talk?" Kate tried.

But Madison smiled and shook her head. "I want to listen."

Kate didn't want to push her, so she played her song, messing around a little with the chorus, while Madison listened intently. Or seemed to, anyway. But she had a pretty faraway look in her eye.

After a little while, Laurel's voice cut over the melody. "Okay, we're done for the night." Then she came over and gave Kate's shoulder a little squeeze. "Nice work," she said. "I know it's got to be tough to compose on the spot."

Kate hadn't exactly forgiven her for lack of sympathy about being the opening act for The Faze, but she decided not to show it. "Next time I'll have the lyrics down better," she said. "I won't have to resort to covers."

Laurel smiled. "Don't worry. The audience wants to see the process, not just the product." Then she headed for the door, her coffee cup clutched in a jittery hand. "Bye, ladies." How Laurel slept at night with all that caffeine in her, Kate had no idea.

"See you soon," Kate called. She set Lucinda down, relieved to be done with her for the night. Now she could kick back and turn on the television (and hopefully avoid any ads for *The Fame Game*, which made her heart jump every time she saw them—at first with excitement, but now with anxiety). She was reaching for the remote when Madison cleared her throat.

Kate turned to her. "Oh, I'm sorry—that's so rude of me. I guess I just thought . . ." *I assumed you'd follow the cameras out the door,* she thought but didn't say.

Madison smiled. "You thought I was only here for the screen time," she said. "Maybe I was. But now I want some wine. Got any?"

"Um, yeah, I think so. . . ." Kate loved how direct Madison was sometimes.

Madison let her head fall back against the cushion. "Great. White, if you have it—and a heavy pour, please."

Kate had to rummage around in the refrigerator for a minute, but she found a bottle of pinot grigio behind an old Thai takeout container. She hoped Madison's palate wasn't too refined, because, according to the sticker, the wine had cost $7.99. (She wasn't even sure how it had ended up in her refrigerator.)

She went back to the living room holding the bottle and two big glasses. "I don't know how good this is going to be," she warned. "Someone left it here."

"Oh, thank goodness. Glad you didn't have to shell out the eight dollars yourself," Madison said drily. "Bottoms up." But she just took a delicate sip. "I've had worse," she said. "I think."

"Sorry," Kate giggled. "I don't go into my fridge much."

"Beggars can't be choosers." Madison shrugged, fishing a piece of cork out of her glass.

"I'm sure you have something better in your apartment," Kate said. There, now she'd know if Madison was back there or not!

"Can't deal with that at the moment," Madison said. "I stopped in before I came here, and Jay's over. He's standing in our kitchen with his shirt off, Kate. What kind of animal hangs out in a girl's apartment with no shirt on? It's so . . . crass."

"Maybe he thinks that bike-chain necklace he wears looks better on bare skin," Kate said.

Madison nearly choked on her drink, which made them both crack up. "And he literally speaks in grunts," she said when she'd caught her breath.

"But Gaby really likes him?" Kate asked.

"Yes. Although if he's male, has a pulse, and drives a sports car, Gaby likes him."

Kate sighed. "Well, at least she's easy to please."

Madison snorted. "I wouldn't even bother with the 'to please' part."

Kate burst out laughing again. "But seriously," she said when her fit of giggles was over. "This whole dating thing is freaky. Did you know that Laurel basically ordered me to start dating someone? She said the show needed more romance."

Madison raised an eyebrow and Kate imagined she could see the wheels turning: *If I find a boyfriend, will I get more screen time?*

Kate went on. "And I'm like, it's not that easy. And then she said she'd 'send me some options.' As if I can pick out a boyfriend like I order a hamburger."

"Believe me, it's been done," Madison said. She leaned forward and poured more wine into her glass. "But if romance is all you've got to worry about, count yourself lucky. At least you're not slaving away in some disgusting animal shelter all day long." Madison sniffed at her fingertips. "I swear, the smell of that place never leaves me."

"Is it that bad?" Kate asked. "I always just imagined a room full of puppies and kittens."

"It's awful. You can't believe how depressing it is in there. All these sad, messed-up animals. And the guy I work with—my boss, I guess you'd call him—is horrible." She looked glumly at her wine. "He's hot. Really hot. But I hate him." Suddenly she hit the arm of the sofa in frustration.

Kate jumped; Madison was usually the queen of control. "Do you want to talk about it?" she asked hesitantly.

For a moment, Madison didn't answer. She gazed down

at her toes, which were painted in pale, glittering gold. But then suddenly she began to speak. Words poured out of her as if she'd been uncorked, just like the second bottle of bad wine Kate had uncovered.

And Kate heard about Lost Paws, about Sophia's apparent love affair with her yoga instructor, about moving back in with Gaby, about Gaby's stash of prescription drugs . . . in short, about everything and everyone except for Charlie and the necklace.

When Madison finally stopped talking, she looked deflated but slightly happier. "So, that's my life in a nutshell," she said, smiling wryly. "What's going on with you?"

But Kate suddenly didn't want to talk. She picked up Lucinda and began to strum. Her tongue loosened by wine and laughter, the words now came easily.

"Lost in love, then lost without you"—*okay, back to the original line on that one*—"I just wonder what leaving cost you / The stories that we shared, the dreams that we dared / I don't understand the reason that we're through. . . ."

She closed her eyes and let the music flow out of her. It felt like the notes were born in her fingers and the melody was borne out in her heart, and her words gave them shape and form in the cool night air.

Okay, maybe she was a little tipsy. But it felt good!

When she was done, Madison clapped loudly. "That was amazing. Do it again," she demanded.

And so Kate did, and when it was over Madison tossed

her iPhone onto the couch by Kate's bare feet. "I videoed it," she said. "Check you out!"

Kate watched herself on the tiny screen. She looked passionate, soulful, inspired. She looked like a real musician.

"It's not terrible, is it?" she asked happily.

"No way," Madison said. "It's fantastic."

And so, in a moment of enthusiasm and tipsiness, Kate posted it on YouTube.

9

MAKE IT RIGHT

Ryan was standing in the doorway of Lost Paws, tan arms crossed in front of his broad chest. He looked pointedly at his watch as Madison approached. "You're late," he said sharply. "Again."

"By five minutes," she retorted. "That's not actually late."

"Ten," he said.

Madison ignored this. The truth was, it hurt her pride to be late. She used lateness—rarely—as a way of building tension. But in today's case, she was late because she'd been packing up the rest of her shoes, clothes, and toiletries (there was so much of everything!) in order to officially move back into her Park Towers apartment that night.

By dinnertime, the little bungalow she'd found for Charlie would be empty of everything that had made it feel homey and welcoming. Nick, her agent, had sent an intern over to wait for the Designer8 people, who were coming to pick up the rented beds, couches, tables, and lamps. (Saving Madison this particular hassle was about the only thing Nick had done for her lately.)

She sighed, thinking about another day spent vacuuming up dog hair or scrubbing down painted cinderblock walls at Lost Paws. Why couldn't someone get her out of this?

Ryan cleared his throat. "Well?" he said.

"I'll stay late," she said.

"Great," he answered. "More time for us to spend together."

She had to bite her tongue to keep from making a sassy retort. Ryan hadn't moved out of her way yet, so she was still on the step beneath him, gazing up at him from below. It wasn't a good angle for most people, but Ryan didn't seem to have a bad one. Madison noticed how his skin was paler beneath his chin. How he had one single freckle near his clavicle. How his Adam's apple cast the faintest shadow on his neck. How—*Oh, please stop, Madison,* she thought. But it wasn't fair that he was so good-looking. He was such an asshole, and not in a charming way.

Ryan turned around and pushed hard on the door. As it swung open, Madison caught the unmistakable whiff of caged animal. It smelled like urine and fear. She fought the urge to dry heave. Even after a week of coming here, she wasn't used to it. She was glad Trevor had stopped sending the *Fame Game* cameras along. She didn't want to have to relive these days when she saw them on TV.

Hazel (or was it Ivy?) sat at the front desk, helping Glory figure out how to print on the new printer. She sneered at Madison.

Ryan faced her with his hands on his hips. "Time's wasting," he said. "Come on."

Madison ducked her head, ignoring the glare from whichever twin it was, and silently followed after Ryan. She had never been this meek in her entire life! But even in this moment of uncharacteristic humility, she couldn't help it: She admired the breadth of his shoulders and the way his jeans hugged his slim hips. She knew she should ignore him completely, but still, she took in the tan, muscled length of his arms, the soft waves of hair that barely brushed his collar. Why did he have to be so hot?

Of course Ryan would choose that very moment to turn around. His eyes met hers and narrowed. "You going to critique my outfit?" he asked. The expression on his face said he knew exactly what she'd been thinking.

Madison flushed and looked away. "That's professional advice. I don't just give it away for free," she said.

"Well, can't say I'm surprised by that," Ryan muttered, turning back around.

"You know what I mean," she called out.

Ryan didn't look back this time; he just shrugged his broad, beautiful shoulders. "Whatever."

Madison vowed never to make eye-to-eye contact with him again. Or eye-to-shoulder, or eye-to-pecs . . .

When Ryan got to the supply closet he reached in and

retrieved a familiar pair of plastic gloves.

"Seriously with the gloves again?" Madison asked. "Am I back on cage duty?"

"No cages, princess. Today you're in the laundry room." He gestured toward a damp, cinderblock room with two industrial-strength washers and dryers, each the size of a Mini Cooper. Blankets and towels lay in heaps on the floor. Here the air smelled a little different. *Like urine and bleach,* Madison thought grimly.

"You know how to do laundry, right?" Ryan asked. "I mean, besides putting it in a heap and waiting for your cleaning lady to take care of it?"

Madison glowered at the piles. "I know how," she said. What Ryan didn't know—and what she certainly wasn't going to tell him—was that she'd started doing laundry at the tender age of seven. Since Sue Beth Wardell had generally neglected laundry, vacuuming, and cooking (or anything else that didn't involve a remote control and a bottle of cheap whiskey), Madison had learned that if she wanted clean clothes each day, or dinner each night, she had to take care of it herself. (And, to make things more difficult, Madison hadn't even had a washing machine in her cozy double-wide in Briar Rose Trailer Park in Armpit Falls, NY. It was the public Laundromat or the sink for little Madelyn Wardell.)

"Well, have at it, then," Ryan said. "There's a radio in the corner there. You can turn on music if you want."

Madison could have strangled him. Was listening to

Katy Perry on Kiss FM going to make this task any more tolerable? She could have a live performance in front of her and she would still be in her own personal hell.

She spent the next five hours in that room, washing, drying, and folding the animals' laundry: the dog-bed covers, the cat blankets, the towels soaked with who knows what. (She was suddenly thankful for her hazardous-waste gloves.) Again, no one came to ask if she was hungry, or if she would like five minutes of fresh air.

She felt like Cinderella, except without the ball and the lost shoe. Or the prince.

She thought about her other castmates, who were doing things like writing songs and starring in movies and making out with guys they met in bars, and she felt, for the first time, that she would trade places with any of them.

And she thought, too, about Charlie, even though she tried not to. How she had no idea where he was, or if he was okay, or why he had done what he'd done. How she was just going to have to wait for him to reach out to her. (And considering he'd failed to call her for a decade, what could she reasonably expect? A collect call sometime around her birthday next year?)

As furious as she was at Charlie, Madison still missed him; she couldn't help it. And she couldn't explain it, either—not even to Sophie. Her sister had been so young when Charlie left that she barely remembered him; the fact that he was gone again didn't seem to mean that much to her.

Or else, Madison thought, Sophie was simply too self-involved to notice that they were once again fatherless. Too busy practicing tree pose, or laughing-cow pose, or whatever. Honestly, Madison would never understand yoga. *Why stretch,* she used to say, *when you can shop?*

But of course she couldn't shop anymore, because every spare nickel was going to Luxe, to pay them back for the necklace, which was—Madison prayed—still in her father's possession or handed over as some kind of barter to someone he owed money to. Because you couldn't just take something like that to a pawnshop, unless you wanted a free ride to the nearest police station.

Try as she might, Madison couldn't shake a tiny glimmer of hope that Charlie would understand how badly he had screwed her over (*again!* said the little voice in her head) and would come back to make things right. But how that was going to work out, she had no idea. She hoped he knew what he was doing. But taking past experience into consideration . . . well, it didn't make her feel very confident.

"I just wanna throw my phone away / Find out who is really there for me," Katy Perry sang on the radio.

Madison almost laughed. *You and me both,* she thought.

At the end of a long and exhausting day of laundry, Madison was in the lobby, finishing off a bottle of hand sanitizer, when a woman brought in a skinny, shivering animal with dirty, matted hair and one paw wrapped in a filthy bandage.

"Oh dear," whispered Glory. "That poor . . ." She shuddered.

"I found it tied up in the backyard of a house no one lives in," said the woman. "I can't keep it—or him, or her, or whatever it is—but I couldn't just leave it there, right?" She shifted nervously from foot to foot, as if the good people of Lost Paws weren't going to take this thing off her hands. "I mean, it would starve."

"It looks starving already," said the twin.

It was maybe the ugliest animal Madison had ever seen. If a wolverine had mated with a dirty yarn mop, and the resulting baby had mated with a giant rat—well, this dog would be the end result.

No one wanted to touch it. Not even Stan, aka Forearms, who was the person Ryan called to pull plastic bags out of Tootsie the poodle's behind after she got into the trash.

The skinny, trembling little dog gazed up at Madison. One sad, cloudy eye met hers; the other looked off to the side. As she watched, it whined, lay down at her feet, and licked, ever so hesitantly, the tip of her shoe.

And Madison burst into tears.

"What the—" breathed Ryan. "Are you kidding me? It's just a little dog saliva. Your shoes will survive."

But she was already running out the door.

★ ★ ★

A few hours later, Madison was standing in the living room of Charlie's former bungalow, with the last suitcase of toiletries by her feet. The furniture, the rugs, the throw pillows, the lamps: All of it was gone, and the rooms suddenly looked small and dark and cold. Madison's footsteps echoed on the gleaming oak floor as she made one final check around the house. There was no trace of her now, and none of Charlie, either. She'd looked hard, but there was nothing—not even a single button or cuff link that had rolled into a corner and been forgotten.

Before she left, she sat one last time on the porch swing. The bright blooms of the bougainvillea were fading, turning brown, and dropping to the sidewalk. She picked at a fleck of paint that was peeling from the railing.

She was exhausted from her day at Lost Paws: by the laundry duties, by tension with Ryan, and by her bizarre emotional outburst. The embarrassment of being a janitor (and—ugh—having to dress like one) wasn't getting any easier to take. She was bitter that she had to crawl back to the apartment she'd shared with Gaby in order to get airtime, save money, and get Trevor off her back. And she was mad at herself for getting into a mess like this—a mess so big that, for the first time, she wasn't sure she'd be able to dig her way out of it.

She flung the paint chip into the yard. (Three thousand a month and they couldn't even paint the damn porch?) But . . . what if she were to come clean? What if Madison

104

decided that it wasn't worth it to protect Charlie, and she just up and told the truth?

For a moment, her spirits lifted. Life would return to normal!

But she quickly realized that if she did tell the truth, there was no way anyone would believe her. She'd have to convince Luxe to release the security footage of Charlie taking the earrings, and then she'd have to explain that Charlie took the necklace, too. And then Luxe would have to admit they lied to get publicity. And then Madison would probably be prosecuted for perjury. And then she'd get more community service—or maybe they'd send her to jail this time.

No, it would never work. Oh God, what an incredible mess she'd created. . . .

She shook her head fiercely. Enough of the pity party. She stood up, checked the lock one last time, then strode down toward her car. She gave a final look into the mailbox and there, along with a cable bill and a mass mailing from a roofing company, was a postcard. The front was a picture of a tree silhouetted in the setting sun. The back was addressed to her.

Maddy, I never meant to hurt you. I will make it right, okay? Just give me a little time. Love, Dad.

Madison almost crumpled it up and tossed it into the street. But then, her heart softening, she picked it up and slipped it into her purse. She had no idea how Charlie planned to make it right, and in a way, she doubted that he could. But just seeing his handwritten promise made her feel a little less alone.

10

ON–SCREEN AND OFF

The silhouette of a man, high atop the stone wall, looked small against the blue sky. A woman's voice cried out, "No! Noooo!" as the man, teetering on the wall's edge, lost his balance and plunged down to the ground.

Smack. Carmen winced at the impact, and then watched as the man got up from the inflatable mat that had broken his fall and brushed his light brown hair back from his face.

"Oh for God's sake," Colum McEntire said. "That blasted pigeon got into the shot. It flew right in front of him. Can someone handle that? Or is that too much to ask?"

Carmen and Luke exchanged a nervous glance. Colum McEntire had a legendary temper—he'd once fired Rio Lockhart, his starring, A-list actress in *Far from Her*, midway through production for some tiny infraction that neither would discuss. (That had required some serious script rewriting!) Some days were worse than others, and today was looking like one of the bad ones. He'd already brought three different PAs to tears. And, as Luke had noted, "two of them were dudes."

Carmen watched as Luke's stunt double drank from a bottle of Gatorade and had his nose powdered by the makeup lady. He did not look particularly like Luke. But they shared that tanned, Hollywood handsomeness—which, if Carmen was honest, was just a little bit generic. It seemed like everyone looked like a Hemsworth these days. Was there some sort of farm that grew guys like this? Maybe somewhere down in Australia, a mad scientist was breeding a new crop of leading men.

Luke scooted his chair closer to Carmen's. "Do you know my double did all the stunts in *Deadman's Driveby*? He broke his leg in one of the crash scenes and cracked a rib in another."

"Impressive. If only there were two of you in real life," Carmen mused, "then maybe Kate wouldn't be mad at me, because there would be enough yous to go around."

"Let's not talk about that," he said.

"Does the heart heal so quickly?" she asked, smiling. It was one of her lines from the movie.

"Actually, no," Luke said. "That's the problem—I think about her a lot. And I start missing her. But then I stop myself, because I know I need to be focused on this role." He gestured to the set before them, a futuristic-looking fortress pockmarked with holes and craters from the explosives that had supposedly struck it. There was a puddle of fake blood near a fake dead tree. (It seemed like only the roses under Julia's window were real.)

"My Romeo, on-screen and off-," Carmen said lightly.

"Romeo is traditionally unlucky in love," Luke noted. "I don't know if you've read the whole script, but . . . it doesn't end well."

Carmen clasped her hands to her heart. "'Love is never easy—love destroys things. It breaks hearts. It tears apart families. But it is the one thing that makes everything better. Love itself is perfect—it's just that those of us who feel it aren't.'"

Luke laughed and put his arm around her. "If you don't stop quoting your lines at me, I'm going to poison you."

"Like Roman poisons himself! How perfectly in character of you," Carmen said, laughing, too.

It wasn't so hard to pretend to love Luke.

But Laurel, meanwhile, was contemplating candidates for Carmen's next fake love interest—one who'd let himself be filmed for *The Fame Game*. She wanted to set Carmen up with Cayden Taylor, lead singer of The Silver Moons. Carmen had never met him, but he'd been in Laurel's class at Palisades Charter High. He'd recently broken up with his model girlfriend and was—for the moment, anyway—still on the lower rungs of the ladder to fame. "He's hilarious. You'll love him," Laurel had said. "And so will Kate."

"And so will the camera, presumably?" Carmen had asked. "And he'll love it right back, I'm sure."

Laurel had shrugged noncommittally, but Carmen knew the deal. "No thanks," she'd said. "I'm happy in my current fake relationship."

Laurel had been undeterred. (Tenacity was important in a producer.) "Okay, well, I'll keep thinking on it," she'd said. "We want someone who'll film. Do you think I should get a Venti, or will a Grande suffice?"

"Venti with an extra shot," Carmen had said, joking. But Laurel had nodded and ordered it.

"Hey," Luke said now, squinting toward the edge of the set. "Is that—Fawn?"

Carmen turned to follow his gaze. It was Fawn. What was she doing here? Catching sight of them, Fawn waved and hurried toward their perch on the sidelines of the set, nearly turning an ankle in her Rochas platform sandals.

"Hey, you guys," she said, slightly out of breath.

Her cheeks were rosy. And, Carmen noted, she'd gone a little overboard with those Kate Somerville tanning towels she liked so much.

"Hey yourself," Carmen said, hearing the surprise in her voice. "How'd you get in?"

Fawn grinned. "Like a locked set is any sort of challenge for me? I told them I was your new assistant. And look, see, I brought you a coffee! Your favorite: dry half-caf cappuccino from Joan's on Third." She held it out.

"Thanks," Carmen said, touched. "That's so sweet." But then she took it and noted that it felt a little on the light side. "Uh, did you drink half of it?"

"I had like two sips!" Fawn said. "You don't mind, do you?"

"Oh! Um, no, of course not," Carmen said. "Here, have a seat."

Suddenly the air was filled with yelling, as Colum McEntire read the riot act to one of the extras for screwing up his blocking.

"Wow, he's . . . intense," Fawn noted.

"Ya think?" Carmen asked drily.

"His bark is worse than his bite," Luke said mildly.

"I'm not so sure about that," Carmen said. She took a sip of the coffee Fawn had brought her and then made a face. It wasn't even that warm.

"I also brought you the latest issue of *Gossip*," Fawn said, having lost interest in Colum's temper tantrum. "Aren't I thoughtful? You should check out page thirty-nine."

"Why?" Carmen asked, already flipping to it.

Fawn smiled mysteriously. "You'll see."

Fawn had folded down the corner of the page—and, it seemed, spilled coffee on it. A FAMILY AFFAIR, read the large black headline. In the middle of the spread was a picture from the other night, when Carmen and Luke had walked off the movie set holding hands. They were smiling brightly, and they looked, Carmen thought, like an actual couple. Good for them! No one would ever guess they weren't totally in love.

And next to their picture—of course—there was a picture of Cassandra, looking happy and radiantly beautiful. *Cassandra Curtis, in Céline, comes to pick up Carmen,* said the caption.

"Pretty cool, huh?" asked Fawn. "I mean, it's kind of a bummer that your mom's picture is so much bigger than yours, but whatever, right? She's been famous forever."

"Uh, yeah," Carmen said, feeling vaguely annoyed—though at whom, she wasn't quite sure. Her mother? Fawn? Herself for caring that Cassandra's picture was at least thirty percent bigger?

"She's so pretty," Fawn added. "Wouldn't you just kill for that hair?"

Carmen, whose hair was in fact pretty much exactly like her mother's, didn't say anything.

"Do you think she's seen these pictures?" asked Fawn.

"Probably not, since she doesn't read celebrity magazines," Carmen said. She shut the magazine and tossed it onto an empty chair. "God, I have to call her. I owe her like six phone calls."

Thanks to her crazy shooting schedule, Carmen hadn't spoken to her mom since the night she'd just relived in the pages of *Gossip*. Cassandra had probably left her messages, but Carmen had only told her about a million times that she never checked voice mail.

Fawn nodded knowingly. "I bet she wants to talk to you about your lunch."

"What lunch?" Carmen asked.

"Oh, whoops," Fawn said, reaching into her pocket and pulling out a crumpled piece of paper. She made an attempt to smooth it out and then handed it to Carmen. "I had coffee with Laurel and I got your shooting schedule for the week for you. You're having lunch with your mom on Sunday."

Carmen read over the schedule in disbelief. Her mom? On *The Fame Game*? That didn't make sense at all.

For one thing, her parents had specifically said they didn't want to be involved in the show, even though Trevor was dying to feature them. And for another, hadn't Cassandra gone out of her way to talk about this as Carmen's show, and Carmen's chance to shine?

And what the hell was Fawn doing having coffee with Laurel?

"So, what are you up to tonight?" Fawn asked, interrupting Carmen's thoughts. "Do you want to check out Whisper? I heard Girl Talk is going to do a surprise show there."

"Good thing they're keeping it a surprise," Luke joked.

Fawn winked at him. "You can come, too, cutie."

"Actually, Luke and I have a date tonight," Carmen said quickly. They didn't, but they ought to. They hadn't been seen in public together since their photo op, and if they didn't hit the town soon they were as good as broken up in the blogosphere. As Trevor was always telling her, control of information was key.

"We do?" Luke said. "Sounds fun. What are we doing? Going to a secret Girl Talk show?"

But Carmen didn't answer. She was still thinking about her mother. Her beautiful, talented, and media-savvy mother.

Carmen was a rising star, but compared to Cassandra, she was still a small one that didn't sparkle very much. And Fawn was just being Fawn, she guessed. She was grasping at her chance to shine, too. Weren't they all?

Carmen shook her head in wonder. Had her relationships always been this strange?

Luke stood and held his hand out to help Carmen up. "C'mon, fake girlfriend. We've been summoned by his Royal Scariness."

Fawn waved them off. "I'll just sit over here and wait . . . like a good little assistant!" Then she turned and fluttered her eyelashes at the director of photography, who was walking by. "Let me know if you need any extras," Carmen heard her coo.

11

QUIET TIME

"So I had to interview this chef guy—I forget his name, but he has this famous restaurant in New York," Gaby said, her voice slightly muffled by the massage-table headrest. "And he was talking about cooking with foods that people don't normally like to eat. Like sweetbreads. And I was all, 'Duh, of course no one wants to eat sweetbreads. No one in L.A. does carbs or sugar.' And then he looked at me like I was the crazy one."

Madison laughed, then gasped as her masseur dug his thumbs into her lumbar spine. His name was Sven, and he was very strong. "Ow. Sweetbreads aren't sugary bread, Gab," she said. "It's the pancreas from veal." Madison had briefly dated a well-known chef (or, more accurately, she'd been his mistress), so she knew a thing or two about foods that gourmets seemed to love and normal people wouldn't touch. "FYI, that's a baby cow."

A horrified squeak came from Gaby's direction, followed by what sounded like a stifled laugh from Timothy, her masseur. "I think I'm going to throw up into my aromatherapy bowl," Gaby said.

Madison looked down at her own bowl, which Sven had positioned beneath her headrest after filling it with rosemary leaves, cedar needles, and lemon slices—the spa's Rejuvenating Blend.

Personally, she thought it smelled like Pine-Sol. But Madison knew she shouldn't look a gift horse in the mouth; this double massage was part of a whole spa day that Gaby had bought for them. "To cheer you up," she'd said. "To get some good girl time."

Of course it wasn't just girl time—it was also screen time. The PopTV camera was stationed in the corner of the room. And today was the day that Madison would give Trevor what he wanted: She'd talk about What Happened to Charlie. But only for a second. And it would be vague.

Gaby babbled on about her job as a host of *After Dark*, the local late-night show that came on after the late-night shows that people actually watched, and which currently had a viewership of about twenty-five people. Madison listened, gladly welcoming the distraction.

"So then, after the interview, he was like, 'I'm going to get a drink at Sky Bar. Would you like to join me?'" Gaby giggled. "And I was all, 'First of all, what is this? 2003? And second of all, how old are you? Like, forty? Do I look like I have daddy issues?'"

Sven cleared his throat. "May I suggest," he said gently, "a few moments of quiet time? If you focus on your breathing, I can release more of the tension I'm feeling in your muscles."

"Great idea," Madison said. PopTV could just snip out these moments in the edit room. She closed her eyes and inhaled her Pine-Sol aromatherapy.

"Breathe in for three counts and out for six," Sven urged her. "Clear the mind. Let it all out. . . ."

Madison tried to do as she was told—tried to pretend, for a moment, that she was alone and relaxed—but it was impossible to shake the weight of her worry and fear. Her life had been turned upside down. Gone were the days of shopping, of sleeping late, of lounging in a cabana at the Beverly Hills Hotel (or even by the pool in her apartment complex). The invites to Hollywood parties had slowed. Club promoters were now sending her mass texts, like she was some random, semiattractive ho they'd spotted lunching at Urth Caffé. She wasn't some club rat—she was Madison Parker! She had once been paid fifteen thousand dollars to walk into a club, and then was allowed to walk right out the back door. How dare they treat her otherwise? The other night, she'd actually had to wait in line to get into Whisper. It was only for a minute, but still!

Free clothes were no longer arriving on her doorstep daily. She'd become the butt of Twitter jokes: *Hey, designers, no need to send @MissMadParker free clothes: She'll just take them!* And the late-night monologues were even worse. She was a walking punch line. Meanwhile, Madison had noted the complimentary designer duds piling up on Kate's couch. (It wasn't fair: That fantastic velvet mini by Alexander Wang was wasted on that petite Midwesterner. It was one thing to be thin, but pancake butt looked good on no one.)

Nick, her agent, wasn't returning her calls. Avon had canceled her contract to promote GlamourGirl, their newest fragrance. And the endorsement deal for Jergens self-tanner? It had gone to some chick from *America's Got Talent*.

The only emails she'd gotten lately were new-shoe announcements from Endless.com and last-chance adoption notices from Lost Paws. As if going there every day wasn't enough, they'd added her to their mailing list. She suspected Ryan had done it just to mess with her after hours, too. Apparently bursting into tears in front of him hadn't won her any sympathy points.

It was all just so unpleasant; she could feel herself getting more agitated by the second.

"Breathe," Sven whispered.

"You breathe!" Madison blurted. Then she squirmed against the six-hundred-thread-count sheets that were covering her naked body. "Sorry," she said, contrite. "I guess there's still a little more tension to be worked out."

Sven's fingers fluttered at her neck. "People often experience emotional release as a result of bodywork. Because you can feel safe and supported here, you might be able to work through some of the feelings that are causing you tension."

But Madison didn't need to listen to New Age BS from anyone besides Sophie. "What was that you said about quiet time? Let's keep doing that."

"But being quiet is boring," Gaby exclaimed. "I'm about to fall asleep over here."

"Then talk," Madison said. "I just can't guarantee I'll listen."

"I saw your sister yesterday, you know. We met at Runyon for a hike."

Madison grimaced. Runyon was where people went to be seen in their American Apparel crop tops and full makeup while walking their tiny dogs. Then they pretended to be caught off-guard when photographed by the paparazzi who always staked out the base of the hill.

Producers loved locations like this, but Madison knew from experience that filming a hike was usually more effort than the results were worth. The poor cameramen had to hike backward and uphill in front of their subjects, while holding heavy camera equipment and baking in the L.A. heat. Meanwhile the girls would be stopped so often to keep the cameras ahead of them that it'd be impossible to even break a sweat.

"Runyon. How fascinating," Madison said.

Gaby chattered on. "She's taking me to this new vegan place tomorrow. And she wants me to come with her to Kula Yoga. She's going to set up a private lesson for us so PopTV can get it."

Madison gritted her teeth. She was reality TV's reigning

queen—and yet instead of hovering around her, the PopTV cameras were following Sophie all over town. *Here's Sophia shopping! Here's Sophia practicing tree pose! Here's Sophia eating a tofu burger on a sprouted spelt bun while Gaby stares into space, chewing ice! Here's Sophia being barefoot in public!*

Now Madison, too, felt like vomiting into her aroma-therapy bowl. But maybe listening to this was better than what she knew was coming. Any minute, Gaby was going to ask about Charlie so that Madison could say on-camera that he was away on business and she wasn't sure he'd be coming back to L.A. for a while. That would satisfy Trevor's need to wrap up the Madison's Long-Lost Dad story. But for some reason thinking about it made her stomach feel knotted and weird.

"Supposedly her teacher lived in Indonesia for, like, ten years and got enlightened or something," Gaby said.

"So he came to L.A. to teach private lessons on a reality show?" Madison asked. "Yeah, he sounds super-enlightened." She groaned. "Yes, Sven, right there. Ow."

"Have you heard from your dad lately?" Gaby asked suddenly. (She was never any good at segues.)

"Yeah," Madison said, careful to keep her voice casual. "He has some out-of-town business interests, so he had to leave for a little while."

"What sort of business?"

"Just business, Gaby. I'm sure you wouldn't understand the details."

"Is he coming back?"

"Of course. As soon as he can."

That was supposed to be the end of the conversation. But it wasn't.

"How soon will that be?" Gaby asked.

"I don't know," Madison said, her voice chilly.

Gaby sighed. "I know it must be hard, Madison," she said. "It's hard for me, too."

What did she mean by that? Madison would have liked to know. Hard to follow Trevor's instructions to keep going on about Charlie?

"Whatever," Madison said. "Life's hard."

"Can I interrupt to point out the irony of that statement, seeing as how you're in the middle of a ninety-minute massage?" Sven asked.

"No, Sven," Madison said. "This is a private conversation. Just rub my damn shoulders."

"I've been thinking," Gaby said.

"Well, that's new," Madison muttered.

"About those diamond earrings of mine . . ."

Madison tensed again. Maybe she should have expected Gaby to bring them up. But for one thing, Gaby usually stuck to her lines. And for another, what with all the missing diamonds lately, she'd sort of forgotten about Gaby's.

"I had them that day your dad came over, and then I didn't anymore?" Gaby's voice was hesitant.

Madison said nothing, but she could feel her pulse quickening. Was this Gaby's idea? Or had Trevor told her to push the issue?

Gaby sighed. "I've turned my room upside down looking for them, and I sort of have to wonder. . . ."

Madison sat upright suddenly, wrapping the sheet around her body and brushing Sven's hands away. "You know what? This isn't what I signed up for. I give you guys everything. I ask for this one little thing to be left alone, and you can't do it. You have like twenty fucking writers in that room every day. You really can't come up with a better story line?"

No one reacted to the fact that Madison had just broken the fourth wall: The unwritten rule that restricted talent from addressing crew (and vice versa) had just been violated. Still, the camera kept rolling, because everyone knew that this was where most of the best footage came from. When the talent lost their shit. Which was precisely what was happening. The always-composed Madison was about to spiral, and it was exactly what they had all been waiting for. Madison knew this, but she couldn't stop it.

She pointed at Laurel, who was seated in the corner. "This is the best you can do? I don't see you guys addressing Gaby's apparent eating disorder or dependency on pain medication that she clearly no longer needs. Her nose has healed, people! For the second time. And what about the fact that Carmen is pretending to date the guy that Kate was sleeping with? Yeah, that's not worth talking about. Instead, let's focus on poor Madison and her father's disappearing act. Has it ever occurred to any of you that maybe it's none of your business? Why won't you just move on already?" She was screaming by now, and her fists were clenched. She could almost hear her heart pounding in the room that was otherwise utterly silent.

Gaby reached out a hand. "Don't get mad at Laurel. She just—"

"Why are you standing up for her? God, Gaby, you are such an idiot. You think she's your friend? She's not. She's your producer. It's her job to get you to trust her so she can take advantage of you. So she can tell you what to do and say, and you'll do it and say it because you are just that freakin' stupid."

Madison stopped suddenly. What was she doing? She looked around the room. Everyone was staring at her like she was some sort of circus attraction. She needed to get out of there. She reached up and took the diamond studs out of her ears. "Here, just take these and shut up," she said to Gaby.

Then she ripped off the mike that had been taped to her chest, grabbed her clothes and bags, and marched toward the locker room, shoving her mike pack at Laurel's chest on her way out.

The room was silent. And then, as the door shut behind her, Madison heard Gaby say, "Ohhh . . . these are Cartier!"

12

MYSTERIOUS CONTRADICTIONS

"I think you should write a song about working in a restaurant," said Brad, one of Stecco's line cooks. Then, to the tune of Gotye's "Somebody That I Used to Know," he warbled, "Now you're just some parsley that I used to chop. SOME PARSLEY!"

Kate laughed as she stood at the giant stainless steel sink, trying to scrub tiny pieces of that very herb out from under her fingernails. "Oh, I'm sure that'd be a huge hit," she said, reaching for the nailbrush. "Now you're just some chicken that I used to roast," she sang. "SOME CHICKEN!"

Brad made a faux serious face. "Totally," he said. "Girl, you can be a star."

"I'll take that into consideration," she said as the final bits of parsley swirled down the drain. "Meanwhile, I hope that you have loads of fun here. I'm done for the night." She dried her hands and headed for the door that led to the back alley.

"You sure you don't want to meet up with us later?" Brad yelled to her as she left. "We're going to Birds."

"I've got a gig," she called back. "But thanks. I'll see you soon."

Too soon, she thought. Her next shift was the day after tomorrow—a day she'd hoped to spend with Lucinda and a pad of paper, working on another new song.

Her legs hurt from standing for six hours straight, and she'd cut her fingers twice chopping parsley. Though she liked Brad, as well as most of Stecco's other employees, Kate did not enjoy working at the restaurant. (And that was putting it mildly.) She wished that Trevor had let her quit Stecco instead of the Coffee Bean—pulling shots was so much easier than dealing with celebrity diners and stoned busboys.

But, come to think of it, why couldn't she have just quit both? Why did she have to be the only person on *The Fame Game* who had an actual menial job? Gaby's *After Dark* duties were a joke, though her endless aesthetician appointments practically counted as part-time employment. Sure, Carmen was working, but on a huge future blockbuster, so that didn't compare. Madison had her community service, but that was court ordered.

Kate, meanwhile, had been working steadily since she was fourteen years old. Her first gig: babysitting her next-door neighbor's twins, who were undeniably spawns of Satan. Her second: selling hot dogs at the Columbus Zoo. Her third: delivering pizzas in her used Toyota Camry. Or was that her fourth? And then there were those ill-fated months she'd spent as a Denny's hostess. . . .

Whatever. The point was, she'd worked a lot, while certain other people simply sat back and waited for fortune and fame to be served to them on a silver platter. (Which would match the silver spoon that Carmen was born with in her mouth . . .)

The last time she and Trevor had spoken, she'd told him that she was going to quit Stecco. Because where, in her *Fame Game* contract, did it say she needed to work in a restaurant? She certainly didn't need the eight bucks an hour anymore. But Trevor had shaken his head. "You're our 'everygirl.' With your story line, we're highlighting the economic pressures faced by young people."

"I don't want to be your token member of the middle class," she'd retorted.

"But you are," Trevor had said. "And you're going to stay that way."

She wouldn't let it go, though, and so, as a concession, he agreed to let her cut her shifts. Instead of working five days a week, she could work two. But she didn't want to chop herbs any day a week, and she still didn't see why she should have to.

She checked her voice mail as she turned into the traffic of La Brea. She was hoping she might hear from Madison, seeing as how they'd sort of bonded the other night. (Hadn't they?) But the only message was from—surprise!—Ethan Connor, her ex-boyfriend back in Columbus. Though he and Kate still emailed now and then, they never talked on the phone anymore. What could he possibly want?

"Hey, Little Miss Hollywood," Ethan said, and Kate could hear the smile in his voice. "I saw that video you posted on YouTube the other night. You wrote a song about me, huh? Do you miss me that much? Maybe I should come to visit." He laughed. "I liked the line about 'autumn's lonely ache.' It made me think of that fall we took a drive out to Lake Michigan. . . . Well, uh, yeah. Okay. I hope you're doing good. Call me sometime."

Kate stared at her phone as if it might have other information to impart to her. Like: Why in the world did Ethan think that song was about him when they'd broken up ages ago?

But it wasn't a question she could worry about right now. She needed to forget Ethan, and forget Stecco, and just start focusing on her music. She hummed a few notes of "Lost in Love," the song Ethan mistakenly thought was about him. Yes, the line about autumn was nice, and the melody was melancholy and sweet. But it needed some work still. Maybe she'd test it out as part of her set later.

Even thinking the words "set later" made her heart speed up. She wished it were with excitement, but actually it was with a combination of anxiety and dread. She took a few deep breaths and reminded herself that she had a hit song and a lot of fans. Just yesterday, Ryan Seacrest had described her as "cute as a button—a very talented button" before playing her song on his radio show.

Yes, she was going to be fine.

You're going to be fine. You're going to be fine.

She'd been saying that like a mantra for the last three hours, so why wasn't it working? The panic had set in the moment she arrived at the venue and saw her name in big pink letters on the promotional poster. Backstage, waiting to go on, she'd thought she was having a heart attack.

"Breathe deeply," the nice sound guy had said, gently patting her shoulder. "You're going to be great. As soon as you get onstage all your fear is just going to—poof!—vanish."

But of course he didn't know what he was talking about. The adrenaline rushed through her veins; her breath came fast and quick. Her palms were hot and clammy and she could feel the color draining from her face. Her heart literally ached with fear.

Then, all too soon, Kate was alone on the big wooden stage, almost blinded by the spotlights. Almost, but not quite. She could still see the rows and rows of expectant faces. She saw the PopTV cameras positioned about the room. She couldn't see Drew—her lone ally—but she knew that he was somewhere in the wings, rooting for her. She wished she could turn to look. A simple smile would lift her spirits.

She offered the crowd her own faint smile, took a deep breath, and began to play "Starstruck." Her hit, the chorus of which practically every teen girl in America could sing along with. "Lovestruck, starstruck, stuck in all those yesterdays / Holding on as tight as we can before the bright light shines our way. . . ."

As she played, her heartbeat seemed to slow to match the beat of the melody. And—miracle of miracles!—the song went off without a hitch. When it came time for the final chords, she strummed them happily, gratefully. She'd done it. The audience applauded loudly and Kate blushed, wondering if it might be possible for her to actually enjoy a live performance. Maybe she was finally getting over her stage fright.

You're fine, she whispered to herself. *Just fine.*

Her next two songs went well, too. (Her playing wasn't perfect, but it was just fine!) But then the lyrics to her fourth song, the new one about breaking up with Luke, suddenly disappeared from her mind. And unfortunately they did so right in the middle of the first verse, as if they'd been sucked up by some cosmic vacuum. "Lost in love, then lost without you / I just wonder what leaving cost you. . . ."

Oh my God, then what?

Kate had absolutely no idea. Her heart began to pound again, harder this time. She hummed a bridge, her palms beginning to sweat in panic. How did it go? What came next? Strumming, desperately strumming, she wished for a tornado or an earthquake or a fire—anything to get her off the stage.

She glanced to the wings, as if hoping some stagehand

would dash out and pull her off. And that was when she saw Drew, leaning against the backstage scaffolding. He nodded and smiled his big, goofy smile at her. *No big deal,* he seemed to be saying. *It's going to be okay.*

It made her feel a tiny bit better. Barely.

But she still couldn't remember the lyrics to the song.

So, not knowing what else to do, she performed a tricky little key change and began "Starstruck" again. Luckily for her, the spotlights, which seemed to have gotten even brighter, made it impossible to see the confusion that was no doubt on everybody's faces.

When she'd strummed the final chords, she leaned toward the mike. "I had so much fun with that song the first time, I just wanted to play it again." Then she smiled, ducked her head, and fled the stage in humiliation.

She ran right into Drew, who was standing with his arms open. She buried her head in his big, warm chest, so thankful that Laurel had wanted him to be in the audience.

"Oh my God, oh my God," she said. "That was horrible."

Drew held her for a few moments before he said anything. Then he put his hands on her shoulders and pushed her back so that he was gazing right into her eyes. "You were great on seventy-five percent of your songs," he said. "That's not horrible at all!"

"But I screwed up so badly," she wailed.

"Who doesn't screw up once in a while?" Drew asked. "And just think: At least now, no one's ever going to accuse you of lip-synching."

"That's definitely looking at it glass half full," she said, kicking glumly at a mike chord.

"Yeah. It is. And this is just part of paying your dues. Getting better. You should have seen Carmen when she did her first play. She completely blanked on her lines at one point."

Kate didn't say anything. She wondered why Drew had to bring up Carmen so often. Did he feel the need to remind her of the friend hierarchy—that Carmen, "his" Carmen, came first?

"You don't want to be just a studio musician, do you?" Drew went on. "Don't you want to connect with an audience?"

"I guess?" Kate said uncertainly. "In theory?"

Drew laughed and put his arm around her shoulders, leading her past the PopTV crew toward the safety of the green room, where Laurel was waiting for them. (Kate would likely get a sympathy pat from her, too. But it probably wouldn't feel quite so comforting.)

"I love the fact that you're on a huge TV show that millions of people watch every week and you don't seem fazed by it at all," Drew said. "Yet even thinking about being in front of a small room of people makes you break out in hives."

Kate wiped a tear from the corner of her eye and tried to smile. Drew was trying so hard to make her feel better, and in a way, he was. And for that she was really, really grateful. "What can I say, I'm a woman of mysterious contradictions."

He laughed and gave her a squeeze. "You know? I like the sound of that," he said. Then he bent down and kissed the top of her hair, sort of the way a big brother would.

13

FAME IS FAME

Madison plucked a lardon from her frisée salad and placed it gently on her unused bread plate. Lately it seemed like people were putting bacon in everything, and bacon was on Madison's Do Not Eat list, along with white flour, processed sugar, most dairy products, and any sort of crustacean. (Ewww. She dealt with enough bottom-feeders on a daily basis.)

Across the table at Breed, the most recent of the farm-to-table restaurants taking over L.A., Sophie was slicing into what looked like a flattened piece of Silly Putty. Apparently it was something called a tempeh steak. "Fermented foods, like tempeh, kombucha, and kimchi, are excellent sources of probiotics," Sophie said, chewing happily.

"Fascinating," said Madison. She had no interest in Sophie's lectures on nutrition, yoga, crystals, or whatever alternative thing she was into this week. And she was distracted by the glances she seemed to be getting from the restaurant's servers. Madison was used to attention, but not of this particular sort. It reminded her, unpleasantly, of the looks she got after Sophie outed her on *L.A. Candy.* She kept catching the eye of one willowy brunette in particular, who was staring at her as if she ought to be wearing a prison uniform instead of a Chloé blazer.

"Healthy gut bacteria is—"

Madison held up a hand to interrupt her. "Please just stop," she said. How come Sophie was incapable of talking about anything real? Madison needed her support! She was skipping her Lost Paws duties in the wake of her on-camera freak-out, hoping desperately for a sympathetic ear, and Sophie wanted to talk about tempeh.

Madison's phone buzzed in her purse, but she ignored it. She was remembering how, when they were little girls, she and Sophie used to talk and giggle late into the night, tucked into the bunk beds in their tiny trailer bedroom. They'd been best friends and confidantes—for a few years, anyway. Then, more recently (thanks to Charlie's arrival), it had seemed like they might be on their way to getting some of that closeness back.

"I just want you to be healthy, physically and spiritually," Sophie was saying. "I mean, you're blowing off work today. That's not healthy behavior."

"I called in sick," Madison said. "What, I'm not allowed to take a day off from hair balls and kitty litter?"

Sophie shrugged. "All I'm saying is that you might want to consider a change in diet—"

Madison slapped her own forehead in frustration.

"Why is it impossible to have a normal conversation with you, Sophie? Can you quit with the bullshit for, like, five seconds, so that we can discuss the fact that our father betrayed us again? And that I am the only one who seems to be suffering because of it?"

Sophie visibly bristled. "You didn't have to take the fall for him," she said. "That was your own genius idea."

Now that sounded a little more like the Sophie that Madison was familiar with.

Madison pushed at a piece of hard-boiled egg with her fork. "I'm just saying, I could use your support. I don't have anyone else to talk to about this."

"And how would you like me to support you, sister?"

Madison sighed. "You could start with some empathy," she said. "I'm sure you've learned about that in your Buddhist spirituality classes or whatever. Also"—and this mattered more than empathy, frankly—"you could help me get back a little camera time."

A small smile flickered on Sophie's lips. "And how would I do that? It's not like Trevor consults me when he's drawing up the shooting schedule. He thinks about who he wants to see on-camera, and then he films that person. It's as simple as that. I've just been lucky enough to be on his mind a lot lately."

"I'm sure you are," Madison said. "All I'm asking you to do is spread that luck around to your favorite sibling."

"Hmm," Sophie replied. Then she closed her eyes and breathed slowly in and out for half a minute.

Madison drummed her fingertips on the table. What the hell was Sophie doing?

Sophie opened her eyes and took one more deep breath. "I actually wanted to talk to you about that," she said. "It's just . . . well, I hate to add to your problems, Maddy. But since we're on the subject, I think you should know that Trevor's kind of questioning your commitment to the show right now." She paused, frowning with concern. "He might be a little angry with you."

Madison felt the breath catch in her throat. She knew that there would be fallout from storming out of the shoot last night. And here it was. The price for standing up for herself was Trevor's wrath. "So I lost my temper yesterday," she said. "I apologized to Gaby already. I mean, getting mad at her for being dumb is like getting mad at the sky for being blue."

But Sophie didn't laugh. "Maybe you ought to apologize to Trevor, too."

Madison stared down at her hands. Her nail polish was beginning to chip off; she needed a manicure. Badly. And for the first time since she could remember, she couldn't really afford one. "You know what?" she said. "Screw Trevor."

Sophie shrugged. "It's your funeral. I hope you like your newfound anonymity." She held out her fork. "Are you sure you don't want to try a bite of tempeh?"

Madison glanced around the restaurant and once again caught the eye of the brunette server. A table of young men and women also kept looking in her direction. She held her head a little bit higher. "I'm not anonymous—I'm infamous. And fame is fame. Right?"

"I don't know, Madison." Her sister looked up at the ceiling, then directly at her. "Listen, I hate to do this when you're in such a low place—I can feel how negative your energy is—but . . . I can't film with you anymore."

"What?" Madison said. "What do you mean?"

"I just don't think you're good for my image right now," Sophie continued. "I need to be around people who are a more positive influence."

"Are you kidding me?"

"I'm in a sensitive place right now," Sophie said. "Both in my career and in my emotional journey."

"Your career? What exactly is that again?" Madison's fork and knife clattered to the table. "You are so unbeliev-ably selfish," she whispered.

Sophie only blinked her lovely blue eyes. "I hope some-day you'll understand," she said. Then she smiled wistfully and stuck a piece of tempeh in her mouth.

When Madison got home, the apartment was empty—and yet it was far from quiet. The next-door neighbors were having a party again. She sighed. She could hear muffled shouts and bursts of laughter through the wall, which annoyed her. Then someone turned up the ste-reo, and all Madison could hear was the thumping bass of Maroon 5. Even more perturbed, she retreated into her room, shutting the door behind her.

Her bedroom had always been her refuge. Even when she had to share one with Sophie in the Wardell family trailer, she'd kept her half of it perfectly neat and tidy. She'd saved her pennies in order to buy a pretty comforter from Sears, and in the spring and summer she'd always placed a vase of fresh wildflowers on her windowsill.

Her bedroom now was a decorator's dream: walls covered with pale blue vintage wallpaper and contrasted with vibrant pink accessories (her favorites: the matching end tables on either side of her California king bed) and lacquered white accents. The color scheme was bold and glamorous—perfect for someone like Madison.

She'd missed this room, she realized. Living with Charlie had been great (while it lasted), but the furniture and décor she'd rented had never been her style.

She sank down onto the tufted chaise longue and closed her eyes for a moment, trying to let her anger and frustration diffuse. Letting the peace and cleanliness of the room calm her. *Relax,* she thought. *(That ungrateful brat.) No—stop thinking that. Relax. (That faux hippie bitch.) Relax. Like Sven said: breathe.*

Her phone buzzed again, reminding her of the various calls she'd already ignored. The screen showed an unknown number. Was it someone from Luxe, checking to make sure her next payment was coming on time? Was it Andy Marcus, Esq., wondering whether or not she was going to pay the remainder of her bill? Or was it someone from the shelter making sure she was going to show up in the morning? Whoever it was, she didn't want to talk. She let that call go to voice mail, too.

Then she noticed, propped on her windowsill, a legal-sized envelope with her name on it. Next to it was a note from Gaby (*At The Vilige Idiot for happy hour. Come on over!!!! XOXOXO*). Madison crumpled up the note and tossed it into the silver-plated trash can in the corner. She didn't want to go to happy hour. If she'd thought that spending time with people would make her feel better, her lunch with Sophie had proved otherwise.

She gazed at the manila envelope. Was Luxe calling her *and* sending her letters? She sighed again. (She'd been doing a lot of that lately.) As much as she'd like to vanish, she should probably just deal. With all of it.

She decided to listen to the voice mails first. There was one from Laurel, saying she needed to talk about her shooting schedule, since there were changes Trevor wanted her to be aware of. *Great,* Madison thought. Because lately, very few of the changes in her life had been good.

Then there was a message from Kate. "Hey, girl," Kate said. "Heard about your little blowup with Gaby. If it makes you feel any better, my show sucked, too. Call me if you want to commiserate. Talk to you soon. . . ."

The final message confused Madison at first. There was the sound of music in the background, and a murmur of voices. Then came Ryan's voice: "Oh, hello, Madison. I guess you're too sick to pick up the phone. Well. I just called to say that I hope you're feeling better enough tomorrow to come do your job. . . ."

She gritted her teeth. What, she wasn't allowed to take a day off? Why couldn't anyone leave her alone? She was doing the best she could.

Madison hung up the phone and set it on the windowsill beside the envelope. Might as well see what pleasure that was going to bring, she thought, and reached for it.

But inside the envelope was not a bill or a threatening letter from Luxe: It was a DVD, with a Post-it stuck to it.

Here's a rough cut of The End of Love's sneak peek. Before you go storming out of a shoot again, I thought you should see what one of your castmates is up to.

—T.L.

Madison didn't like to be reminded of the movie. At Trevor's insistence, she'd auditioned for a part, bombed completely, and been pity-cast as someone who spoke one line and then died. She hadn't heard anything about the role since, though, and she wondered if she'd been cut before she even had a chance to walk on set.

She got up, propped herself up against a bunch of pillows on her bed, and slipped the disc into the slot on her laptop. For three minutes, she was practically mesmerized.

After watching it, Madison realized two things: (1) It wasn't going to be nearly as terrible of a movie as she had hoped it would be; and (2) Carmen Curtis was a really, really good actor.

It pained her to admit it, but Carmen's talent was undeniable. Madison could accuse her of being a Topanga Canyon silver-spooner, a daughter of Hollywood royalty, and blah blah blah all day long—but she could no longer pretend that the girl wasn't gifted (when it came to acting, at least).

She closed her computer and leaned back against her silk pillows. "Shit," she whispered, as the message Trevor was trying to send dawned on her loud and clear. Carmen was amazing, and Kate was, too (the way she could just riff on melodies, the way lyrics seemed to pop into her head!).

Carmen and Kate were artists. They were devoted to a craft, and they used their gifts to give something to the world. Meanwhile, what did Madison have to offer it besides a crowd-pleasing ruthlessness and an enviable body? What skills did she possess, other than courting publicity? She didn't like to think about the answer to those questions. She'd never had to ask them before, and that, she felt, was how it ought to be.

She closed her eyes. "Shit," she said again.

She thought back to her days in Armpit Falls, and for the first time in years she heard her mother's voice echoing in her mind. *Maddy isn't good at much. Too bad she's not pretty like her sister. Might make things easier for her.* When Sue Beth was especially drunk, she'd blame Madison for Charlie's leaving. *You weren't worth sticking around for. You're just a burden. Every time I look at you, I think about all the mistakes I made in my life.*

Was it any wonder she'd cut off contact with Sue Beth?

Success had a way of silencing those old, cruel voices.

And Madison had come to believe that her career would be long-lasting. She didn't need acting talent; she would create a brand and multiple product lines (clothes! perfumes! lotions! deep-conditioning hair treatments!). Then she'd marry rich and live the life she'd always dreamed of. She had it all figured out.

Maybe now was the time to reconsider this. She was a reality-TV star. Who were the people who'd experienced stardom like hers in the past, and where were they now? Some were spokespersons for off-brand skin-care lines. Some traveled around the country, making appearances at sporting events and county fairs for a few thousand dollars, trying to capitalize on what little recognition they still had. The rest had just simply disappeared. It was sad. But in a way, it was also inevitable. How naïve she'd been to believe she would be the exception.

She sank down farther into the bed, then pulled the downy white covers over her head. No, she was not going to deal anymore. Not tonight. She wasn't going to call Laurel, or Kate, or Ryan. She wasn't going to go drink with Gaby. And she was calling in sick to Lost Paws again. Tonight, Madison Parker was officially out of service.

14

IN A PARTY MOOD

The party was up a narrow, winding road in the Hollywood Hills, and by nine p.m., Carmen could tell it was going to be what Drew liked to call a rager. Even with the crowd still relatively thin, there was a wild, excited energy in the air. Several guys had taken their shirts off—not because they'd been in the pool, but because they felt like it—and by the looks of it, a few girls were getting ready to shed theirs, too.

The truth was, Carmen hadn't wanted to come. She was burned out from filming; her ideal plan for the evening would have involved a book and a bubble bath. And solitude. Sweet, sweet solitude.

But Trevor had arranged for—aka forced—the entire *Fame Game* cast to attend the party, which was being thrown by a friend of Fawn's named Ned something or other. Ned's mother was the last in a long line of Hollywood beauties who now had a skin-care line on HSN and had married the man who had invented the frozen burrito or something. . . . There was some backstory Fawn had mentioned, but Carmen had forgotten it. Fawn was friends with about a million rich party kids, and she was always living it up at some fancy house in the Hills or out in Malibu. It was difficult to keep them all straight.

Carmen had brought along Lily Ray, her makeup artist from *The End of Love*. They'd become friendly thanks to all the time they spent together on set. And since Lily was newly single, she was always looking for something to do.

"This place is huge," Lily said now, looking around the room and nodding approvingly. "This is going to be fun."

Carmen hoped Lily would have enough fun for the two of them.

Though the rest of her castmates were huddled around Laurel, waiting to be miked, Madison was MIA. Laurel, Carmen noted, did not look happy about it. Apparently Madison had had some freak-out the other day while they were filming. She hadn't gotten the full story from Gaby, but she knew that it wasn't very smart of Madison to keep getting on Laurel's bad side. Not that Carmen particularly cared; Mad could dig her own grave if she wanted to. It seemed like she was knee-deep already.

Once miked, Carmen and the rest of the gang were instructed to head out to the pool, since that area had been lit already.

"But it's freezing out there," Gaby whined. All of them were clad in skin-baring outfits, but Gaby's, of course, was the skimpiest.

"It's fall in Southern California, Gaby. It rarely drops below seventy. Besides, the view from up here is beautiful," Laurel said. "Trevor specifically asked for it in the shot."

"But why would we all be hanging out outside on a cold night?" Gaby persisted.

Laurel smiled. "You can't tell it's cold on film, Gaby. Think warm thoughts."

For a while they huddled near the doorway, half-inside and half-out. A band was setting up in the corner of the vast, sunken living room, but for now the music was being provided by a dreadlocked DJ in a Hello Kitty T-shirt. (Carmen prayed he was being ironic.)

Fawn came over, looking excited. "Oh my God, did you see? That's Mink River," she said. "He DJ'd at Paris Hilton's birthday party last year."

"Mink River?" Carmen repeated. "Is that his real name?"

Fawn looked at her blankly. "Um, no?" Then she noticed Lily, who was shyly taking everything in with her large, dark eyes. "Oh," Fawn said coolly, giving Carmen a nudge. "You brought a surprise guest. Aren't you friendly?" She didn't sound pleased.

"Well, I didn't think this was an RSVP kind of thing," Carmen said. "This is Lily. Lily, Fawn."

"Nice to meet you," Fawn said, obviously not meaning it.

Carmen wished that Fawn would be a little nicer, but

she'd always been sort of prickly and possessive. It was just the way she was. In any case, Lily didn't seem to notice. She smiled and shook Fawn's limp hand.

"Do you want something to drink, Carm?" Fawn asked.

Carmen shrugged. "Why not. When in Rome . . ."

"Come on, the bar's over here," Fawn said, pulling Carmen away from Lily and back into the house.

Laurel had requested that the cast members stick together as much as possible; the more shots they were all in the better. But there didn't seem any harm in slipping away for a moment. Certainly any hole that Carmen's absence created in the shot would be quickly filled by other party guests, all of whom were more than eager to sign releases to be filmed.

Half of them were probably hoping they'd be discovered in the footage and contacted to join the cast. It seemed like everyone wanted on the show these days. Between her mother "finally relenting" to be filmed for a lunch date and Fawn showing up whenever the cameras did, Carmen was beginning to feel like a pawn in *The Fame Game*—in more than the intended way. It was ironic that the one person she wouldn't have minded being forced to hang out with on camera still didn't want to be anything more than a peripheral presence on the show; Luke was still not interested in that part of her life.

"Here," Fawn said, shoving a red cup at her. "This will put you in a party mood. Now let's go back and find your friends."

My friends, Carmen thought wryly. Even though they'd been spending eight to twelve hours a day together, she didn't know Lily that well outside of work, and these TV-show girls weren't really her friends, either, were they? Sophia's only true friend was her own reflection; Gaby was wrapped around Jay, who definitely needed to lay off the Drakkar Noir; and as for Kate . . . Well, Carmen still didn't know what was going on there. She'd planned on going to Kate's show the other night, but Colum had kept everyone until midnight again. She'd heard from Drew that it hadn't gone well (which was confirmed by a quick check of the gossip blogs), and that it was all caught on film. Poor Kate. She had to deal with that stage-fright issue.

Fawn took hold of Carmen's hand and led her back toward the cast (and the cameras). Then she proceeded to position herself right in the sight line of the nearest lens. She acted as if she didn't know it was there, but she obviously did. She kept touching her hair, the way a girl does when she's trying to flirt. *The camera's not a guy, Fawn,* Carmen wanted to say. *You can stop tossing your head like a pony.*

Lily had fallen in love with the way the house was decorated and had vanished to go Instagram it room by room, and Kate was the only other person who seemed to be having a good time—as long as she wasn't talking to Carmen, that is. When they'd first arrived at the party, Carmen had told her how cute she looked. Kate had acted surprised at first, and then had barely huffed out a surly "thanks" before turning away and striking up a conversation with Gaby. It was sort of how their last break-fast shoot had gone. Once they'd covered the ground they were supposed to—a mention of Kate's upcoming performance and, weirdly, whether either of them knew where Madison's dad had disappeared to—Kate had looked over at Laurel and said snottily, "Okay, are we done now?" Clearly Carmen's emailed apology (*I never meant to hurt you or be dishonest with you, and I hope that we can get past this,* etc.) had not done its intended job.

But Kate was looking pretty happy tonight. And as the party progressed, she got tipsier and tipsier, until eventually she had a champagne bottle gripped in one hand and the bicep of a tall blond guy in the other. "Oh my God," she was saying, "the baked crab handroll at Katsya is to die for. Have you been? No? Shut up! We have to go there tomorrow. Seriously. We're all going!"

She was flushed and giggling and flirty. Didn't she used to claim she was shy? She certainly wasn't acting like the Kate that Carmen and Drew had met back at the open mic at Grant's Guitar Shop. As Carmen watched Kate knock back another cocktail, it occurred to her that Kate was acting more like the girls who Carmen had gone to high school with—girls who she'd never really liked that much.

Carmen could feel herself getting judgmental, so she tried to put herself in Kate's position. How weird it would be, to be plucked from utter obscurity (well, there was that YouTube video, but there were belching five-year-olds with more views than her) and then thrust into one of the brightest spotlights imaginable: your outfits critiqued, your private life speculated about, your every offhand remark televised for an eager nation. Your song loved and sung and hated and parodied. Your friend publicly dating your secret ex. Your breasts and abs and cellulite discussed in public forums. Your live performance skewered on Twitter and Tumblr. (There was already a gif of Kate with the caption *Oops, I forgot my own song!*) Kate's mind was probably being blown every single day. So it was understandable that she was acting a little crazy. And maybe, too, she wanted to shed a bit of her innocent, good-girl image; maybe she wanted to show Trevor and, by extension, the rest of the country, that she wasn't just some naïve girl from a flyover state.

That didn't seem so unreasonable to Carmen. And at least Kate still had her shirt on.

Carmen felt an arm wrap around her waist, and she looked up to see Reeve Wilson, whom she'd met on the set of a music video back when she was in high school.

"Well, if it isn't Little CC," he said, giving her a big sideways hug. "How the hell are you? I haven't seen you in ages."

Carmen laughed, surprised and happy to see him. "I don't know if you've read any of the headlines lately, but I'm quote-unquote 'not Little CC anymore.'"

Reeve took a step back. "What do you mean?" he asked, acting shocked.

She rolled her eyes. "Oh, for God's sakes, Reeve, I

know you're, like, all indie and whatnot, but please don't tell me that you've never seen a copy of *Gossip* in the grocery store or heard about the show."

He put his hand over his heart. "I don't own a TV," he said. "My mind is pure."

"If your mind was pure, you wouldn't be at this party," Carmen retorted.

He clinked his glass to hers. "Touché," he said. "So wait—what is this thing you mentioned?"

"I don't actually want to talk about it," she said. "But basically I'm on TV. And well . . . so are you." She motioned to the closest camera. "I mean, I assume you signed a release to come into the party."

"Oh, was that what that was? I didn't know they were here for you. They handed me a piece of paper and I signed. I just needed to get to the bar."

"You shouldn't make a habit of signing things you don't read," she said. "Consider that my Friday-night PSA."

Reeve sighed. "I know, I know. My dad's a lawyer. He has two rules: Don't sign anything you don't read, and don't make a sex tape."

"By the look on your face I'm guessing you broke both of them," Carmen said.

"I plead the fifth," said Reeve. "Did I mention how fantastic you look?"

Carmen felt herself flush, even though Reeve was a congenital flirt and meant probably ten percent of the compliments he paid. "Thanks," she said. "You're looking pretty good yourself."

Just then a guy with a shaved head walked up and clapped Reeve hard on the shoulder. "Wilson, dude," he said. "I've been looking for you. That chick Stacy—" At this moment, he noticed Carmen. His eyes lit up. "Oh, hey," he said. "You look familiar. I know you. Were you at Damien's party the other night?"

Carmen shook her head firmly. "No, I was not."

Reeve introduced them. "Carmen, Vic. Vic, Carmen."

"Pleasure," Carmen said insincerely. There was something about Vic that rubbed her the wrong way immediately. (Maybe it was the leer he gave her, or maybe it was the wallet chain hanging from his way-too-skinny jeans.)

Vic reached out and took Carmen's hand and kissed it. "Delighted," he said. He gave her hand another kiss for good measure, and might have gone for number three if she hadn't tugged her hand away. "Dude," he said to Reeve. "Your friend is hot."

"Dude," Reeve said. "She can hear you, you know. But I agree with you. She's smokin'."

Carmen laughed. She had to admit, she sort of liked the attention. And she was happy to see Reeve Wilson again, who had given her her first Death Cab for Cutie album.

"Wait a second," Vic said, suddenly looking as if a lightbulb had been turned on in his mind. "You're Carmen Curtis."

Carmen ducked her head. "Guilty as charged."

"You're starring in that Romeo-and-Juliet movie."

Carmen nodded again.

"Oh, wow," Reeve said. "That's the director who fired Rio Lockhart. He's supposed to be a total dick."

"Well—" Carmen began. She had to be careful what she said, since the other day she'd received a grumpy phone call from Trevor Lord about a TMZ item he'd come across. CARMEN CURTIS THE LATEST TO CALL COLUM MCENTIRE "ASSHOLE"? the headline had read.

"We cannot have things like this popping up on the internet," Trevor had said sternly. "So watch your mouth, all right?"

Carmen didn't specifically remember calling Colum an asshole, but probably, in a moment of frustration, she had. Not to him, of course, but maybe behind his back. So the question was: Who would have been around to hear it? And who would have then speed-dialed TMZ? That was the mystery.

"Dude," Vic said. "Aren't you dating Luke Kelly? Your costar?"

"Well," Carmen said again.

But Reeve wrapped his arm around her waist. "Who cares about Luke? Love the one you're with!"

And Carmen, banishing all thoughts of TMZ and Colum McEntire, had to laugh. She had been so busy lately she had forgotten how much fun male attention could be. Unsurprisingly, her fake relationship had been preventing her from having a real one—and until she ended it, that wasn't going to change. Even if she tried to secretly date someone for real, the second they were spotted together she'd look like she was cheating on Luke.

"You know," Reeve said, smiling at her, "I always had the biggest crush on you. It's too bad you have a boyfriend—otherwise I'd love to take you out sometime."

Carmen flushed. Maybe it was the questionable cocktail she had just finished, or maybe it was her resolution to be more honest, but in that moment, she knew what she had to do.

Not only would it clear the air with Kate, it would also score her points with Trevor. He'd be thrilled if she filmed a romantic evening or two, and it would get him off her back about how busy she'd been lately. And now that Carmen thought about it, Reeve would be perfect to film with. He was charming and funny, and he would look great on camera (at least for a couple dates).

"Well, it's a good thing I don't have a boyfriend, then." Carmen smiled back at him. "Gossip magazines love a good on-set romance, but Luke is just a friend."

Reeve looked surprised at first, and then happy. "So . . ." he began.

Carmen held up a hand. "I'll be right back," she said. "Don't go anywhere."

She ducked and wove through the groups of party guests until she found herself in a small, quiet room off the back of the house, its walls painted dark gray and hung with black-and-white photographs. It was then that she remembered: Ned was both a frozen-burrito heir and the son of a famous photographer. Before dialing, she reached around to the mike pack secured to her waistband and flipped the power switch off. She gazed at a picture of a forested gulch, sliced through by train tracks, as she waited for Luke to pick up his phone.

"Looooover," he said when he answered.

"Dude, I thought we were done with that word," she said.

"Did you just call me 'dude'?"

"I didn't mean to. Someone here at the party kept saying it. That word is like a communicable disease."

"I'm sure they have an antidote for that. What's up?"

"Well, actually—I have to break up with you."

"What?" He sounded genuinely surprised.

"I can't do this fake-dating thing anymore. It's not fun for me."

"I'm insulted," he said teasingly. "I'm such a good looooover."

"Seriously—"

Luke interrupted her. "But haven't we been over this? The publicity is good for both of us."

Carmen paused. Yes, they had been over it. And she'd felt funny about it then, as well. "I just don't want to play the game right now. I want my fake life to look more like my real life. Doesn't that make sense?"

Luke laughed. "Poor you! It's all so complicated, isn't it?"

She bristled slightly. "I'm playing three roles here," she said. "Julia. Carmen on *The Fame Game*. And Carmen in my own life. So yes, it is complicated."

Luke sighed dramatically. "All right. Well, I can't force you to stay in our fake relationship. But do me a favor, okay? Let the breakup be mutual. My agent says I might be in *People*'s Fifty Most Beautiful People issue, and I don't want the blurb about me to say something about how you broke my heart. Okay? Because that would sort of dent my reputation."

This sounded reasonable enough to Carmen, so she agreed. They chatted for another minute or two and then said good-bye.

"Have a nice time at the party, ex-looooover," Luke said. "See you tomorrow. . . ."

The moment she hung up, she emailed Sam, so she could feed the news to *Gossip* or another weekly. She used the words "amicable" and "friends" and said something about them both wanting to focus on their careers.

Then she hurried back out to join the party. (She'd gotten a text from Laurel: WHERE R U??) Reeve was nowhere to be seen, so Carmen went right up to Kate. "I broke up with him," she blurted. "The fake relationship between me and Luke is over for real."

And Kate gave her a giant, drunken grin and flung her arms around Carmen's neck. "I'm ssso glad to hear that," she slurred. "You're the bessst."

Carmen smiled and hugged her back. They were friends again.

She just hoped that when tomorrow came, Kate would remember that.

15

A MUCH BETTER PLACE

Kate sat in the waiting room at Beverly Hills Medical, biting her nails and fidgeting. After her disastrous show the other night, Trevor had summoned her to his office for a "quick check-in." And quick it was: She'd sat in traffic for over an hour to get to a meeting that lasted all of fifteen minutes.

"Kate," he'd said, not without sympathy. "Your stage fright isn't going to magically disappear. You need to deal with it. For the show, and for your career. I know you're getting calls from record labels—you should get a manager, by the way—but you're never going to have a career if you can't sing in public."

What Trevor didn't say (because he didn't need to—Kate could hear it in his voice) was that he might have picked a different girl for *The Fame Game* had he known that public performances turned Kate Hayes into a quivering mess.

But in her defense, she hadn't known how bad it was

going to be. Back when she was auditioning for the show, stage fright hadn't affected her that much because she didn't go onstage that often. Now that performances were a part of her life—a necessary part of her life—it was starting to have a bigger impact. In addition to the preperformance panic attacks, she also had postperformance insomnia. And the sudden fame certainly wasn't helping anything.

So Kate had taken Trevor's words, spoken and un-, to heart; she resolved to conquer her fears. On film (naturally). He and Laurel had mapped it all out for her. Day One of Operation Eliminate Stage Fright was meditation class, in which she and three other people lay in a circle, their eyes closed, and listened to the sound of a waterfall while a woman told them to visualize their fears as clouds of dense, thick smoke, and then breathe the smoke out "into the farthest reaches of space." Day Two was acupuncture, which—contrary to what everyone said—hurt. When the guy put a needle in Kate's Heart Five spot (which for some reason was on her forearm), she yelped in pain. "Breathe it out," he'd urged. Kate felt like sticking him with one of his own needles. "That's what the meditation lady said," she'd huffed. Day Three was yoga, which was fine but hardly life-changing, followed by EFT, which stood for Emotional Freedom Techniques. This involved tapping herself on various pressure points while talking about how she loved and accepted herself despite her fears and anxieties. She'd had a hard time keeping a straight face for that one.

Maybe, just maybe, some of the things would have been helpful. But how was Kate supposed to relax into her meditation with PopTV cameras filming her? Did Trevor truly think she could tap her way to emotional freedom with a giant lens in her face? She needed privacy, for one, which maybe she could get, and time, which she couldn't.

She explained this to Laurel, who had nodded knowingly and given Kate Dr. Garrison's number. "Psychiatrist to the stars," Laurel had said. "He'll know how to take care of you."

So here she was in the pale-blue-and-cream waiting room, hoping for a solution that would work a lot faster. And she was alone for once: Apparently PopTV drew the line at filming psychiatric evaluations.

She gazed at a signed photo of Shaun White on the waiting-room wall and wondered what sort of doctor would choose a picture of a professional snowboarder for his office décor. Did that say anything about his medical competence? Or was it just a reflection of his interest in extreme sports, or even his questionable decorating taste?

She was still mulling this over when the doctor called her into his office. He was in his late fifties, probably, but dressed more like he was in his early thirties, and his hair was messy with product. He held out his hand. "I'm Dr. Garrison." Then, studying the paperwork in his hand, he said, "And you're Kate Hayes."

"That's me," she said, feeling suddenly more nervous.

He motioned for her to sit down. In contrast to the

sterile waiting room, Dr. Garrison's office was full of books and bonsai plants; it looked like it should belong to a college professor. "It's nice to meet you. So tell me. What can I do for you today?"

Kate picked at a cuticle until she recalled that her manicurist had scolded her for the habit. "Well, I'm filming a show," she began.

Dr. Garrison nodded encouragingly.

"And it's a lot of work, a lot of pressure, a lot of everything." She proceeded to tell him about the anxiety she felt buzzing through her veins—a buzz that turned into a roar whenever she got near a stage. That was definitely the worst thing. But there were plenty of other complications: She felt far away from her family; she owed Natalie about twenty phone calls; and she still couldn't help thinking about Luke. Sure, he was officially single now, but she was still on his manager's Do Not Publicly Date list.

Speaking of dating, Trevor was still pushing Kate to find a love interest; he'd said, his voice all paternal-sounding, that she needed a little romance in her life. But that, she quickly learned, was code for the fact that *The Fame Game* was lacking romance in its episodes.

And as if that weren't enough, there were all the relationships with her costars to navigate. Like, did drunkenly making up with Carmen mean things were suddenly good between the two of them? And what was up with Madison? Why wasn't she returning Kate's phone calls . . . again?

Kate was on a roll—she could have kept going for

hours. But then she saw Dr. Garrison glance at his watch. She wrapped it up quickly after that. "So, um, yeah," she said, then looked down at her feet. "It's mostly the stage fright, but then it's everything else, too, y'know? Well, I guess I was hoping you'd have something that could help me with the anxiety."

Dr. Garrison sat down on the edge of his desk and looked at her intently. "There are certainly ways in which anxiety can be medically addressed," he said. "But let me ask you, have you first tried any behavioral coping strategies?"

"What does that mean?" Kate asked, confused.

"Behavioral coping strategies. Things such as yoga. Meditation. Exercise."

Kate laughed. "Yeah. I tried them all. It wasn't really helping." Was he going to send her home with a prescription for yoga? Because she was pretty sure she needed something stronger.

Dr. Garrison nodded. "Life's taken a slightly different turn than you expected, huh?" he asked.

"Has it ever," Kate said.

"Well, let's give you a little something for the stage fright. Some people like beta-blockers, but I only give those to my cat. She has heart problems." He wrote something on a piece of paper.

Kate nodded as if this made sense to her. "Great," she said. "I really appreciate it." Then she flushed slightly. What was there to appreciate? It wasn't like he was doing her a favor; he was simply performing the duties of his profession.

"Xanax will also help you with the day-to-day stresses that you're understandably experiencing," he said. "It'll put you in a much better place. Is there anything else you need?"

Kate suddenly felt so relieved that she said, "I don't know. Do you have a lollipop?"

Dr. Garrison looked at her blankly.

"My pediatrician used to give me lollipops," she said. "I was just trying to make a joke."

His smile was thin. "Check with the receptionist," he said. "I was referring to other psychological issues you might be experiencing. Any trouble sleeping? Sometimes that comes with anxiety."

Kate nodded. "Yes, now that you mention it. I do have a hard time sleeping. Is there something for that, too?"

"We have something for everything," Dr. Garrison said. And just like that, he handed her another prescription. "Enjoy," he said. "But not too much."

On her way out of the medical building, Kate, feeling better already, decided to focus on the upside of everything. For one thing, the weather in L.A. was amazing. It was October and seventy-five degrees! For another, her music was going really well, at least in private. She and Drew were hanging out more and he'd offered to help her with some songs. He was back in school at UCLA now, but he was still interning part-time at Rock It! He said that once they got a few songs recorded, he would take them to his bosses and see what they thought. If they wanted to sign her, it'd be a big deal for both of them. Scratch that—a huge deal. (Rock It! was her dream label, but so far they hadn't exactly been knocking down her door. She knew Carmen's dad wasn't a fan of *The Fame Game*, but that wouldn't prevent him from offering her a deal if he genuinely liked her songs, would it?)

Then Trevor could hardly complain about Kate finally getting her way and quitting Stecco, because a newly signed recording artist would never keep her waitress job. Of course, she had to film a few "working" scenes there in the meantime to make it seem like she was still employed there. Laurel said that Bill Shapero, Stecco's owner, was giving them a break on location fees for the continued exposure.

In the bright fall air, Kate squinted against the glare of the hot sun on sidewalks and car hoods. She reached into her bag for her sunglasses, couldn't find them, and realized that she'd lost yet another pair, which put her loss total at six pairs in three months. She wondered if there was a way to surgically connect them to her body; it seemed like the only way she'd ever hold on to them.

She noticed a sunglasses shop halfway down the block and decided she could treat herself to a new pair. She was headed in the direction of the store when she heard someone shout her name.

"Kate," cried a girl's voice. "Kate Hayes!"

Expecting to see someone she knew, Kate turned around quickly, a smile on her face. But instead of a friend, she saw a group of three high-school girls, practically hopping up and down in excitement.

"Oh my God," said the tallest one. "It's you! I can't believe it's you." She turned to her friends. "You guys, can you believe it? I told you it was her!" Then she turned back to Kate. "You're so pretty! Can you please take a picture with us?"

Kate flushed and stammered. "Ah—sure—wha—where . . . ?"

The girls quickly gathered around her excitedly, a couple of them wrapping their arms around Kate. (Apparently personal space wasn't something that concerned them much.) One girl stood back and quickly took their photo with her iPhone. They all smiled, and before Kate had even looked at the camera, the girl glanced down at the screen and nodded, letting her friends know that she'd gotten the shot.

"Oh my God, you are the best," gushed the tallest one, who was apparently the only one gifted with speech. "You're totally my favorite on *The Fame Game*. Team Kate!"

"Team Kate!" echoed the other girls.

And just as quickly as they had materialized around her they were gone, rushing off in a fit of giggles.

Kate paused before continuing on to the sunglasses

shop. It was an odd feeling. None of the girls had introduced themselves, and only one had made eye contact with her. They really only seemed interested in getting a photo that they could upload to their Facebook profiles within minutes, if it wasn't there already. *I mean, they couldn't even wait for me to smile at the camera,* she thought indignantly.

She shook off the slight, though, and went into the store. She found two pairs of large, dark sunglasses, and alternated trying each one on, deciding which pair she liked more. Then she shrugged. She was on a hit television show. It was time she start acting like it.

She grabbed both pairs and walked toward the register. While Kate waited for the clerk to acknowledge her existence, she glanced at the cover of the magazine the girl was reading. There was a little picture of Luke and Carmen with a jagged line running between them. *The end of love in more ways than one,* the caption read.

"Good news travels fast," she muttered.

The clerk looked up. "Huh?" she asked. "Oh, hey, can I help you?" She seemed profoundly bored.

Kate smiled at her. Unlike the three girls outside (who had returned and were peering in the window at her), this one had no idea who she was. Which was fine with Kate. She had two new pairs of designer sunglasses and a fresh prescription that was going to solve all her problems. She felt like kind of a badass.

16

A BAND-AID ON A BULLET WOUND

Connie Berkley, a community service supervisor for the L.A. County court system, fixed Madison with a steely gaze. "Three days," she said. "Three days." She knocked her hand against a manila folder, which, Madison presumed, contained her Lost Paws attendance and performance reports.

Madison gazed at the wall above Connie's head. Why was it that all government offices had to be painted the same horrible shade of beige?

"Do you have anything to say for yourself?" Connie asked.

"I was sick," Madison said.

Connie raised her eyebrows. "Too sick to return a call from your supervisor?"

"Yes. Deathly ill."

Madison hadn't actually been sick, of course—or at least not suffering physically. It was more that she was sick of life: sick of *The Fame Game* (and frankly, a little sick of the fame game . . .). Sick of Lost Paws. Sick of her money problems, of Sophie, of the decision she'd made to take the blame for Charlie . . . and sick, in the end, of herself. All she could do was lie in bed and watch reruns of *The Golden Girls*.

"May I be blunt, Miss Parker?" Connie asked.

Madison shrugged. Connie could be whatever the hell she wanted to be and it wasn't going to change the fact that Madison felt like shit.

"I've worked here for ten years," Connie said. "I used to see only regular people. And by regular people, I mean regular lawbreakers. You know, guys who stole their girlfriend's mom's minivan and used it in a robbery attempt. Girls who got drunk and smashed their car into a building. Normal people doing normal bad stuff." She leaned back in her chair. "But now, you know who I see? People like you. A new one every month, it seems. People whose money and fame goes to their heads and screws them all up." She circled her finger around her ear. "It makes you crazy," she whispered.

Madison yawned. Was it possible that time moved slower inside a government building?

"Oh, so is what I have to say that boring?" Connie said, an edge coming into her voice. "Let me tell you something. I know your kind and I don't think too highly of them. But, as a decent human being, I feel it's my duty to try to impart a little bit of the wisdom I've gathered in my fifty-three years."

"Funny, you don't look a day over fifty-two." Madison smirked.

Connie ignored this. "Point number one: The rules always apply. You may get special attention at 'the clubs,' but the law gives preferential treatment to no one."

"I think there are quite a few people who would disagree with you on that," Madison noted.

Connie held up a hand. "Listen! Don't talk. Point number two: Everything comes to an end. Beauty. Fame. All good things do, it's like the saying goes. Point number three: Be prepared. That comes from the Boy Scout handbook, but people ought to tattoo it on their foreheads. Especially people like you. What I'm saying, Miss Parker, is that you better get your shit together. Find a skill. Do something with yourself. You've been on three reality shows. Is that what you're planning on doing with your life? Are you aiming for *The Real Housewives of Reality TV*? Then maybe *Plastic Surgery Nightmare*? Don't be one of those women, Madison. You're smart—I can see that." She held up the manila folder. "Even your supervisor has a note in here about you being more on-the-ball than he'd expected. Do something worthwhile with that brain of yours. It's probably the one thing that's real about you, the one thing that hasn't been enhanced or altered to fit some Hollywood ideal."

Still processing the fact that Ryan had written something almost-nice about her—a backhanded compliment was still a compliment—Madison looked at Connie with a mixture of anger and grudging respect. It wasn't any of Connie's business what she did with her life. But the woman was voicing some of the very thoughts she'd been trying to ignore the past few days.

It made her wonder what it'd be like to have a mother who actually gave her advice. Well, advice that she could listen to.

Connie was on a roll. "Do you know who Marlise Simone is?" she asked. "No? Well, that just goes to show you. She was huge five years ago—she was on one of those MTV shows. And then she got into drugs, and then she got into shoplifting. And then she got caught. And now she's back at home, living in her parents' basement. In Wyoming." Connie looked at Madison intently. "That's cautionary tale number one, and I have a whole book of them. Care to hear more?"

Madison shook her head. "No thank you," she said.

"What about Iris Williams? She didn't get in trouble with the law, so I haven't met her personally, but I read the magazines. Anyone can see that she had an unfortunate run-in with her plastic surgeon. She's got a pair of lips like a duck bill and I'm sure it's because she thought her mouth looked small on television. Now nobody will hire her." Connie reached out and poked Madison's hand. "This stuff warps you," she said.

Madison offered Connie a small, tight smile. "I'm not going to be like those girls," she said. "Some of us escape unscathed."

Connie looked doubtful. "I'm gonna say you're already scathed. What with this criminal record and all."

Madison stood. "Listen, I do appreciate your taking the time to lecture me. But can we be done now? Consider me duly warned. I'll be back at Lost Paws on Monday, ready to work."

"Good," Connie said. "Because I don't want to see you again."

"Believe me, the feeling is mutual," Madison said.

Madison sat curled on her couch, paging through one of the old photo albums that Sophie had brought with her from Armpit Falls. Only weeks ago, Madison had regarded the album as a prop—just some old thing for her, Sophie, and Charlie to gather around while the PopTV cameras filmed them trying (and mostly failing) to recall some shared happy memory. But now she looked through the pictures more carefully, and more sadly.

There she was, age six, perched on top of a slide at the park behind the supermarket; there she was at seven, proudly holding up a ribbon she'd won at her school's Field Day; and there she was at eight, fixing a dinner of Hamburger Helper while her mom was out of frame, smoking in her La-Z-Boy. (Sophie, age five, had taken the picture; the focus was terrible.)

If Madison had stayed—if she'd never run away, never renamed and remade herself, never set her eyes on fame and fortune—she'd probably still be in that trailer park; if not living with her mom, then living a few doors down. If she thought her life sucked now, she should think about that for a moment.

But this exercise in comparison didn't make her feel better for long. Madison had begun facing an ugly truth. She left her home because she wanted to be somebody. But what, exactly, had she made of herself? She was fake: all surgery, fillers, and extensions. She was silicone and acrylic and paint and dye.

She set her jaw defiantly. Frankly, she could deal with that stuff. She'd chosen it, and she wasn't sorry. A girl did what a girl had to do to get ahead.

But she didn't like being a criminal in the eyes of the world. She hated the position that Charlie had put her in. That she'd let him put her in.

And she felt utterly alone. In the past, she could have given one single come-hither look to a rich man, and within the hour she'd have companionship, gifts, whatever she wanted. But she didn't know any guys who wanted a convict for a girlfriend.

She put her head in her hands. *Alone,* she repeated. *Alone.* She wished she had someone to call. But that was just one of the prices she paid to be Madison Parker: She didn't let people get close, and if she did, she didn't let them stay for long.

She was gazing at a picture of herself and Sophie standing on a tall snowdrift beneath a clear blue sky. They were waving at the camera, Madison wearing only a sweater because she'd outgrown her coat and Sue Beth hadn't managed to get her a new one. Madison remembered the cold brightness of that day—how they had come into the trailer, noses red with cold, and Sue Beth, in a moment of rare maternal concern, gave them a hot chocolate and ran a warm bath.

"Oh, look at you! That picture is so cute!"

Madison started: She hadn't heard Gaby come in. She closed the album. "Yeah, well," she said, "it was a long time ago."

"I can't believe you grew up with snow," Gaby said, giggling. "That's so . . . freaky." Gaby had never been east of Las Vegas or north of Big Sur.

Madison noticed that her roommate's eyes were oddly glassy. "Gaby, are you on something?"

"Oh, yeah, maybe something," Gaby said, weaving a little. "I forget. It's a blue pill. Jay gave it to me."

Madison frowned. "Why?"

"He said I was being uppity and I needed to take a chill pill." She flopped down onto the couch and closed her eyes.

"He did not say that." Madison didn't think it was possible to dislike Jay any more, but here she was, wrong about something else.

"His exact words," Gaby said with a little laugh, letting her head fall back against the cushions. "He went out, though. So now I'm nice and chilled and he's not even here."

She gave an exaggerated pout and slowly slid down until she was lying on the couch. In another moment, she was asleep, with her shoes still on. Madison looked at her frail roommate and remembered when they first met. Gaby had been a girl-next-door type herself, with a healthy figure and a closet full of button-downs. Now she lay with her thin arms crossed and goose-bumped, a shadow of her former self. What had happened to the sweet, not-too-bright girl who just wanted to have a good time and gossip about boys?

Madison stood up, pulled a cream-colored chenille throw from the couch, and placed it over Gaby. Then she picked up Gaby's Balenciaga off the ground and fished out several prescription bottles. She made her way into her bathroom and opened her medicine cabinet to survey her various supplements. After a moment, she carefully selected a few. Then she emptied each of the bottles she'd taken from Gaby's purse and replaced them with the supplements she thought most resembled the pills: some vitamin C, a little vitamin D, and some baby aspirin. She secured the tops back onto each bottle, walked back into the living room, and slipped them back into Gaby's purse.

She knew this was only a gesture—like placing a Band-Aid on a bullet wound. But maybe it would slow Gaby down a little. (This little trick had worked sometimes on Sue Beth Wardell once she developed her taste for Vicodin.)

Madison gave the covers over Gaby one more little tug

so that she'd stay warm, and then, after watching her sleep for a moment, she slipped on a pair of sandals and left the apartment.

She didn't know where she was going; she just walked. A moment later, she found herself inside the wrought-iron gates of the Park Towers pool. It was late, and no one else was around. The deck chairs were empty, the umbrellas closed for the night. The still water was glowing turquoise. It looked beautiful. Clean.

Madison never swam in pools. Chlorine was bad for the skin, and water messed up the hair and makeup. But almost before she knew what she was doing, she had stripped down to her underwear (a lacy black La Perla set). She stood for a moment on the pool's tiled edge—then she dove in.

The water was a delicious shock to her skin; it felt somehow both warm and cool at the same time. She swam almost the whole length of the pool before surfacing, gasping and shaking water droplets from her hair. It was amazing—why had she never been in it before? She ducked under again, swimming down until she touched the bottom, and then rocketing back up. The night was silent except for the sound of the splashing water and the song of one lone cricket. For an hour, Madison swam from one end of the pool to the other, feeling almost as if the water was washing her clean of sadness.

17

PLAYING TO THE CAMERAS

It was one of Carmen's rare days off from *The End of Love*, but instead of spending it in bed, or on a hammock by a pool, or anywhere else she could be idle and horizontal, she was hurrying to meet her mom for lunch at Saburo's in WeHo. And PopTV would be there to capture this loving family moment. . . . Ugh. She still couldn't believe that after everything her dad had said about the show, and all the objections he'd raised to it, that her mother was going to be on it. When she'd tried to talk to her mom, Cassandra had acted like she was doing Carmen a huge favor by deigning to be on the show, and that, like their legendary shopping sprees, it was one more thing they had together that Philip would never understand. Carmen hadn't known how to tell her that wasn't exactly how she saw the situation, but now definitely wasn't the time to bring it up again.

First, though, she would be getting a phone call from Fawn. Laurel hadn't told her what it was about, just that it was part of the day's filming.

She was walking toward the restaurant entrance when Fawn called. "Hey, Fawn," Carmen said. "I'm just heading to lunch. What's up?"

"You've got to check out *D-Lish*," Fawn said, sounding even more excited than usual. "There's a bunch of pictures from that party in the Hills we went to."

"Really? Pictures from the party?" Carmen asked, dropping her car keys into her purse. She knew to repeat what Fawn said, since Fawn's side of the conversation wasn't being filmed. "On *D-Lish*?" She was interested, of course, but it wasn't like she'd never been in party pictures before.

"Yeah, check 'em out now," Fawn said. "Love you! Bye!"

Carmen pulled up the website on her iPhone. The pictures were right at the top of the page—and they were horrible. Carmen gasped. Who in the world had taken these pictures, and how the hell had they managed to make her look so awful?

She stared at the picture of the girl with the shiny nose and the double chin, with the cocktail in her freakishly overlarge hand. It wasn't just the unflattering angles and unfortunate lighting, either. One photo showed her with her arm draped around Reeve Wilson, and in another she'd been caught midblink and looked wasted. If the girl in the photos hadn't been wearing her new Kimberly Ovitz dress, Carmen never would have recognized herself.

Below the photos was a rude blurb about her looking

like a hot mess, and below that were dozens of comments: *Gross! No wonder Luke dumped her,* someone wrote. *He could do so much better.* Someone else called her a cow; still another accused her of being a bloated celebutard.

Carmen felt her throat constricting. Why would Fawn tell her about this on-camera as if it were some fun thing? Why would Laurel have her do it? One of them should've warned her! These photos felt like an attack. Sort of the way that the "anonymous sources claim Carmen not happy with Colum" tidbits had felt like an attack. Or the way the "was the break-up really mutual?" items had. Now her bad press was part of the show?

Carmen shook her head as she hurried toward Saburo's. She couldn't think about this now—she had to keep filming. When she entered the restaurant, frazzled and late, she gave her lipstick a quick touch-up and fixed a smile on her face. "Reservation for Curtis?" she said to the hostess.

The woman nodded, her face a mask of lovely blankness. "Right this way, miss."

Carmen followed the hostess (and the PopTV camera followed Carmen) past a living wall of water bamboo and into the restaurant's quiet side room, which overlooked a courtyard full of fountains and cherry trees. There was a glare from the windows, so her mother, already seated at their table, appeared only in silhouette. Her head was turned away and Carmen saw her fingers drumming lightly on the tablecloth.

"Sorry I'm late," Carmen said, approaching, trying

not to look at the other camera that was protruding from the tree next to their table. Should she say why? Give the cameras what they wanted? Even though every lens in the world seemed to love Cassandra Curtis—for real, she'd never taken a bad photo in her life—she had, occasionally, been the subject of rude internet commentary. Maybe she'd offer some good advice. "I was looking at awful pictures of myself online," Carmen added.

"Oh, darling," Cassandra said, smiling up at her. "Tell me all about it. Sit, sit!" She waved for the waiter and mouthed the word "tea."

Carmen immediately collapsed into the chair. "Someone sent in really ugly pictures of me to *D-Lish,* and they got posted."

"Darling, you could never take an ugly picture," her mom said, beaming at her. Cassandra was in her late forties, but she didn't look a day over thirty-five. People who didn't know the Curtises—people who apparently lived under rocks or in caves, with no access to a radio or television—often thought the two were sisters.

"Um, unfortunately that's not true," Carmen said.

Suddenly, out of nowhere, a small man clutching an iPhone appeared at the edge of their table. The camera flashed in Cassandra's face, and then he dashed away, pursued by a waiter.

Smooth, thought Carmen, shooting eye-daggers at the man's retreating back. But of course even *that* photo of her mother would be beautiful.

Cassandra shook her head and *tsk-tsk*ed. "Always with the flash. Don't they know how annoying it is? Here, have some tea."

Carmen took a sip of the warm liquid and tried to smile. Despite the timing of Fawn's call, her job now was not to complain. She'd been given her assignment, and it was to ask her mother about her work. Plus, she didn't really want to talk about the awful pictures. Or the fact that *D-Lish* suggested she'd hooked up with Reeve Wilson at that party, "only moments after being dumped by Luke Kelly." Ugh!

"So how's your new single coming?" she asked.

Cassandra flashed her trademark megawatt smile. "It's going to be incredible," she said. "I can't wait for you to hear it."

"Do I get to before it's out and on endless repeat on Kiss FM?" Carmen teased.

Cassandra laughed. "You're the one who never has time to talk to your old mom."

"Sorry," Carmen said, meaning it. "I've been so crazy busy." She had a hard time not reacting to Cassandra referring to herself as her "old mom," though. She was definitely playing to the cameras with that one.

Her mother patted her hand. "Of course you have. You've got a lot on your plate. And it's all so exciting." She leaned in close and spoke low and conspiratorially. "Speaking of exciting, let's talk about your love life," she said, winking.

This, clearly, was a Trevor Lord talking point. Carmen would have known it even if her mother hadn't given such an obvious lead-in.

"I don't know that 'exciting' is the right word." Carmen, who didn't particularly want to go down this conversational road, tried to steer the subject back. "I mean, it's certainly not as exciting as a future number-one single."

Her mother waved a hand dismissively. "Oh please."

"Right—you've had so many of those. What's one more?"

"That's not what I meant, darling. I meant let's talk about you. How are things, really? How is it working with Luke now that you guys have split? I'm sure you saw the magazines. There were so many awful puns about 'the end of love.' . . ."

Carmen had to fight the urge to roll her eyes, since Cassandra knew perfectly well that she and Luke were never actually together. But apparently Cassandra was a bit of an actress herself. This lunch/scene was starting to feel like one of those exercises in Carmen's acting class, where two people get thrown together and each has been given a direction that conflicts with the other person's. "Actually, I haven't seen much of him lately. I've been filming scenes he's not in, so he's had a few days off."

"And you're sure you're okay?"

Her mother looked so sincere: Was it possible it wasn't an act? Had Cassandra (who, admittedly, could be sort of self-centered) somehow forgotten that Carmen's relationship with Luke was fake? Had she disregarded her own rule of not believing what she read in *Life & Style*? Maybe she was suffering from early-onset Alzheimer's or some other form of dementia.

"I'm fine, Mom," Carmen said.

"Well, that's probably for the best," her mother said. "Playing lovers while dating—that could get complicated. So. Tell me, then. Do you have your eye on anyone else?"

"No," Carmen said, feeling annoyed at her and Trevor both. "No. I'm way too busy."

"You shouldn't work too hard, honey. You're young—you need to go out and have fun!" Cassandra tossed her ebony hair and smiled her beautiful smile, and Carmen could sense the camera moving in for a close-up.

She gritted her teeth. She was so sick of living in her mother's shadow, so sick of having everyone think they knew her because they knew her mom. She should have changed her name, the way Nicolas Cage did; it separated him from his famous relatives, made him find his own way at least a little bit. (*But then you couldn't cash in on your name,* a small voice whispered. Not that she had lately! But being a Curtis had definitely greased some important wheels—she couldn't deny that.)

Cassandra reached across the table and patted Carmen's hand. "Carm? You've got a thousand-yard stare. What are you thinking?"

Gently Carmen eased her hand away. But she smiled at

her mother. She was not going to let her mother or Trevor back her into some weird corner that made for good TV. She was an actress, damn it, so she was going to act: act as if she was grateful to her mother for her on-camera support. Act as if she did miss Luke, but that she knew their breakup was for the best. Act as if this restaurant, which was the latest B-list celebrity hot spot, did not remind her of some tricked-out Sushi Express.

"I'm just really tired," she said. "I'd forgotten how hard filming is. The days are so long, and you're always running over the scheduled shooting time, and even when you're trying to relax in your trailer someone's always poking their head in." Luke was one of the worst offenders on that front, and he was still calling her "ex-looooover." Not that she minded the company (and in fact, when he didn't stop by, she missed him).

"Look on the bright side," Cassandra said. "At least you're not moving from one country to the next every three nights."

Carmen closed her menu. She was going to have the seaweed salad and that was it. "Are you saying that touring is harder than filming? Because if you're here to support me, let me point out that you are not doing a very good job." She laughed, but she meant what she said. She was annoyed. Clearly Cassandra was feeling like she wasn't in the spotlight quite enough lately, so she decided to borrow a piece of her daughter's. Album sales did require promotion, after all!

"Oh, no, silly," Cassandra said. "I'm sure that filming is just as hard. I was only trying to think of one thing that might be easier about it."

"Gotcha. Well, thanks. I'll keep that in mind."

"Do you want to talk about you and Luke? About how you're feeling?"

Carmen took a deep breath. She'd write the lines in her head as she was saying them. "You know, Mom, I feel okay. I mean, it's not exactly enjoyable to break up with someone. Especially not when you have to work with them every day. But sometimes it's for the best. Luke and I are still friends. We're committed to that."

She sounded strong but not cold. All in all, she was happy with her response.

Her mother nodded. "You're a wise girl," she said. "You always have been."

"Well, you and Dad raised me right, I guess," Carmen said, offering a slightly forced smile.

She was playing the Good Daughter to the hilt. She deserved a SAG award for this lunch.

For the next half hour, she picked at her salad and made small talk with her mother. It felt weird. She was familiar with her mother's behavior when she was "on," but it had never been directed at her before. It was the Cassandra Show today, and Carmen was merely an extra. How many times had her mom managed to mention her album *Everything or Nothing*? Oh, only about five. Thousand.

And then, when it came time to leave, Cassandra

took off her microphone, graciously said good-bye to the starstruck crew, and made her grand exit, hounded by paparazzi all the way to her car. Only two of them stuck around to follow Carmen.

18

GOING ROGUE

By the time Kate found parking, she was over an hour late for shooting the latest installment of Operation Eliminate Stage Fright. She could see the PopTV van parked outside of Ocean Park Hypnotherapy, and a small knot of bystanders had gathered, trying to figure out what was being filmed. The PAs stuck with the standard "we're shooting a mayonnaise commercial" answer to avoid crowds. She had on her new pair of sunglasses, so she was able to slip past them unrecognized.

Laurel and the PopTV crew were in the waiting room, which was decorated with giant crystals and pastel paintings of beaches at sunset. Their expressions ranged from bored to annoyed.

"Kate," Laurel said sternly, standing up with her hands on her hips. "Your call time was an hour ago. I've been calling you. Do you not have your phone on you?"

Kate stopped short. When had Laurel become such a schoolmarm? "Um. It's on silent. I had a hard time finding a parking spot."

Laurel took a sip of coffee, grimaced, and then said, "And you expect me to believe that you were driving around for an entire hour looking for one? Why wouldn't you just call me? I could have had a PA find you a spot."

"Well, I might have gotten a slightly late start, and there was crazy traffic on the 10," Kate admitted. She tried to scoot around Laurel. She hated to be reprimanded; it made her feel nervous and itchy.

Laurel stopped her. "Look, I don't want to have to talk to you this way, but this is your job, Kate, and it costs us thousands of dollars if people don't show up. Next time you wake up late? Call and let me know."

Kate shrugged her off. "So I screwed up," she said. "I'm sorry."

"The role of *Fame Game* screwup has already been taken by Gaby," Laurel said drily. "Though being late is not actually one of her flaws. Don't let it become one of yours."

Kate felt like this lecture of Laurel's had gone on long enough. "I said I was sorry. I'm tired. So give me a break, all right?" She tossed her purse down onto a side table; it gaped open and a Luna Bar wrapper fell out. Rather than picking it up, she kicked it under a chair. She was annoyed that she had to tape this hypnotherapy episode—hadn't the yoga and the acupuncture and the EFT BS been enough?

Kate knew the answer to that, of course: No, they hadn't. Trevor was going to make the most of Kate's stage fright, turning a liability into a dramatic bonus. He'd film her performance at the El Rey tonight—which, thanks to the Xanax, would go great—and make it seem as if all this woo-woo crap had fixed what ailed her.

But Kate knew what really worked: pills. She and Drew had gone to an open mic the other night in secret, and Kate had rocked it: three songs played to perfection and a standing ovation (well, half of one, since some audience members were too cool to get up from their seats). She'd never played that well in front of a crowd in her entire life.

She couldn't wait to tell Trevor that she was cured, but as it turned out, she didn't even get the chance. Someone had posted a video of her on a local arts and culture blog, along with a glowing write-up of her performance. (*Kate Hayes: dreamy lovechild of Carole King and James Taylor with some Katy Perry pop chromosomes mixed in?*). And Trevor, whose spies had seen the article immediately (damn you, Google alert!), had been as annoyed as he was pleased. He was glad his star wasn't going to die of a heart attack before a performance, but he didn't like having to play catch-up. He didn't like his girls going rogue.

But Kate was getting tired of being at Trevor's beck and call. Sure, he'd finally let her quit Stecco, but then he'd forced her into these stupid therapy sessions. And what about the dates she kept having to go on? Lately it seemed like every day Laurel sent her another email with a photo attached: *What do you think of this guy?* she'd write.

Cute, right? He knows how to play bass! Or *He grew up in Indiana!* Or *He's addicted to sushi, too!* As if any of that mattered.

Last night's date had been some aspiring model who Trevor had met at his gym. The guy was cute, and the date was fine, but Kate definitely didn't feel a connection with him. Nor had she felt one with the previous two guys, either. When she'd mentioned this to Trevor, he'd only shrugged. "Well, there's more where they came from. Besides, even a bad date makes for good TV."

Which made Kate wonder: Did Trevor have a Rolodex of hot, single guys? And if he did, wasn't that a little weird? Sure, she really could have used that back when she was looking for a prom date, but right now, she sort of wished he'd stop pushing the whole dating thing. Especially since some of the guys were a little strange. It almost felt like Trevor was sending her on dates he assumed would fail because he thought they'd be more entertaining.

Laurel reached down and picked up the Luna Bar wrapper. "You dropped this," she said.

"Oh, you can throw it away," Kate said breezily. "I don't need it." Then she gave Laurel a small, insincere smile that said *Lecture me all you want, but don't forget who's the talent and who's the crew here.*

Laurel narrowed her eyes. "Be careful," she said.

"You don't need to worry about me," Kate answered. "I'm great. I'm ready to go. Let's get this show on the road!" She clapped her hands sharply, startling the camera guy. She laughed. "Sorry!" She was starting to have a little bit of fun. She hoped Barry, the hypnotherapist, wouldn't make her too calm, because she was enjoying her new-found edge.

The El Rey was bigger than Kate had expected, and everything—walls, carpet, seats, booths—was brilliant bloodred. A giant chandelier glittered above them, sending out sparks of light that danced around the room. Kate gripped Drew's elbow, giddy with excitement. "Wow. I feel like I've time-traveled back to the 1930s," she said. "This place is so cool."

"I know, it's awesome, right? I love Art Deco. Carmen and I used to come here to see shows in high school all the time."

Kate was too nervous to wonder what qualified as "all the time." Or if any of these shows had felt sort of like dates to Carmen or Drew. But anyway, she reminded herself, Drew was talking about high school. That was all of . . . well, less than a year ago for Carmen.

Drew pointed them toward the sound technician, a pale, long-haired guy mostly hidden behind giant monitors. "Here—you have to meet Joe. He's going to make you sound amazing."

Kate shook Joe's cold hand. He looked as if he'd never set foot outside. Like he spent his days in a basement, listening to heavy metal, and his nights running sound inside the all-ages club.

"So you're the opener, huh?" Joe asked, sounding friendly but unimpressed.

"The opener for the opener, actually," Kate admitted.

Joe nodded, now looking even less impressed. "Everyone starts somewhere," he offered.

Drew put his arm around Kate's shoulders. "She's going to the top," he said. "You're going to be able to say, 'I knew her when . . .'"

"Oh, yeah, man," Joe said.

Kate couldn't tell if he meant it or not (and she ought to assume he didn't), but she flushed anyway.

"All right," Drew said. "Nice to see you again, dude. We're heading backstage."

"Right on," Joe said, and flashed them a peace sign.

Kate followed Drew down the edge of the long, red room to a door that led backstage. "Do you think he liked me?" she asked. "Do you think he thinks I'm a one-hit wonder?"

"No, of course not. But he's a pro. Even if he hated your guts, he'll still make sure you sound amazing." He paused before the door leading backstage. "This used to be a movie theater, you know," he said, motioning her in. "Crazy that I saw Lana Del Rey play here last week, and tonight I'm going to see you."

Kate gulped. "Right!" she said, trying to sound brave. It was definitely time for her Xanax. Because that whole hypnotherapy thing she'd done earlier? That was a load of crap.

Backstage, it was dim and cluttered. "When's sound check?" Kate asked, leaning Lucinda against the wall and reaching into her purse for the little blue pill.

"In a minute," Drew said. "Relax, why don't you?"

Kate smiled and sat down on top of a speaker. "I'm trying," she said, knowing the pill she'd just swallowed would help. But she wanted to stay just a bit nervous: It would keep her on her toes.

When Joe was ready, the headlining band did their sound check. It was some Canadian group she'd never heard of, but obviously they were bigger than she was since it was their name on the marquee, not hers. After listening to them for a few minutes she'd decided that at least they weren't as terrible as The Faze. Next came the opening indie duo—a guy on a guitar and a girl on a violin—and they did their sound check. When it was Kate's turn, she got all of three minutes: She had time to plug her guitar into the amp, check to see that the sound came through the monitors, and make sure she could adjust the mike stand.

"Joe didn't give me much time up there," she said to Drew when she stepped offstage.

He nodded sympathetically. "Don't worry. When you headline, you'll have all the time in the world."

She scoffed at that. Her days as a headliner were still a long ways off.

Before Kate knew it, it was time to go on. She waited for a moment, hidden behind the heavy red curtain, and then watched as it opened to reveal a room crowded with people. She felt her heart flutter, but—just as she'd expected—there was no hard knot of panic. She offered a small smile, and then began to play.

She played six songs, two of them brand-new, and she didn't forget a single word, didn't flub a single chord. The audience sang along to "Starstruck," and a lot of them seemed to have heard her YouTube version of "Lost in Love," too, because she definitely wasn't the only one singing the chorus.

When it was over, the audience applauded thunderously, and Drew gave her a giant hug.

"I knew you'd be awesome," he said.

"I didn't mess up," she said happily, hardly daring to believe it. "Oh my God, I love you, Dr. Garrison."

"Huh?" Drew asked.

"Oh, nothing, never mind," Kate said. "I'm starving. Can we please go get a burger?"

Drew patted his stomach. "Of course," he said.

Gaby came running up to her and gave her a big hug. "Kate! Oh my God, you were amazing!"

Jay gave Drew what Kate referred to as a "bro handshake" then said to Kate, "Way to go, Kate Hayes. You didn't choke this time."

Drew gave her a look that said, *Yes, this guy is the douchiest of douche bags.* Then he grabbed Kate's hand and squeezed it. "We've gotta head out."

"Where are you guys going?" Gaby asked.

Kate would have told her, but she'd bring Jay along, which would definitely ruin her celebratory mood. So instead she pretended as if she hadn't heard the question.

"Thanks so much for coming, Gab," Kate said as she let Drew pull her away from them. "See you soon, okay?"

As they made their way out of the El Rey, Kate was suddenly mobbed by teenage girls. All of them were clamoring for her autograph, and as she signed their little books, they took pictures and begged her to follow them on Twitter.

Drew hovered protectively by her side, and after the frenzy had gone on for while, he gently drew her away. "Thanks, girls," he called, waving. "Kate Hayes loves you!"

Kate turned back to the knot of giggling girls. "I do!" she yelled and waved over her shoulder. Then she looked up at Drew and smiled. She couldn't tell if she was more exhausted or exhilarated. "Now let's get the hell out of here."

19

A NEW LEAF

On Monday morning, Madison skipped the ninety-minute beauty ritual she'd been performing every day for as long as she could remember. Instead she washed her face and smoothed on a bit of tinted moisturizer. She applied two thin coats of mascara and slicked the barest hint of pale pink gloss on her lips. Then she pulled her long blond hair back into a simple, loose ponytail.

Traffic on the 405 was strangely light, and she got to Lost Paws twenty minutes early. She was sitting on the steps, sipping her green tea and watching the seagulls peck at a mound of old French fries, when Ryan arrived.

An odd look came over his handsome face. "Welcome back," he said. He glanced at his watch. "Turning over a new leaf?"

She smiled politely at him, ignoring the implied insult of her past performance. No, she wasn't going to take the bait, and she wasn't going to bitch or whine. She was simply going to do her work and go home, and then come back tomorrow and do it all again. Today, she hoped, would be a day free of drama.

Possibly her first. Ever.

Ryan stepped past her and unlocked the doors, and she followed him inside. The smell of pee was, by this time, familiar to her. She hardly even noticed it anymore.

"I'll go ahead and get started," she said, "if you want to tell me what I'm doing today."

"We have a bunch of dogs who need a flea bath," Ryan said. "How's that sound?"

Of course, he didn't actually care how it sounded to her at all; she understood that. "Sounds fine," she said. "Show me the way."

He looked at her quizzically once more and shook his head. "Come on, then."

Madison spent the morning hosing down, soaping up, then rinsing off shivering dog after shivering dog. She was bitten twice, peed on once, and shed upon constantly. Her clothes were ruined. The wellies that Ryan had given her were full of water. Even with gloves on, she could feel her hands burning from the chemicals in the flea shampoo. But she didn't make a single complaint. (If only the PopTV cameras could see her now!)

After four hours of hard labor, Ryan appeared in the doorway. He watched as Madison gave Samson, the hideously ugly mutt who had moved her to tears a week ago, a final rinse.

Madison pretended she didn't know he was there.

"You're doing so good, Sam," she said soothingly to the dog, who stood trembling under the spray. "This is going to make you feel so much better." She washed the last bits of lather from his fur and then guided him to the corner and wrapped him in a worn but soft towel. "There," she said, rubbing him vigorously. "Now you're nice and clean."

Samson whined and tried to lick her. A haircut and bath had helped, but he was still pretty unfortunate looking. "Oh, you," she said, smiling. "Keep your tongue in your mouth. You're just like all the other guys."

Ryan came over and squatted down beside them both. "We want him to look as good as he can," he said. "We're taking his Last Chance shot today."

Madison put her hand protectively on Samson's head. She didn't like the sound of that. "What do you mean?"

Ryan reached out and rubbed Samson under his chin, and the dog practically purred—oh, to be petted by two people at once! But Ryan's voice was grim. "We take a photo and send it out in an email blast. It's the last thing we can do for him before . . ." He trailed off.

Madison paled. "You aren't going to kill him, are you?"

Ryan shrugged, unhappy but resolved. "We do the best we can, Madison. But Lost Paws isn't a no-kill shelter."

She gazed at Samson. He really did look so much like a mop crossed with a rat. One ear stood up and the other flopped down, and he would probably always look mangy. Who in the world would adopt him? "You can't do that," she said, her voice catching in her throat. Samson whined and looked at her with his cloudy, sad eyes.

"We can't save all of them, Madison," Ryan said. "That's the hardest thing about working here." Then he stood up. "We'll make him look great for his picture; don't worry. And maybe someone will adopt him. And you— you've done a great job with him. Thanks."

An actual, in-person compliment from Ryan Tucker— you could have knocked Madison over with a feather.

But it didn't matter. For one thing, Samson's life was on the line. And for another, it didn't change anything about Ryan and Madison's tense relationship. There was no way Ryan was going to go easy on her just because she wasn't complaining for once. No, she thought gloomily, she and the dog were both basically doomed.

After lunch, Ryan sent Madison to clip the nails of Lost Paws's cat population, a task that would have been unpleasant enough if they were friendly house cats. Which they weren't. Some of them were wild-eyed strays from the building site of Jungle Bar, the new nightclub Gaby had reported on before she got fired from *Buzz! News*. Gaby had called them "fearful cats," because she didn't know the word "feral." But that's what they were. Feral. Savage. Like tiny tigers.

Madison's arms were covered in scratches by the time she was done. And while in the past she would have run to Ryan, claiming unsafe working conditions and preferential treatment to those horrible, greasy-haired twins, Hazel and Ivy, today she said nothing at all. She got her Bacitracin and her Band-Aids and took care of business.

Madison didn't even blame the cats. She felt only sympathy for them. Because now, like them, she knew what it was to be unwanted.

"You really don't have to do this," Ryan said. He was leaning on the counter in the Lost Paws reception room, watching as Madison filled out a clipboard full of Xeroxed forms.

"I know," Madison said. She scanned down the page. No, she didn't have a fully fenced yard; she lived on the sixth floor of the Park Towers apartments. No, she didn't have experience with pet ownership. (Sue Beth had allowed her to keep a turtle for a while, but then Sophie let it out to play in the yard, and that was the last anyone saw of Puddles.) No, she didn't have a relationship with a vet—but she knew how to Google one. Same thing. Yes, she understood that a pet was a great responsibility. She had been taking care of Gaby for years. How could this be much different?

She glanced toward the hallway that led to the dog wing. Somewhere back there, a freshly groomed Samson was locked in his little cage. He was probably curled in the corner, licking sadly at the rawhide bone that every Lost Paws dog was given upon arrival. Madison smiled to herself, thinking about it: He no idea that his life was about to change. If there was a dog lottery, Samson the mutt was about to win it.

"You could always just foster him, you know," Ryan said. "That's a big deal, too. And a great help. We always need foster homes."

Madison didn't answer. She was writing down the names and addresses of personal references. It was dumb that she had to fill out all the forms—it wasn't like she was some random stranger off the street, after all—but she wanted to do this right.

"The nice thing about fostering is that it's not a long-term commitment," Ryan went on. "I fostered one of the Great Danes for a while. . . ."

A part of her appreciated his skepticism. Madison knew she didn't look like the doggie type, and certainly not the mangy-shelter-mutt type. Ryan was trying to make things easy for her—to let her know that she could help grant Samson a death-row reprieve without actually signing up for twelve years of responsibility. But she knew what she was doing. Samson needed an ally. He needed her. And no matter what he did, she wasn't going to abandon him the way his previous owners had.

"Really," she said, filling in answers to questions such as *How do you discipline your pets and why?* "I'm sure about this." She wondered if she would rename Samson something more . . . mediagenic. It really was too bad he wasn't some darling teacup poodle—something she could carry in a handbag or dye pretty colors. Something that would look good in *US Weekly*. (Paris Hilton's dog had looked so cute when it was pink, even if PETA didn't agree.) But he needed her.

Ryan pushed himself off the counter and came over to stand beside her. "I'm not convinced you are really thinking this through," he said.

The tone of his voice made her look up from the forms. "What do you mean?"

"A dog isn't an accessory, Madison," he said (as if he'd known what she was thinking!). "It's a living being. It needs to be walked and loved and fed and cared for. I don't know how much you understand about it, but pet ownership is not a game."

He looked as if he was going to keep going, but Madison had had enough of his patronizing lecture. "You think I don't know that? You think I'm not capable of taking care of him?"

"I don't know. You seem like you might be better at taking care of yourself. Isn't that your thing—looking out for number one?"

Madison scoffed. "You think you know me because of what you've heard about me—because I'm sure you're way too cool to ever watch PopTV—but let me tell you: You don't know the first thing about me."

Ryan laughed mirthlessly. "Actually, I have seen you on TV. And you forget that we've spent a lot of time together in the last couple of weeks. When you actually show up to work, that is."

Madison bristled. "First of all, we don't spend time

together. It's not like you come to the laundry room to fold towels with me! And second of all, you don't have to get on my case for missing work; Connie already did. Do you have any idea how humiliating it is to be yelled at by a middle-aged woman in Crocs?"

Ryan raised a hand. "Look, I'm not trying to start a fight—"

"Oh really? Because you're doing an excellent job of it."

"I'm just concerned about Samson."

"Three hours ago you were talking about killing him, and now you're acting like sending him home with me would be worse," Madison yelled. "You're a hypocrite, Ryan Tucker. You act like you're God's gift to the animal kingdom, when really you're just an asshole."

Ryan took a step back. "Whoa," he said. "Maybe you should calm down a little."

Madison lowered her voice. "I'm perfectly calm," she said. (A lie.) "I'm taking Samson. And if you don't let me adopt him, I'll have to steal him."

"Of course you will," Ryan said snidely. "How could I forget that if you want something, you just take it."

That, really, was the last straw.

Madison picked up a paper coffee cup that was sitting on the counter and threw it at him. "I didn't do it!" she yelled. "I didn't even take that necklace, so you just shut up, you arrogant prick! You don't know what the hell you are talking about."

She stopped and clapped a hand over her mouth. Her eyes were wide. Then she fled from the room.

"Hey," Ryan called after her. "Hey—"

He caught up to her on the steps outside the shelter. "Wait! What do you mean you didn't take the necklace?" he asked, half out of breath.

"I mean that I didn't take it," Madison shouted bitterly. She couldn't believe she'd let him goad her into confessing. "How much clearer do I need to be?"

Ryan whistled low under his breath. "No shit," he said softly. He sat down on the top step and gazed up at her. "Okay. Wow. Then why would you say that you did?"

Madison felt the sting of tears brimming in her eyes, but there was no way she was going to let herself cry. She gazed up at the cloudy sky; she couldn't look at Ryan. When she finally spoke, her voice was cool and controlled. "It's a long story, and one that I don't particularly like talking about."

"Maybe it'd make you feel better," he offered.

"You've been a jerk to me since day one. Why would I confide in you?"

"For the pleasure of proving that I was wrong about you?" Ryan suggested.

Madison finally looked at him. "Do you think I care what you think of me? Because I don't. I know who I am, and that's all that matters."

Ryan sighed. "I'm sorry. I'm sorry if I jumped to conclusions about you. I'm sorry if I haven't been very nice. I will admit that I have certain . . . prejudices against people like you."

"People like me? What does that mean?"

Ryan shrugged. "People who crave fame and attention. It just doesn't make sense to me."

"Just because you don't understand it doesn't mean it's wrong. You know the shithole I came from—everyone does. Doesn't it make sense I'd want to live a different life?"

Ryan nodded slowly. "I guess. But I still want to know about the necklace. Will you tell me? I won't tell anyone."

Madison dropped down onto the step next to him. She was so tired of keeping the secret; she really was. She was sick of everyone looking at her like she was a criminal. Maybe telling Ryan Tucker would make her feel a little bit better. (There was a first time for everything.) She'd already blurted out the truth; what was wrong with filling him in on a few details?

"Pretend you don't hate me," Ryan urged. "Come on, pretend I was never a jerk to you. You may find this hard to believe, but lot of people think I'm a nice, pretty sympathetic guy."

"You're right; I do find that hard to believe."

"Just tell me," Ryan said softly.

Then Madison surprised herself, and she did. By the time she was done telling him—about Sophie, about her dad, about their painful history—she felt five pounds lighter.

"So," she said, flinging her hands up in the air. "That's that."

Ryan was speechless for a moment. Then he simply exhaled with a "Wow."

Madison felt almost giddy with relief. "Yeah, wow," she repeated.

But then reality came rushing back and she felt terrible again. What good had telling Ryan done? None.

Ryan reached out and touched her arm. "I'm really sorry," he said. "For everything that you've gone through. And for misjudging you."

"People have been misjudging me my whole life," Madison said. "What's one more?"

"Well, I won't do it anymore. There's a different Madison Parker than the world sees, and I just met her."

Madison held out her hand. "Hi," she said wryly. "Nice to meet you."

Ryan shook her hand, but instead of releasing it, he kept it wrapped in his.

"Nice to meet you, too," he said.

20

LET THE HATERS HATE

Carmen sighed happily as she sank down at the edge of the mineral pool. Slipping off her flip-flops, she submerged her feet and felt the warm water swirl around her ankles. She closed her eyes for a moment, and let out an involuntary "Ooooohhh . . ."

Birds were chattering from the eaves of the Hope Springs Resort, and the sun was setting over the desert in a blaze of orange and red. Carmen was only two hours east of L.A., but it felt like a different world entirely. A quieter, simpler, prettier world. She kicked her feet in the water, thrilled to be taking a break from the city—from the traffic, the smog, the paparazzi, the PopTV cameras . . . from all of it.

Carmen and the rest of the *End of Love* cast and crew were in the desert for a few days to film scenes of Roman and Julia trying to live off the land (which, like nearly everything else in their story, was not going to go well for them). Today's shoot had been long and exhausting;

Carmen was sunburned, not to mention blistered. (Those boots Alexis Ritter had designed were really not comfortable.) And her call had been at five a.m.—five!—because she had an hour of makeup with Lily before she could get into her wardrobe and film. Which meant that Carmen was probably getting up just as Gaby was crawling into bed with Jay after they'd spent the night partying at Whisper and then who knows where.

But overall, the day had been great. Colum McEntire hadn't yelled at her once, and in fact he'd even paid her a compliment on a line she'd improvised. Her scenes with Luke were raw and intense; at times they'd felt so real that she almost believed she was starving in a post-apocalyptic desert.

Yes, things were good. It was nice to have a moment of peace and solitude to remember that.

But Carmen only enjoyed solitude for so long. There were some people—Kate, maybe (she seemed like the nature type)—who could watch the sun go down solo, but Carmen preferred to share it with someone. Even someone who was hours away. So, because she missed him and she hadn't talked to him in forever, she called Drew.

It was a Friday night, and she thought there was a chance he was over at her house for dinner. Maybe he'd be peeling carrots for one of Cassandra's salads, while her dad talked his ear off about some new band he'd seen at Slim's when he was in San Francisco. But Drew didn't pick up. Instead of leaving him a message, she hung up and sent a text. I MISS U. U STILL EXIST, RIGHT?

Then she got up and walked over to one of the lounge chairs. She spotted Lily in the lobby staring intently at her iPhone, probably choosing between filters for an artsy picture of rocks she'd taken. Carmen had never met someone so obsessed with Instagram. A string of lights suspended from the courtyard trees illuminated the stack of magazines she'd brought from her room, all of them bookmarked to the articles about her. She opened the nearest one to see a picture of herself paying for a coconut water and an apple at Whole Foods. *Carmen Curtis tries to keep fit with healthy snacks,* read the caption.

Huh? she thought. *"Tries" to keep fit?* Carmen had struggled with various things in her life—algebra, her mother's fame, a tendency toward oiliness in her T-zone— but fitness had never been one of them. Where were these stories coming from?

"Reading up on yourself again?" said a voice, and Carmen, startled, looked up to see Luke grinning at her. "Are you curious about what you've been up to lately? Because, you know, you could just ask me." He sat down next to her and picked up a towel to dry his wet hair. "The indoor pool is too hot, by the way," he said. "It's like a giant bathtub."

Carmen shut the magazine and smiled at him. Even after a whole day together, she was still happy to see him. "Someone's been talking to the press about me," she said.

"So what else is new?" Luke asked. "I mean, you're a public figure. They take pictures of you feeding your parking meter. Saw one of those the other day, in fact."

Carmen crinkled her nose. "I still got a ticket, though." She picked up another tabloid and tossed it at him. "I mean, look. There are all these stories that are wrong . . . or sort of mean."

But Luke didn't open the magazine. "Don't pay any attention to this stuff. It's not worth your time. This is what these magazines do. You know better than anyone."

"Easy for you to say," Carmen answered. "No one's calling you overweight or spoiled or undeserving of your success."

At that moment, as if he had some sort of conversational ESP, Drew texted Carmen back. I'M NOT THE ONE WHO'S FALLEN OFF THE FACE OF THE EARTH, MISS TABLOID QUEEN!

If I'd fallen off the earth, you wouldn't see me all over the tabloids, dope, she thought, setting the phone on top of *Gossip.* Carmen would have liked to text him that retort, but suddenly it felt like too much effort. She was so tired!

"You've worked hard for everything you've gotten, and you deserve it all," Luke said. "Let the haters hate."

Carmen sighed. "I just want to know who the haters are."

"Maybe it's me," Luke said. "Maybe I'm secretly trying to sabotage you because you're a better actor than I am."

Carmen laughed. "Yeah, that makes sense. Seriously, though—I want to know who's doing it. At first I thought it was just tabloids being tabloids, but some of these 'sources' know personal details that no one else could know." Her first thought was Madison Parker. After all, the girl had a history of interpersonal sabotage. (Poor Jane Roberts! She was probably still scarred from Madison's betrayal. . . .) But she quickly realized that in this case, Madison was innocent. "It had to be someone who was with me at the party in the Hills—"

"The one you broke up with me from," Luke interrupted, poking her with his foot. "Heartbreaker."

Carmen was too absorbed in her thoughts to laugh. "Yes, that one. Assuming this is all the same "source," the person had to be there, because that's where the hideous pictures came from. And he or she also heard me complaining about Colum McEntire . . . which I don't do to that many people. I hope." She bit her lip—had she been less careful in her conversations than she'd thought?

"So who could it be?"

"Well, it's either Kate or Fawn or Gaby . . . or Laurel," Carmen said, ticking off the possibilities. Then she looked over at the lobby. "Or Lily."

"Kate would never do something like that," Luke said.

Carmen shot him a look. He was pretty quick on Kate's defense, wasn't he?

"You know what you should do?" Luke went on. "Plant fake information with each of them. Then you wait to see what comes out in the press."

"Um—"

"Hang on, run with me here. You confide in Lily that you're going to get lipo and tell everyone you're going on a vacation somewhere. Then tell Fawn you're going to start exploring Scientology. Tell Gaby . . . well, she probably won't remember whatever you tell her. I don't think you have to worry about Gaby being the secret source. And tell Laurel that I was your one true love." He smiled winningly. "Because I am so very desirable." He flexed a bicep for comic emphasis.

Carmen laughed. "Sure, and I can tell Kate that I'm going to sing backup for Taylor Swift. I do sort of know Taylor, you know."

"You don't need to test Kate. She would never do something like that," Luke said again.

Carmen thought about this. Luke was probably right. For one thing, Kate hardly seemed like the lies-and-deception type. And for another, it wasn't as if Carmen had done a lot of confiding in her lately, so how would she know about the Colum business? So, great: She could rule out Kate Hayes. But why did Luke have to look so moony whenever he said her name?

If Carmen thought Luke looked moony then, though, it was nothing compared to the way he looked when the next text came in. Drew had sent a picture of Kate, smiling and holding up her guitar over her head in triumph. Behind her was a blur of teenage faces. Fans. THE FAMOUS KATE HAYES SAYS HI, he'd written. COME BACK AND SEE US SOMETIME.

Luke, reading this, had flushed—then gazed off into gathering dusk.

"You've got a Roman expression on your face,"

Carmen said, nudging him. "All wistful and yearning."

Luke took a deep breath and smiled. "Well," he said. But then he was quiet again.

Carmen flopped back against the deck chair and closed her eyes. She felt a strange and unpleasant twinge of jealousy. Was Drew into Kate now? Is that why she hadn't heard much from him lately? Suddenly it felt like all the guys she knew had a crush on Kate. And she was so not into that. She was used to them all having crushes on her—and she liked it that way.

21

YOU KNOW ME BETTER THAN THAT

A cool October wind blew as Madison and Ryan strolled down the Santa Monica beach, Samson trotting along behind them. There were still a few brave sunbathers dotting the sand, but Madison shivered and pulled her cashmere cardigan closer around her shoulders. Samson, too, wore a cashmere sweater, with blue-and-white stripes, from Coach's canine line. It had been a splurge, but it was worth it: He looked . . . well, almost cute. (Maybe if he'd been wearing the sweater when Gaby saw him for the first time, she wouldn't have screamed, "Rat! Rat!" and gone running from the room.)

"You should see your face," Ryan was saying. "It's like you'd rather be tortured."

"Going to the Santa Monica Pier *is* being tortured," Madison said. "I had to go there once for the show and I vowed never to do it again." She shuddered, remembering the smell of fried food, the white glow of tourists' new walking shoes, and dirty kids running around screaming.

"I can't believe you actually like going there."

"I used to go when I was a kid," Ryan said, clearly unembarrassed by his suggestion that they go ride the Ferris wheel at the pier. "I guess it's nostalgic for me. Also they sell churros."

"Yeah, I don't get that whole nostalgia thing. Maybe you have to have a happy childhood for that."

Ryan laughed sympathetically. They'd been hanging out a lot lately—ever since their fight had cleared the air between them—and by now he'd heard plenty of her horror stories from back home. "Yeah, or maybe just weird taste. I mean, I still think it'd be cool to work at the Rusty's at the end of the pier."

"I'm sure five minutes of actually doing it would change your mind," Madison said. "Trust me. I've been a server before."

As they drew near the pier, Madison reflected on the fact that she could be coaxed into that tourist trap—if it were filmed for PopTV, and if Ryan were with her. It'd be a nice counterpoint to the episode in which Charlie had tried (and failed) to win her a stuffed animal at the air-gun booth. But Ryan had made it clear that he had no interest in being on TV.

She didn't understand it. What did he have to lose? Unlike Luke, he had no "A-list actor" image he was trying to cultivate. Also unlike Luke, he had a cause he could promote. If he mentioned Lost Paws on an episode of *The Fame Game*, donations would come pouring in; Madison was sure of it.

She'd taken to telling him about her shoots, as if to prove how fun they could be. There was the shopping excursion she'd had with Kate, and the redecorating scene she'd filmed with Gaby at their apartment . . . Of course, Madison left certain details out. For instance, that Kate had been snooty at Kitson, and that Madison had been forced to lock Samson in her bathroom because Trevor refused to allow the dog on camera. (Madison would have liked to fight Trevor on the point, but she didn't have much leverage these days. She had to play nice.)

"Are you sure you don't want a churro or something?" Ryan asked, looking longingly at the amusement park.

Madison elbowed him. "Tell me you know me better than that," she said.

Ryan laughed. "All right, I guess I do. Sorry."

She smiled back at him. He was so easy to hang out with, and she never would have guessed it when they first met. He'd picked on her then; he'd worked her like a rented mule. (Of course, he still made her work, but now the disgusting jobs were distributed more fairly among the Lost Paws employees and volunteers.)

She found herself thinking about him a lot when she wasn't with him. She wondered what he was doing and who he was with, and whether or not he might be thinking about her, too.

They weren't dating, because they weren't making out. But they spent so much time together—surely they were more than just work friends?

Or maybe they weren't. Madison wasn't very

experienced when it came to being friends with guys. This was new territory. She'd always seen men as . . . well, as a means to an end. A rich boyfriend meant fancy gifts or a nice apartment to stay in. An actor meant more publicity, more pictures of her in the tabloids. A chef meant delectable meals and a trip to Paris or something.

But what did she want from Ryan? He certainly wasn't the kind of guy she ought to be interested in. He wasn't a director or a producer or a CEO or a TV personality; he was her boss from her court-ordered community service! He was so not anyone who could help her get to the next level of her career. He wouldn't even film.

But already he'd introduced her to parts of L.A. she'd never bothered to go to: the farmer's market in Venice, the rose garden in the Palisades, LACMA. (Madison never thought she would willingly enter a museum, but she had actually enjoyed it.) It was as if the two of them had lived in different cities, as opposed to different neighborhoods. Hanging out with Ryan, away from the tourists on Melrose or photographers on Robertson, Madison felt herself relaxing. One afternoon she ate an ice-cream cone. (A tiny one, but still.) Another time she went into the Gap.

"So do you want to grab dinner?" he asked.

Madison laughed and gave him a little shove. (She was always finding reasons to touch him!) "It's barely six p.m. Who are you, my grandpa?"

"There's that seafood place—I forget what it's called. But they make really good ceviche."

Madison bent down and picked up Samson. He could only walk so far before he got tired and even sadder looking. "Will they let Sam sit outside with us?"

This wasn't what she used to ask about when it came to restaurants—she used to only care if she and her date could get the best (i.e., the most visible) table. And the comped champagne. And the owner to come out and thank her for her patronage, etc.

Ryan reached over and scratched Samson's ears. The dog closed his eyes in pleasure. "Sure they will," he said. "Who could resist a face like this?"

Madison smiled. It really was strange. The more time she spent with Ryan, the less she thought about the things he could or couldn't do for her. What did she want from Ryan Tucker?

Maybe she just wanted him.

22

KEEP ME STANDING

Kate and the rest of the *Fame Game* cast sat in the green room, along with a handful of presenters for the PopTV Movie Awards, touching up their makeup and waiting for their moment in front of the cameras and the spotlights. The *Fame Game* girls were featured guests of the ceremony, invited to plug their show and present the teaser for *The End of Love*. Of course, they were already being filmed by the PopTV cameras as they loitered backstage, and Gaby was playing around with her new mini digital recorder, too. "Hey, guys, say something funny!" she kept crying, but everyone was pretty much ignoring her. Even Madison, who hadn't been on-camera with them much lately and should have been trying to monopolize every inch of film, was sitting quietly in the corner, texting on her phone.

It was going to be the day of a thousand cameras, Kate thought, sidestepping a thick mike cord lying on the ground. She'd been eating handfuls of M&Ms from the snack table in her nervousness, but probably she should just have a Xanie. She'd grown fond of those little blue pills; they made so many things so much easier. Like, for instance, the fact that Ethan, her ex, had started emailing her ten times a day. What did he want from her? She was certainly never going back to Ohio.

And just the other night, completely out of the blue, Luke had called. Maybe, if she'd been thinking more clearly, she wouldn't have answered. But she saw his number on the screen and said, "Hello?" in a voice that she knew must have sounded almost breathless. As if she'd been waiting for his call. For weeks.

But she hadn't! She was doing all sorts of things—she'd hardly been thinking about him at all!

Or that's what she kept telling herself in the first few seconds of the phone call, before he'd even had a chance to say why he was calling. Though she practically felt like hyperventilating, she made her voice sound casual. "Hey, you. Long time no talk."

"Hey back at you, Kate Hayes," Luke said. She could hear the smile in his voice—and was there anything sexier than an Australian accent?

He sounded so relieved to be talking to her that she didn't feel stupid for her own excitement. He told her he missed her and that he wanted to see her. "Tonight," he'd said. "What are you doing tonight?"

Luckily she already had plans with Drew to work on some new songs, so she couldn't drop everything and go to Luke. Which, honestly, she had kind of wanted to do. It was all so confusing. She wished she could've talked to Carmen about it, but—well, that wouldn't really help, would it? Everything was such a mess.

Of course, the next day, when she got the script for their PopTV Movie Awards appearance, she understood why Luke had called: She was about to see him. On TV. He'd wanted to break the ice first. How gentlemanly of him.

Kate felt a hand on her shoulder and she nearly leapt.

"Whoa!" It was Carmen. "Didn't mean to startle you. Jumpy much?"

"Sorry. I guess I'm a little anxious."

A guy with a large set of headphones wrapped around his neck poked his head in the door. "Twenty-five minutes to air," he said to Laurel, and then he vanished.

Kate experienced a tiny jolt of terror. Cameras. A big studio audience. A live broadcast. Yes, she definitely needed a Xanax. She reached into the pocket of her purse, where she always kept it. But nothing was there.

"Oh shit," she said. Panic rose in her throat.

"What?" Carmen asked.

Kate bit her lip. "Um—well—you know how I get stage fright?" Carmen nodded, smiling sympathetically. "Well, I got a prescription for Xanax. And it's been great. The problem is, I left it at home."

Madison glanced up from her phone. "Ask Gaby," she said. "She's like a walking pharmacy."

Kate turned to her, eyes full of hope. "Gaby, do you happen to have any Xanax for me?" she asked.

Gaby nodded enthusiastically. "Sure. How many do you want?"

"One," Kate said. Then she thought about the live audience again and the millions of people watching at home and Ethan back in Ohio, and Luke, who was in the building somewhere, and Carmen . . . and said, "No, actually, two, please."

Gaby tipped two pills into her palm, and Kate quickly tossed them into her mouth. (She felt uncomfortable taking medication from Gaby with others walking around them, even if she did have a prescription of her own.) Carmen handed her a mini bottle of Evian and she swallowed.

"Phew," she said. "Okay. Awesome. Things are going to get a lot easier."

"No doubt," Madison said, raising one perfect blond eyebrow.

Gaby held out the bottle to her, too. "Want one?" she asked.

Madison shook her head. "No thanks."

"It's one of the few vices she doesn't have," Carmen whispered to Kate, who giggled.

Gaby put the bottle back in her purse. "Hey, where's your sister?" Gaby asked Madison. "Isn't she presenting with us?"

Madison shrugged. "Who knows," she said, sounding bored. "Maybe she's running late."

"Why, is she at a Maxi Skirts Anonymous meeting?" Carmen laughed.

Madison laughed back. Like a real, true laugh. It was nice, Kate thought, to hear her join in the fun.

"Sophia's still a supporting character," Laurel noted.

"It's just you four today." Her phone rang, and she ducked out of the room to take the call.

"Well, I'm pretty psyched not to smell that patchouli of hers," Kate said.

Carmen smiled. "Or listen to her talk about the color of my aura."

"The color of my aura," Kate heard herself repeat. "The color of my aura."

It took her a moment to remember what the word "aura" meant. She laughed at the sound of it. Aura. It was sort of funny, wasn't it? Aura aura aura. She blinked her eyes, and realized that her eyelids felt a little heavy. When she looked around the room, she felt slightly dizzy. Her heartbeat began to speed up a little. She leaned toward Carmen and whispered, "Is it kind of warm in here?"

Carmen gave her a strange look. "Um, no. I don't think so." Then she touched Kate's arm. "Are you okay?"

Kate thought about this for a moment. "I'm not sure," she said. She bit the tip of her fingernail uncertainly.

"Gaby," Carmen said, sounding a little alarmed, "what did you give Kate?"

"Xanax. Just like she asked for."

"Let me see the bottle." Carmen took it and showed it to Kate. "Does this look right?"

"Oh shit," Kate whispered as she squinted at the label. It had taken her a second to focus, but when she finally did she realized that the pills had four times as many milligrams as hers did. Which meant she'd just taken eight times her normal dosage. "Oh shit. Shit. Shit!"

"What?" Carmen asked.

Kate shook her head. *Eight times!* She'd be having a panic attack right now if she were capable of it. "Shit," she said again. Then she began to laugh. This was bad. Really bad. She tried to stand and felt a little uneasy on her feet. She dropped back onto the couch, laughing still.

The guy with the headphones opened the door again. "Almost ready, ladies?" he asked.

"Yeah. Just need to powder our noses." Carmen smiled at him, then whipped back around. "Can you make yourself throw up?"

"It's already in her system. There's no point," Madison said.

Kate clutched Carmen's wrist. "You have to help me," she whispered.

Carmen put her arm around Kate's waist. "You're going to be okay," she said. "I'm going to help you through this. Just don't freak out."

"Ummm, what is wrong with her?" Laurel said sharply as she walked back into the room. Her eyes were locked on Kate in horror.

Kate giggled, and Carmen turned to Laurel. "I think she took too much Xanax. Like, way too much."

Laurel visibly paled, then immediately started dialing numbers. She was probably calling Trevor. Or maybe she was calling a doctor. Kate kind of felt like she might need a doctor. "Paging Dr. Garrison," she whispered, leaning against Carmen's shoulder. On the other hand, though, maybe she didn't need a doctor. Her head was made out of clouds and her body was made out of lead . . . and maybe that would be fun!

"Just try to hold your head up and smile," Madison said as they hurried down the hall to the stage. "It'll be okay." She looked amused now, Kate thought, but perhaps not maliciously so.

As they waited in the wings for their cue, Kate dimly recalled that each of the *Fame Game* girls was supposed to say something about her *Fame Game* life. Gaby was going to mention that silly after-hours show of hers, and Carmen, obviously, was going to talk about her role as a modern-day Juliet. Kate knew that she was meant to say something about her music, but what exactly it was, she couldn't remember. Each girl's lines would be displayed on the small prompter in front of them, so she hadn't bothered to memorize hers, but suddenly Kate could barely make out any of the words on the screen.

In the glow of the lights, she noticed how much makeup her castmates were wearing. Did she have that much makeup on? She touched a hand to her cheek; she hadn't really paid attention when she was getting touched up. What if she looked as clownish and painted as they did? She was palpitating her cheek until Carmen pulled her hand down and gave Kate's fingers a reassuring squeeze.

The MC was some Jimmy Fallon type with a cleft chin and blindingly white teeth. "And here's the clique you'd kill to be a part of, PopTV's own It girls," he was saying.

"The ladies of *The Fame Game* need no introduction! But since they tell me that's part of my job tonight, let me introduce Kate Hayes, Gaby Garcia, Carmen Curtis, and Madison Parker!"

The applause was deafening as they made their way onstage. Kate felt like she understood what things must be like for Justin . . . Justin . . . what was his name? Oh my God, the one who sang "Boyfriend"?

Carmen's fingers dug into her palm. Kate thought it might hurt, but she couldn't actually feel anything.

She heard Gaby chirp about getting to interview Brent Bolthouse, and Madison say something about finding pleasure in giving back to the community.

Then she heard someone say her name and felt a microphone in her hand. She turned toward the sound, as slowly as if the air were molasses. "Wha—?" she said.

"It's your line," Carmen whispered. "Your success!" She gave Kate's arm a sharp pinch, which woke Kate up long enough to be able to mumble something along the lines of, "I'm sure you've heard my single, 'Starstruck,' and I'm working on some new songs . . ." So many *s*'s in what she just said!

Kate could see the confusion on the host's tanned face. Or was it horror? The air seemed to shift and wave in front of Kate. She bit her lip, hard, but she could hardly even feel it. In the fuzzed depths of her mind she felt a little prayer forming. *Please, God, just let me get through this. Please just keep me standing.*

Carmen, who smiled brightly, grabbed the microphone

from her. "My castmates have all been busy," she said, "and so have I. I've been working on a movie with . . ." And then a spotlight shone on the far side of the stage and out walked Luke, gorgeous in a trim navy suit (no tie) and low Converse sneakers.

The crowd went wild. Luke joined Carmen center stage as a screen came down from the ceiling to project the sneak peek from *The End of Love*. Kate's heart would have begun to beat faster if it could. Madison put her hand in the small of Kate's back. "Offstage," she whispered as she pushed Kate in the right direction. "Time for us to get offstage now."

Kate opened her eyes and blinked rapidly as her bedroom came into focus. She was in bed, under the covers, but it wasn't morning yet. The sky outside was dark. What time was it? What day was it? She put her hands on her stomach and felt satin . . . not the satin of her nightgown, though, but the warm gold satin of the Jay Godfrey dress she'd picked out for the PopTV Movie Awards.

In a rush, the memory—distorted, hazy, horrifying—came back to her. She had taken too much Xanax. She'd gone onstage. She had said . . . something . . . and then . . . ? Carmen and Madison had brought her home, taken off her shoes, and tucked her into bed.

She rolled over in bed and buried her face in the pillow. What had she done?

She wanted to curl up in a ball and disappear. An on-camera meltdown! The fact that it wasn't really her fault meant nothing. She'd made a complete and utter fool of herself.

With trembling fingers, she reached for her phone. Eight missed calls: from Carmen, Madison, and Laurel. Even from Natalie and her sister, Jessica. From Luke. And, most ominously, from Trevor.

She couldn't bear to listen to any of the messages, but she needed to hear a friendly voice. So, after downing the entire bottle of Voss water that Carmen and Madison had left by her bed, Kate called Drew. Not only was he a good friend and pretty much her favorite person right now, he'd seen her screw up publicly before. He'd be able to tell her how awful this was in comparison. He answered on the first ring, which she took to be a bad sign.

"Did you see it?" she asked. She both hoped that he had, and that he hadn't.

"Yessss," he said slowly. "How are you feeling? Are you okay?"

"Oh my God, was it that terrible? You could tell I was loaded."

Drew's voice was immediately reassuring. "It really wasn't that bad."

"I was practically a zombie," Kate cried.

"It really didn't look that bad," he repeated. "I mean, I just thought you were tired until Carmen called me. I'm sure no one thought anything of it."

Considering the number of phone calls she'd gotten, Kate knew he was only trying to make her feel better. But wasn't that why she'd called him? There was something so solid and reassuring about him. She felt like she could trust him. And in Hollywood, it seemed as if trustworthiness was something of a rare trait.

"I wish you'd be on *The Fame Game* with me more," she sighed. "You'd protect me from my own idiot self."

Drew laughed. "I'm fine to be a bit player now and then, but I have no interest in being the focal point of any camera. I just can't see letting strangers into my life like that. I don't know how you do it."

Kate bristled slightly at this. "But I've gotten so much!" She looked around at her big, well-decorated room. "You should have seen the apartment I was living in before this. And designers send me clothes, so I don't look like the total hick I used to. And Trevor said they were going to buy me a new electric guitar. . . ."

She sensed that she wasn't convincing Drew of the wonderfulness of being a reality-TV star, though, so she stopped.

"Sure, now you have better stuff than you did before," he said. "But you've got strangers taking pictures of you and gossip sites dying for you to do something embarrassing. . . ."

"Like I just did," Kate said, feeling glum again.

Drew laughed. "You've got to let it go! Water under the bridge. But what about all that stuff I keep seeing about Carmen? How she doesn't like her director and how she's a diva on set. I mean, it's like you guys are targets now. Targets for attention, and that attention can be either good or bad."

"Trevor said he'd buy me a Gibson," she said, barely registering his words. "Like one that Taylor Swift plays. And have you seen my Facebook fan page lately? Even my old social-studies teacher sent me a letter," she added. "She said she always knew I'd go far."

There was a pregnant pause. "I know things are cool," Drew said eventually. "I'm really glad you're happy. All I'm saying is, everything comes with a cost. I've lived in this town for a while and I've seen it happen."

Kate was silent. She knew that Drew was right. After all, if life was so perfect, what was she doing burning through one prescription for Xanax and another for Ambien? But she wasn't going to admit it. Not to him, and barely to herself.

"If I weren't on *The Fame Game*," she said, "I wouldn't know you. And if I didn't, who would I call in a moment of desperation? Who would help me write my songs and go with me to my gigs and tell me that I didn't make a total fool out of myself when I clearly did?"

"Well, I am pretty awesome," Drew said, "now that you mention it."

Kate giggled. He was awesome, and she was so relieved he was in her life. And if Trevor hadn't sent her a text shortly after she and Drew had hung up, her day would have ended all right. But Trevor had texted. COME TO THE OFFICE TOMORROW. 11 A.M. IMPORTANT.

Kate gulped, and then buried her face in the pillow again.

23

PICKING A WINNER

Trevor drummed his fingers on the desk. Which should he consider first, the good news or the bad? The triumphs or the meltdowns? Because it was a Monday, and because it was still early in the morning, and because he hadn't finished his tall half-skinny extrahot quad shot yet, he chose the former.

The PopTV Movie Awards appearance had gone off almost without a hitch, and the response to *The End of Love* sneak peek had been amazing. After premiering on the awards show, the snippet had been put online; it logged a million views in less than twenty-four hours. A million! Perez Hilton immediately ran a post, speculating that *The End of Love* would be bigger than *Romeo + Juliet*, starring Claire Danes and Leonardo DiCaprio. Ever since Perez had gone nice, and stopped drawing all over stars' faces in posts, Trevor hadn't put much stock in his opinion—but he agreed with this one. EW.com suggested that Carmen's star would quickly and completely eclipse her mother's.

Yes, Trevor thought, the movie was going to explode; the book it was based on had already landed back on best-seller lists with all the news the movie was generating. That was a good sign.

Filming was going to wrap in a few weeks, so he had to talk Colum into letting him shoot more behind-the-scenes footage. Carmen in her trailer, Carmen getting her makeup done, Carmen lounging around with her costars around the craft-service table: That would be TV gold. Carmen had even become friendly with her makeup person, who wasn't bad looking. Trevor was sure he could put that developing friendship on the show if he needed to. And having Cassandra agree to film had been a pleasant surprise. Obviously there were a lot of emotions to mine in that mother/daughter dynamic—that was how it usually went with those "my mom is my best friend" relationships.

He leaned back in his chair and congratulated himself on picking a winner. Were this whole thing really a game, and he had to put money on one of his girls, he'd bet on Carmen for the win. The fact that she'd become tabloid fodder lately, more so than she'd ever been before, proved his point: The brighter the rising star, the bigger the target.

But there was, Trevor thought, a distant chance that Kate could give Carmen a run for the money someday. She, too, was a genuine talent.

But she was also turning out to be a genuine problem. And it was with that particular thought that Trevor came to the end of his good news. He took another sip of his coffee and then got up to pace his office.

Kate had made a fool of herself on national television. That was unfortunate. But in a way, he could call it an honest mistake; she had crippling stage fright. And he'd actually managed to turn it into a good story line, a map for the rest of her season: Paralyzed by performance anxiety, Kate tries all sorts of therapies and would-be cures. Then she has a big performance, which he would milk for all its will-she-screw-up-or-won't-she potential. And then there would be the great footage of her at the El Rey, triumphant after a nearly flawless set.

Actually, the footage from the other night could fit quite well into her story line. If he saved it for the premiere of season two, Trevor could figure out how to make it a ratings event ("Kate's stage fright returns—see what led up to Kate freezing on live TV!"). That was Trevor's job: taking lemons and making lemonade.

It was the attitude of Kate's, though, that was turning out to be the real problem. Demanding to quit Stecco. Showing up late to shoots. Complaining about the dates he sent her on. She was still basically a kid; he knew that—but he didn't need her acting like a spoiled brat.

That was why he was going to send her home.

Not forever, just for a few days. For a little time-out. A reminder to Kate of where she came from (and where she could quickly be sent back to if she didn't watch her step). And—on the more positive side—a chance for the audience to feel like they were getting to know Kate better.

Trevor imagined the local coffee shop that Kate (and the cameras, of course) would visit, and considered scheduling her an acoustic show there. He envisioned the footage they could get at the zoo, where Kate had once worked. Should he interview the girl who used to bully Kate? Should he check in with the twins she used to babysit? (Well, he could check in with one of them, anyway; the other was in juvie after an incident with matches.)

The possibilities were endless. Most of them would end up on the cutting-room floor, but Trevor liked the idea of showing where Kate Hayes came from. It gave hope to all those girls who saw themselves in her.

Yes, Trevor thought as he performed a handful of deep knee bends, Kate's trip home would provide some interesting material. He had told Laurel to pitch it to Kate as a mini vacation. He couldn't afford to have Kate get guarded and suspicious, the way Madison had been lately; it made for dull footage.

Speaking of Madison: There was something going on with her. Trevor didn't know what, but whatever it was, it had put the tiniest spring in her step. Did it have to do with her deadbeat dad? She'd stopped complaining about her community service, and she hadn't even lashed out at him when Sophia said she couldn't film with her. Trevor had assumed such news would send her running back to him, ready to tell the truth about Charlie and begging Trevor to rehabilitate her image.

Sophia, of course, had already spilled the beans—that

girl was too easy. All he had to do was say that he'd consider making her a main cast member for the second season, and she gave up everything. It was a pretty dramatic story, but Trevor hadn't figured out how to make it work for the show. If Madison wouldn't admit the truth to him, he had nothing. And frankly, even if she did, he wasn't sure what good it would do. She'd perjured herself, after all, and while Trevor wanted a great story, he didn't want Madison to get jail time for the sake of it.

But still. Something was going on with her. He had to find out what it was.

Something was going on with Gaby, too, he mused. She never seemed to eat anything anymore, and she was amassing a hoard of pharmaceuticals to rival Gary Busey's. Her boyfriend, Jay, certainly wasn't a good influence, but since he was the only love interest who wanted to film, Trevor used what he could. The episodes that showed how manipulative he was had started to air, and people were talking about Gaby much more than they did when she was on *L.A. Candy.* Everyone had opinions when it came to relationships. Even Madison seemed to be worried about Gaby, judging from what he'd seen of her on-camera meltdown. Which reminded him, he still had to find a way to use that footage. . . .

He picked up the small weight off his desk and began a set of curls. He had a lot to work with—that was for sure.

24

GO IT ALONE

"I think this would fit me perfectly," Fawn said, holding up a Stella McCartney dress she'd plucked from Carmen's floor. "Don't you?"

Carmen watched as her friend turned sideways in front of the mirror. "It'd probably fit, yeah," she said. She was sprawled out on her bed, exhausted from a day of interviews and photo ops. The sneak peek of *The End of Love* had sparked a media frenzy, and suddenly Carmen found herself on a press junket for a movie that hadn't even finished shooting yet.

"Do you mind?" Fawn asked, already slipping off her jeans.

"No, go ahead. Try it on," Carmen said. There was a whole pile of clothes on the floor, and she had no doubt Fawn would work her way through them all. She'd already done a number on the items Carmen had bothered to hang up.

"Sooo, Julia Capsen, what's up with you and Romeo

these days?" Fawn asked, shimmying into the dress. "Oh, this does look good."

"His character's name is Roman," Carmen said. "And nothing's up. We're friends. Coworkers. We broke up, you know." This wasn't exactly the whole truth, but Carmen was starting to wonder if it was smart to tell Fawn the whole truth. If she admitted to crushing on Luke a little, might she read about it on *D-Lish* tomorrow? Carmen didn't like the feeling that she couldn't trust the people around her. Growing up the daughter of Cassandra and Philip Curtis, she had learned to be slightly wary of her fellow humans. But it hadn't made her closed off. At least not until recently.

"Mmmhmm," Fawn said, sounding unconvinced. "I know all about your fakeup—that's my new term for a fake relationship breakup, by the way."

"You are a true genius," Carmen said. "But really, nothing's going on." A memory of Luke, wet from the pool and silhouetted against the desert sky, came to her then, but she quickly brushed it away.

"I can't wait for your breakover." Fawn's eyes widened. "That's the makeover that takes place after a breakup. Oh! Let's get highlights!"

"I think I'm fine, but thanks. Besides, I can't change my hair until the film wraps," Carmen reminded her.

Fawn shrugged this off. "Can I wear this dress to the Susan G. Komen benefit next Saturday?"

Carmen raised her eyebrows. "Are you a supporter?"

Fawn giggled. "Please. I spend my money on myself. It's just that my mom's on the board, and my dad is away, and she doesn't want to go by herself."

Fawn's parents, whom Carmen had only met once, lived in Bel Air. Fawn rarely saw them, it seemed. They were just characters in the background of her life, most useful for their ability to write large checks to their daughter. Fawn had convinced them that an actual job would interfere too much with her acting career. Or perhaps "career" should be in quotation marks still, since Fawn hadn't been doing much to pursue it lately.

Maybe having invisible parents was better than having famous ones. Carmen hadn't seen much of her mother in person recently—after all, she spent fifteen hours a day on the *End of Love* set—but she seemed to be everywhere in the news. She was hyping her new single in every outlet available: *GMA*, *Rachael Ray*, *USA Today*, Facebook, Twitter. There was almost a desperate quality to it, which made Carmen feel both annoyed and sad. The fact that she'd talked to Rachael about Carmen's "love troubles" made her lean more toward annoyed.

"Do you want to go with us?" Fawn asked, interrupting Carmen's thoughts. "It's always a fun party."

Carmen closed her eyes. "I'm too tired."

Fawn threw a silk scarf at her. "It's ten days from now, silly. I think you'll be able to sneak in a nap before then."

Carmen would have liked to sneak in a nap right now. But Fawn showed no signs of slowing down on her closet raid, and plus, Carmen was feeling mildly anxious. Movie publicity was one thing, but it seemed as if every time she turned around there was a new gossip item about her. (*Carm: stress eating?* said the latest caption, beneath a picture of her eating a candy bar—as if it were a crime to enjoy a Milky Way once in a while!)

"Do you think . . ." But she didn't exactly know how to phrase it. "I feel like there's been weird little things about me lately," she said. "You know, on TMZ and stuff."

"Welcome to public life, Carm," Fawn said, pulling another dress off the floor and examining the label.

"I know, but it feels sort of . . . mean sometimes. Like that thing about how Luke was really the one to break up with me because I'm a diva."

Fawn looked at her coolly. "Oh, where was that? I didn't see that one."

"You want to read all my bad press?"

"There's no such thing as bad press," Fawn replied. "I'd kill for someone to write something nasty about me, as long as there was a superhot photo to go with it."

"Easy for you to say. No one's publicly accusing you of gaining ten pounds from stress-eating."

"Oh, poor you. Always in the magazines! It must be rough to have such a famous mom and have so many people care about you."

Carmen sighed. "But there's something weird about it. It's like . . . there's some person out there feeding them stories. Someone who doesn't like me."

At this, Fawn laughed out loud. "Carmen, are you hearing yourself? (A) you're being totally paranoid. And (B) don't you think it's a little self-centered for you to assume that someone is out to get you?"

Carmen sat up. Fawn, in another one of her dresses now, was looking at her with comic disbelief. "Also: a little crazy," she added.

Carmen laughed, a rush of relief flooding her thoughts as she let Fawn's words sink in. "Yeah, you're probably right. I'm being crazy."

"You're a nice person, Carmen," Fawn said. "For instance, you're going to let me borrow this dress, too. And nice people don't make enemies."

Carmen nodded. "You're right. I am nice. And because I'm so nice, I'm also going to let you borrow the Christian Louboutin clutch that matches."

Fawn grinned and did a little victory dance around Carmen's room. "You're the best. I promise to only say good things about you, ever."

Carmen smiled back. Fawn was definitely a bit cuckoo, and she had certain issues with boundaries. As in: She didn't seem to have any. But still, Carmen knew that Fawn meant what she said.

All the lights were off downstairs. Philip Curtis was away in New York for the week, and Cassandra always went to bed early. Sleep, she liked to say, was even better than Restylane when it came to undereye bags.

Carmen slipped off her heels and tossed them into the hall closet. She wished she'd been able to go to bed early. Instead she'd had to film a dinner scene with Sophia, Gaby, and Jay, a trio that came close to Carmen's idea of conversational hell. Gaby she could deal with, but Sophia's New Age obsessions had gotten tired a long time ago, and Jay was simply a jackass. He wasn't even that nice to Gaby. She'd given him a "commitment bracelet" earlier that day, but he'd already taken it off. When Carmen asked him why, he'd held up a wrist encircled with a giant, hideous gold watch. "If it didn't clash with my gold accessories," Jay had said, "I'd totally wear it all the time."

Even Sophia rolled her eyes at that one.

Then, leaving the restaurant, Carmen had been chased by a TMZ videographer. The day before they'd run an item with the title CARMEN CASHING IN ON THE CURTIS NAME. And now they wanted her to comment on the "fame war" between her and Cassandra. Carmen had shrugged them off—"I didn't realize we were in one," she'd said—but they followed her, still peppering her with intrusive questions. Why were people so rude?

Also, how come everyone always brought up her mother? It was getting really, really old.

Carmen padded up the stairs to her mother's room. A light shone under the doorway, but Carmen would have knocked even if it had been off. It was time she and her mom had a talk.

"Carmen?" came Cassandra's voice. "Is that you?"

Carmen pushed open the door and saw her mother in her pajamas, with a sleep mask pushed up on her forehead, in a circle of light from the reading lamp. "Hey, Mom," she said. "Did I wake you?"

Her mother smiled. "No, I was reading." She held the book up, but Carmen couldn't see the title. "It's about what they called learned optimism."

"What's that?" Carmen said. She didn't really care, but she didn't want to be impolite.

"It's this idea that a talent for joy, like any talent, can be cultivated. Like singing or acting or playing music. You practice, and it gets easier—to play a song, or to wake up feeling happy." Cassandra stopped and gazed at her daughter. "What's wrong, sweetie? You look upset."

Carmen walked into the room and sat at the foot of her mother's bed. "I'm tired. And stressed. I should be feeling, like, amazing, but this whole life-in-the-spotlight thing, well, isn't exactly what I thought it would be."

Cassandra nodded. "I know. Maybe I should have done a better job of warning you."

"About that," Carmen said.

Her mother raised an eyebrow. "What?"

"I feel like you should also do a better job letting me do this on my own."

"Excuse me?"

Carmen took a deep breath. "I really didn't appreciate you coming on *The Fame Game*."

"We talked about this," Cassandra said, sounding

defensive. "I thought you were happy about it."

"Well, you were wrong." Carmen could hear the anger in her voice, and the force of it surprised her. "You were so wrapped up in the constant monitoring of your career that you failed to notice I wasn't exactly thrilled with the news. But, hey, you need to move records—I understand that's more important than your daughter's feelings."

"Carmen," her mother gasped. "Listen to yourself! Why would you say such a terrible thing to me?"

"Because lately it seems like that's what matters to you. You've been a star forever, barring that blip of relative calm when I was little. So you've already had one comeback, and you don't want to have another. You just want to stay on top. Am I right?"

Cassandra looked taken aback. "Well, certainly being successful is easier than not being successful," she allowed.

"Admit that you love and crave fame," Carmen said.

Her mother laughed. "Of course I do. But who doesn't? You do, too."

"Yes," Carmen said hotly. "I do. And it's my turn to have it. So I don't want you on *The Fame Game* again, and I don't want you talking to journalists when they call you up to ask about me, and I don't want you meddling in my life."

Cassandra paled. "What is going on with you, Carmen? This is crazy talk."

"No, it's not," Carmen said. "I'm sick of being in your shadow, don't you know that? And the second I come out of it, you move over so I'm right back in it. And I'm telling you, Mom: It's getting old."

Her breath was coming quickly, as if she'd been running.

"I am your mother," Cassandra said quietly. "And you may be a legal adult, but that doesn't mean you know the first thing about the world."

"So you're going to teach me by hogging the spotlight? You know, most mothers would teach their daughters how to cook or manage their money or not kill their house-plants. But all you've taught me lately is that fame is more important than family."

"Is that really what you think?" Cassandra pulled off her sleep mask and tossed it onto the bed. "First of all, let me remind you that you're the one who's been too busy to talk. Second of all, you have always been your father's and my number-one priority. We've given you everything."

"Including the Curtis name, I know. I'm so lucky," Carmen replied sarcastically. "That name has haunted me my whole life. Everything I have ever done is 'undeserved' because of it. That's what they say, you know. My name was handed to me, just like everything else."

Cassandra sat up straighter in her bed. "I am so sorry that we wanted the best for you," she said. "Apparently, though, we're just a burden. You'd be much better off without our name . . . and everything that comes along with it."

Carmen gaped at her. "Wait. What—?"

"Well, clearly us providing you with everything you want has been a huge mistake. So it stops here. The car, the credit cards, the clothes . . . this home."

"That isn't what I meant," Carmen argued.

Her mother's eyes were dark and cold. "I'm going back to bed now, and you should probably do the same. You'll want to get an early start tomorrow morning. Apartments are pretty difficult to find in L.A. Oh, and the rent is absurd."

"You're seriously kicking me out?"

"You want to go it alone? I'm happy to give you that, too. Welcome to the real world, darling," she said.

Carmen stared at her. She couldn't believe how badly this had all gone, but she couldn't back down now. "Why wait until tomorrow? I'll get out of your hair tonight."

"Whatever you want, Carmen," Cassandra said.

Then she turned off her bedside lamp, placed her sleep mask over her eyes, and turned her back to her daughter.

Carmen had quickly packed her Goyard weekend bag and was now sitting in her car, still in the driveway, trying to figure out where to go. She dialed Drew with trembling fingers. He didn't pick up, though, and she didn't leave a message. She tried Kate next. Now that they'd pretty much made up, maybe she could crash at her place for a while. But Kate didn't answer, either. Fawn picked up, but she was between apartments and was house-sitting all the way out in Palisades—way too far away from the PopTV

Films studio. So Carmen called Luke.

"Hey, ex-looover," he said. "Can't wait to see me on set?"

"Can I come stay with you?" she blurted.

"What?"

She told him what had happened. Luke listened sympathetically and then, when she was done with her rant, he said simply, "Come on over. You can have the bed. I'll take the couch."

25

SOMEWHERE BETTER

"PopTV is sending Kate back to her hometown, you know," Madison said, flipping the radio station to 97.1 FM and tapping her foot to the chorus of "Call Me Maybe." "They're going to follow her around while she eats a Grand Slam breakfast at Denny's and tries on a pair of Jessica Simpson boots at the mall. Can you believe it? She gets screen time and a vacation from L.A. and all its craziness."

Ryan laughed as they sped north on the 1. "Well, you're about to get a mini vacation yourself, you know." He paused. "Although when I think about the way my two sisters are going to jump on you, it may not actually be that relaxing."

"I have experience with sisters," Madison said drily. "I'm sure yours will be easier than mine."

Out the window of Ryan's Jeep, Madison watched for glimpses of the ocean. Trees flashed by, and the sky was a deep, cloudless blue. She felt like she was playing hooky from real life, sneaking away to spend the night at Ryan's parents' house in Santa Barbara because it was Ryan's birthday and the Tuckers had promised them a home-cooked meal, a giant cake, and a big stack of DVDs to watch. "You won't even have to move from the couch," Ryan had assured her. "My mom will wait on you hand and foot." The old Madison would have run screaming from such an evening (although the hand-and-foot part didn't sound bad), but the new Madison thought it sounded perfect. It was a break, and she needed one. Badly.

An hour later, they pulled into the driveway of the Tucker home, a large white stucco Mediterranean on a bluff above the Pacific. There was a fountain out front—a nymph, surrounded by birds and fish—and more blooming bushes than Madison had ever seen. Ryan hoisted her Louis Vuitton over his shoulder (she was incapable of packing light) and led her into a vast foyer. A central staircase split in two at the landing and curved up to the second floor. A huge fern dwarfed the entryway table, its green fronds dotted with what looked like tiny, feathery miniature ferns.

"It's called a mother fern," said a voice. "Those little things on the leaves are baby plantlets. You can take one home and plant it."

Madison smiled at the woman who was standing in the doorway to the kitchen, wiping her hands on a tea towel. Her hair was coppery and pulled back in a low ponytail. She had wide, high cheekbones and her eyes were the same lovely green as her son's. "You must be Mrs. Tucker,"

Madison said, walking over and holding out her hand. "It's so nice to meet you. I'm Madison."

"Call me Lucy," she said, taking Madison's hand and shaking it firmly. "Welcome. I hope you're hungry, because I made enough eggplant parmesan to feed the whole neighborhood. I also hope you don't mind small, insolent children, because there are two of them running around." She grinned at her son. "Right? I'm being fair to warn her, don't you think?"

Ryan laughed. "Emma and Rebecca are eleven. They are highly cute and highly obnoxious."

"But so sweet," Lucy said, her eyes going soft. "Hearts of gold."

Ryan turned to Madison. "I might argue with that. But you can judge for yourself. They're probably in the back garden. We eat dinner out there most nights."

"Do you need any help?" Madison asked. She was struck by Lucy Tucker's poise and beauty. Her own mother had been the prettiest girl in Armor Falls, but her looks had faded years ago. And she could never serve up eggplant parmesan, unless it was on a sandwich from Wendy's.

Lucy shook her head firmly. "No, you guys go on out back. Dinner will be out in a minute."

Ryan held out his arm, directing Madison to the back of the house. She passed through a formal living room, then a more comfortable sitting room, and then into a hallway that led to the back deck.

"You have such a beautiful home," she said. She

couldn't keep the wistfulness out of her voice.

"Thanks," Ryan said, seeming slightly embarrassed by its quiet opulence. "It was a nice place to grow up, I guess."

Suddenly two shrieking girls flew out of the bushes and flung themselves at Ryan. Whether they were trying to hug him or tickle him or some combination of the two was hard for Madison to tell; they were a blur of blond pigtails and matching pink sundresses. Ryan, grunting and laughing, managed to capture one under each arm.

"Madison," he said. "This is Emma on my left and Rebecca on my right. Girls, this is Madison."

Immediately the twins stopped fidgeting and an awed look came over their lovely, nearly identical faces. "We loved your show," said Emma. *Madison's Makeovers*. Mom wouldn't always let us watch it because she's kind of strict about TV stuff, but we got to see it over at Heather's house."

Rebecca, whose eyes were slightly darker than her sister's and whose lips were fuller, nodded. "We loved it so much. I can't believe you're at our house!" She elbowed Ryan in the ribs. "How come you never told us you were friends with Madison Parker?"

Madison laughed. "He wasn't. Not until recently, anyway."

"He is such a freak," Emma said. "You think he looks all normal but I'm telling you, he is a total dork."

"All right, all right. That's enough. Let's go sit down," Ryan said, smiling indulgently at them. "But give your hands a rinse first."

The girls scampered off, and by the time they returned everyone was sitting around the table in the back garden, which Mr. Tucker ("Call me Dan") had set with blue-and-white Spode china and delicate goblets that glinted in the early evening light.

Madison listened to the family banter as they dug into their ridiculously delicious food. ("Oh, don't praise me, I just follow Jamie Oliver's directions," Lucy had said.)

Was this what having a normal family was like? Madison wondered. Or was the Tucker family actually an abnormally good one? She smiled shyly at Ryan, who was sitting at the head of the table, looking like he couldn't imagine being anywhere else. She felt a pang of longing, and maybe even envy; it seemed like her entire life, she'd always wanted to be somewhere else. Somewhere better than she was.

But what could be better than this? After dinner, after the cake and the round of "Happy Birthday," Madison and Ryan were left alone to sip iced tea in the rose-covered gazebo. She had given him a wallet, which wasn't a very good present, she knew that. Not nearly as good as the book of Robert Adams photographs his dad had gotten him, or the crazy poster portrait of him that his sisters had made. But she'd frozen up in the Nordstrom aisle: What did you get the guy who seemed to have everything, but who worked in a shelter in El Segundo and dodged cameras like their lenses might steal his soul? Madison had never met anyone like Ryan and she just wasn't sure what to do with him.

Except kiss him, said a little voice. But she couldn't—not without knowing if he felt the same way about her. So she sat next to him, as chastely as if she were in Sunday school. They chatted in spurts, discussing Lost Paws' newest dog, a Great Pyrenees named Chance, and gossiping about whether or not Sharon, aka the Raisin, had a crush on Stan, aka Forearms. Madison regaled Ryan with stories about various disasters on the set of *Madison's Makeovers*, and Ryan admitted that he'd nearly flunked out of college because he had decided, on a whim, to spend two months bird-watching in Thailand.

They had so much to say to each other. As the night grew cooler and darker, and bats began to circle in the air above, Madison tried to remember the last time she'd just sat with a guy. Just talked. In the past, there had always been an undercurrent, a subtext—questions she asked without saying them out loud. *What will you give me? And what do I have to give to you to get it?*

But she never had that thought with Ryan. Instead she thought: *I like you. I like myself around you. Are you ever going to kiss me?* But what if she was completely off? What if they were simply friends and she was reading too much into it? She really didn't know what to think.

"It's so nice here," she said softly. "It smells like roses and the ocean."

Ryan looked at her and his eyes were keen but warm. He seemed almost as if he wanted to say something, or to reach out and grab her hand. But he didn't.

"It's better than Columbus, Ohio, right?" he asked

teasingly. "Even if that's where the cameras are?"

"It's definitely better here," she said. "They don't call that flyover country for nothing."

"Have you ever been to Ohio?"

"No," Madison said. "But I don't need to. I've seen pictures!" Then she laughed at how snobby this sounded.

"Right," Ryan said. "So I guess I don't need to listen to your stories anymore because I've seen you on TV."

Madison knew perfectly well that he was joking, but she felt a tiny stab of worry anyway. What if she was beginning to bore him? They'd never spent this long together before. What if this much Madison was just too much?

Beside her, Ryan yawned and then shifted in his seat. This confirmed her fears. He'd had enough of her and wanted to go to bed.

"Am I getting boring?" she asked. She tried to say it lightly.

Ryan shook his head. "Sorry, it's been a long week. I'm tired." He stretched his long legs out, and Madison noticed that his feet were bare.

She was exhausted herself, but she didn't want the night to end yet. Not until she knew what was going on between the two of them. Just Friends didn't go on weekend getaways together, did they?

"We could go in. . . ." she said softly.

He shook his head. "Don't mind me," he said. "I'll perk up."

"How are you going to do that?" she asked.

Ryan turned to look at her. Madison met his gaze, holding her breath. In the fading light his eyes looked dark, almost black. "I don't know," he said. "Maybe this way?"

He leaned toward her, and his fingers felt their way toward hers, and then they were kissing. No longer sleepy, no longer uncertain, they wrapped their arms around each other, under the roses and the stars.

26

WHAT I WISHED FOR

Kate sat in a cab, across the street from the house in which she'd grown up. She'd sworn she was never going back to Ohio (except maybe for Christmas), and yet here she was. She wasn't really sure how she felt about it. Besides . . . coerced. And nervous, because the 4.6 million viewers of *The Fame Game* (according to last week's ratings) were about to see exactly where she came from.

Her mother had placed two big planters of mums on each side of the front porch, the way she did every fall. The neighbor's dog was barking as usual, and old Mrs. Hennick across the street was peering out her window, the way she did whenever she heard a car turn into their cul-de-sac. Kate's world had been flipped upside down in the last few months, but here in her old neighborhood, everything was exactly the same. Seeing those gold and orange flowers, and that same dumb Thanksgiving flag her mother had hung by the door (a turkey wearing a pilgrim hat)—well, it made Kate feel kind of like a kid again. A kid with strawberry-blond pigtails and a big voice. A kid with a crazy dream to make it as a musician.

She stirred restlessly in the backseat of the cab. The camera crew was set up and ready to film her arrival, but since they hadn't quite finished blocking her shot, she had to wait. She hoped Laurel had alerted the neighbors about the disruptions; otherwise Mrs. Hennick would be dialing 911 any minute.

Beside her, Laurel cleared her throat. "Allergies," she explained. "Leaf piles." She gestured toward the neat mounds of maple leaves that dotted the neighbor's lawn.

"Too bad I'm not Gaby, the walking medicine cabinet," Kate joked. (Too soon?)

"I'll be fine," Laurel said. "You about ready? We're going to start in a few minutes."

Laurel had gone over all of Kate's story points on the second leg of their cross-country flight. Kate knew that she was supposed to tell her mother about how she was struggling to balance her restaurant work (even though she'd already quit) while also pursuing her music career. Then she'd been told to talk about the new friends she'd made in Hollywood, and their different personalities and quirks.

It was silly: They wanted her to talk to her mother as if the two of them hadn't spoken since she moved to L.A., which of course they had. But as Trevor had reminded her, "If it didn't happen on-camera, it didn't happen." So yes, she knew what to do. But she didn't want to think about it, not yet. She had a few more moments of normalcy, and then she'd be on camera. Acting. Playing herself, but still acting.

"We used to play hide-and-seek all around here, because of the cul-de-sac," Kate said, a trace of wistfulness in her voice. She was gazing absently at an elm tree she used to hide in when she noticed a familiar blue car parked in its shade: a beat-up Subaru wagon with a Phish bumper sticker. She gasped.

"What?" Laurel said. "You okay?"

"That's Ethan's car. Tell me you guys did not call my ex-boyfriend," Kate demanded.

Laurel didn't respond for a moment. Instead she took a long drink of her coffee.

Kate lowered her voice, the way her mother used to do when she was disappointed in her. "I've been avoiding him for weeks, and now you're just going to spring him on me? That is so incredibly uncool."

Laurel sighed. "I can't always tell you everything, Kate. This is my job. I would never put you in a position that I didn't think you could handle, but sometimes we just need a genuine reaction."

Kate flopped her head back against the seat.

"I mean, come on," Laurel said. "With the rest of the cast slowly immobilizing their faces with injectables, you're kind of our last hope." She laughed and gave Kate a nudge.

But Kate didn't find it funny. She hated feeling like everyone around her knew a secret and was just sitting and waiting for her to be blindsided. "God," she said, "it's like some kind of mean-spirited surprise party. And, like, there's a giant cake, but instead of a hot guy jumping out, it's my ex-boyfriend."

"It's going to be fine," Laurel said soothingly. "You're going to be amazing. You're a pro."

"Whatever that means," Kate huffed.

"It means that when it's time to shoot, you shoot," Laurel said. "Like right now."

Laurel gave her arm a quick squeeze and hopped out of the cab. She went around to the driver's window and asked that he count to ten before pulling up to the house. She pointed to a PA standing in the street. "Stop right in front of him," she directed. And then she vanished into one of the production vans.

When the driver stopped at his mark, Kate took a deep breath, steeled herself, and got out of the cab. In a matter of seconds, she was opening the door to her childhood home and a life that now felt a million miles away.

In the entryway hung the same pastel seascapes Kate remembered, and the air still smelled like the Crabtree & Evelyn potpourri her mother loved. The living room seemed smaller and dingier, but maybe that was because it was full of cameras, tangled extension cords, lighting equipment, and strangers.

"Oh, honey," her mother cried, coming out of the kitchen.

Kate rushed forward to hug her. "Hi, Mom," she said

into her hair. Kate wrapped her arms around her mother's waist, and she could have kicked herself for thinking it, but she couldn't help it: *Has Mom gained weight?*

Her mom stepped away, holding her shoulders. "Let me look at you, my beautiful girl. Oh, I've missed you!"

"I've missed you, too." And God, what was with those mom jeans? The waist of them had to be six inches above her belly button. Didn't she understand she was going to be on TV?

"Come in, come in," Marlene Hayes said, sounding flustered. "Are you hungry?"

Kate followed her mom into the living room and set her purse on the rocking chair that she used to sit in as she waited for the school bus. "No thanks, Mom. I'm okay."

"Are you sure you don't want me to make you a nice salad? I have some lovely arugula from Hillsdale Market."

"Sit, Mom," Kate said. She heard the impatience in her voice. She didn't want half of teenaged America to see her mother babying her.

Her mother did as she was told. Marlene was obviously nervous, but she was handling herself pretty well, considering. "You have to tell me everything," she said.

What Kate most wanted to do was go upstairs and lie down. Then, after a nap, she'd come down and style her mother for her camera time. She thought of Cassandra Curtis, who was possibly the most glamorous forty-something on earth, and how Trevor had filmed her nibbling sushi at some fabulous Brentwood eatery. Couldn't they have made Marlene Hayes look a little less . . . suburban?

Kate tried to banish these superficial thoughts. Tried to pretend there wasn't a camera three feet from her face, waiting for her to Tell All. What would she do if she and her mom were alone? Maybe she'd crawl into her lap, and have her gently smooth the hair back from her forehead the way she did when Kate was little. Maybe she'd sigh dramatically and tell her mother about all the insanity of her new life: how it was wonderful and awful and exciting and terrifying, and how sometimes, when she looked at herself in the mirror in the morning, she felt as if she were looking at a stranger.

But the camera's red light was blinking, and that wouldn't be what Trevor wanted to hear. It wouldn't be what Kate wanted to show, either.

"Where do I begin?" Kate asked, laughing in a way that she hoped sounded sincere.

"Well, gosh," her mother said, "I don't know." But before she could make a suggestion (and hit her own talking points!), there was a knock at the door. Marlene turned around, trying to look baffled as to who might be stopping by. Kate felt her heart start to beat a little faster. They both knew who it was, but they had to pretend—for the cameras, yes, but even worse, to each other—that they didn't. Her mother bit her thumbnail like a girl.

"Aren't you going to get it?" Kate asked. She wished, for a moment, that she had the guts to defy Laurel and say, *Don't answer it. It's probably just the Jehovah's Witnesses.*

"Ha!" Marlene's laugh was a sharp bark. "Yes, silly me."

Ethan Connor looked better than he used to—that was the first thing Kate noticed as he strode, smiling, into the living room. He had let his dark hair grow so that it curled at the collar of his flannel shirt. He was tan from weekends spent on the river, and it seemed as if he'd grown an inch or two.

"Well, look who it is," he said, his voice booming. "Little Miss Hollywood." He was thrilled to be in a room full of cameras—it couldn't have been more obvious.

She stood up and hugged him, being careful not to hit his mike pack. "Oh my God, Ethan! It's been a while!"

Ethan stepped back and looked at her. "And whose fault is that?" His voice was suddenly cool and his dark eyes glittered. "Certainly not mine."

He had walked in, Kate realized, ready for a fight. She wondered if he was actually mad at her (which, okay, he might have a reason to be) or if his anger was Trevor's idea. Not that it mattered: She wasn't going to get into it with Ethan in front of the cameras. She'd had enough on-screen drama lately.

"Life has been soooo crazy," she said, sinking back down in her chair and wiping her brow for effect. "I hardly know where I am or what day it is."

"I can help you with both of those things. It's Tuesday, and you're in Ohio. Your humble roots." Ethan narrowed his eyes. "Speaking of roots, did you dye your hair?"

Kate put a hand up to the crown of her head. "Just a

little highlighting," she said, flushing.

Ethan gazed at her for a moment. "I think I liked it better before," he said finally.

She exhaled sharply. "Well, thanks for the input. I'm sure my colorist will care." *Whoops,* she thought. *You're not supposed to fight.*

"It's more than that, though. Did you get it straightened, too, or just wash it?"

"So, Katie, dear, tell us about your new songs," her mother interjected.

Kate turned to her gratefully. Why couldn't she have had ten minutes alone with her mother before PopTV started bringing in the exes? She was going to complain to Trevor about this. "Well, I've been writing a lot, and it's been going really well."

"I'm sure it's been going a lot better than your performances," Ethan said. "So that's good."

Wow, was he going to just keep putting her down or what? She would have brought up her awesome El Rey show, but since it hadn't aired yet, it hadn't happened. "So anyway, Mom, I've got basically an album's worth of stuff, and I'm going to see what can happen with it."

"Oh, that's so exciting!" Marlene said. "I hope you'll play me some."

"Of course."

"Has Courtney Love been in touch lately?" Ethan asked.

Kate rolled her eyes. "No," she said.

"Hmmm . . . probably off her meds . . ." he said.

At that point, Kate had had enough. She wasn't going to play nice any longer. "What is your problem, Ethan? Are you just going to sit there and insult me? Look, I'm sorry I didn't call you back. But that song wasn't about you, okay? And I just didn't feel like dealing."

Her mother stiffened on the couch. "Kate, that isn't the way we talk to our guests."

"Have you been listening to what he's been saying to me?" she demanded. "I wasn't the one who walked into the room with guns blazing."

Marlene frowned. "No one said relationships were easy. There was a time you two were inseparable. And now look at you. Ethan may be a little prickly, but you, Katie, need to be polite."

"Excuse me?" Kate said.

"You heard me," her mother said. "Now sit tight. I'm going to go get the cookies I baked and we are all going to be a little better behaved."

Ethan and Kate stared at each other from across the room. "I suppose you're enjoying this," Kate said.

Ethan's posture softened. "Oh, Kate," he said. "I'm sorry. I just—I don't know. I miss you, I really do. But I guess I'm not doing a good job of showing it, am I?"

Kate's eyes widened. Was he sincere? Was he acting? Was he bipolar?

She really had no idea. And frankly, at the moment, she didn't want to know. She was jet-lagged and exhausted and, come to think of it, she actually was hungry. She stood up. "It was a long flight. I think I'll go lie down for a little while," she said. And carefully, so Trevor couldn't accuse her of having a Madisonlike freak-out, she took off her mike pack and left the room, swiping two of her mom's cookies on the way.

"It was awful," Kate said, picking at the glow-in-the-dark star stickers that she'd put on her wall when she was ten. "First there was the whole thing with Ethan, and then they made me film at the Columbus Zoo."

"I don't know, zoos are all right, aren't they?" Drew asked. The connection was bad, and his voice sounded strange and far away.

"They had me at the penguin exhibit, so a crowd of gaping Ohioans could watch me toss fish to the poor things. It's because I used to work there, but I never even did anything with animals. I sold hot dogs and lemonade!"

"All right, that could have been better. What else?"

She finally got a star unstuck and she flicked it onto the floor. "They made me go back to my old high school and say hi to my choir teacher. And tomorrow I have to sing at some party my mom's friend is throwing. I would rather cut off my left hand than do that." She went back for another star; she didn't want their little greenish glow over her head anymore. She was too old for that stuff.

Drew laughed. "But it must be nice to see your mom. . . ."

Kate nodded, as if he could see her. "Of course. It's

great. When she isn't accusing me of having changed."

"Have you changed?" Drew wondered.

Kate gave up on the stars and flopped back onto her ancient comforter. "I don't know! Probably? But I had to. And why is it that whenever someone says you've changed, they mean for the worse?"

Drew laughed. "I don't know if that's always the case."

"But it usually is," Kate insisted. "And okay, I get it. Everything's so different than it used to be, and it's all supposed to be better. But it's also much more complicated." Violet, her childhood teddy bear, was propped on her desk; she picked it up and turned it over in her hands. "People get really weird when fame is involved."

"Yeah, like when your boyfriend wouldn't be seen in public with you." Drew's voice had an edge to it.

Kate felt a pang of sorrow—but not for Luke. She was over him; she knew that now. The pang was for her own self, because she'd gone along with it. "That sucked," she agreed. "More things suck than I would have imagined."

"'This is what I wished for / Just isn't how I envisioned it,'" Drew said.

"Huh?"

"'Famed to the point of imprisonment—'"

Kate was laughing now. "What are you talking about?"

"I'm quoting Eminem," Drew said matter-of-factly. "His wisdom is underrated."

"Wow. I've never heard you rap before." She hugged Violet to her chest. There was a time in her life when she wouldn't let the bear out of her sight. "I don't know if I

262

want to again, either."

"Don't worry. I bust it out on rare occasions. Like when my Kate needs cheering up."

My Kate, she thought, squeezing Violet harder. *What does he mean by that? He used to call Carmen "my Carm."* . . .

"So are you coming home soon?" Drew asked.

Home, thought Kate. *Is L.A. really home now?* "In a couple of days."

"Try to have more fun until then," he urged. "Life isn't as hard as you're making it."

"I know," she said, sighing. "You're right, as usual."

She felt like she'd gotten off track somehow. Dazzled by the spotlights, she'd forgotten who she was and where she hoped to be going. Maybe being in Ohio was going to be better for her than she thought. Maybe she should thank Trevor instead of blaming him. Maybe she shouldn't mind that her mom was so normal. Maybe she still had a lot to learn.

"'So be careful what you wish for / 'Cause you just might get it . . .'"

"Oh my God, are you rapping again?"

"Sorry," Drew said sheepishly. "It's stuck in my head now."

Kate slipped under the covers and cradled the phone against her ear. Yes, it was going to be good to be here. But she couldn't deny the pull she felt back to L.A.

Back to Drew.

27

TALKING POINTS

Carmen leaned over across the banquette table at Walrus, a new, slightly hipsterish bar that had opened earlier that week, and poked Fawn in the ribs. "My dress looks amazing on you."

Fawn grinned. "Sooo amazing that you might let me keep it?"

"Guys," Drew said. "We just finished with the is-Balenciaga's-new-collection-the-greatest-thing-ever conversation. Can we move on to something, I don't know, a little more gender-neutral?"

Carmen laughed and nodded. "Sorry." It was time to change the subject anyway; PopTV was filming this night out and no one had hit their talking points yet. Sometimes it took a while to warm up, though. Plus, tonight's crowd was kind of weird. Carmen, Gaby, and Sophia were the only ones on the shooting schedule, but at the last minute Carmen had begged Drew to come. "For moral support," she'd said. "I need to be around at least one real friend tonight."

Trevor was making the most of Carmen's three-day break from shooting; he'd already had her film a brunch with Gaby and a shopping excursion with Sophia. She'd even gone out with Reeve Wilson and let the cameras come. Trevor obviously hadn't gotten wind yet of the blowup with her mother (or where she was staying); otherwise he would have tried to make her film some tearful confrontation. Laurel knew about it, though, since they'd planned to have a quick shoot of Carmen and her mom in their breakfast nook, with Cassandra offering sage advice about the new wave of attention Carmen was getting. Carmen had told Laurel they had to scrap the scene . . . and then she asked if maybe there was an apartment for her, too, at Park Towers.

"I wish Kate could be here," Carmen said brightly. "She loves this place."

Sophia took her cue. "Where is she, anyway? I haven't seen her around."

"She's back at home. In Ohio. She was basically suffering from exhaustion, so she decided to take a break. Rest up."

Sophia nodded. "Totally. Rest is so essential to mental and physical well-being. I'm always telling Madison that, but I don't think she listens to me."

"How's she doing?" Carmen asked.

Clearly they could hit their lines without any help from Gaby, who had disappeared somewhere with Jay. He hadn't been on their schedule, but his being there was definitely no accident. He was already miked when Sophia, after receiving a text, had pointed him out across the room and said, "Gaby, isn't that your man? Who's that chick hanging on him?" Gaby had gone over to investigate (followed by two cameras) and had never returned.

"Oh," Sophia said in reply to Carmen's question. "She's only got a few weeks of community service left, and then maybe she'll be able to come out and play more."

They talked about Kate's upcoming shows and the fact that Carmen had booked her first monthly magazine cover for the following spring, when *The End of Love* would be coming out.

Drew wasn't saying much—Trevor never gave him any talking points, even when he was on the schedule—but Carmen was glad to have him there. It had been so long since they'd hung out, and she missed him. He was so solid. So grounding.

That was why, after the cameras left (and Sophia had followed them out), she made him stay a little longer. "I'm your ride, remember," she'd said teasingly. "You can either sit with me or you can walk."

The DJ had started spinning bizarre mashups (Adele and the Wu-Tang Clan; LMFAO and the Ramones), and it was hard to hear. She scooted closer to Drew and said, "So—what's up? Tell me everything."

He shrugged. "I don't know. Not much is going on, really." He looked at her carefully. "But you know how I sort of like to keep tabs on you, right? So I know what's up with you even when we don't hang? Well, I saw something kind of crazy on the way here, and I'm sure it's not true, but . . ."

"What?" Carmen asked. "Was there a picture of me walking in front of the doctor's office with the caption *Carmen Curtis Deathly Ill?* or something?" She had stopped looking at anything that was printed about her, so who knew what the gossip sites were saying. She was trying hard not to care anymore.

He smiled wryly. "Basically. It was you, driving and looking sort of pissed, and it was like, *Cassandra Kicks Carmen to the Curb.* Which is crazy. I mean, you did look upset, but you always look pissed when you're driving. Where do they come up with these stories?"

Carmen sighed. The secret was out. She had no idea how, but if Drew knew, then Trevor knew, and he was going to try to make something of it. But there was nothing she could do about that now. "Because it's true," she said.

Drew's mouth fell open. "What?"

"We had a fight. She kicked me out." She said it matter-of-factly, as if it were no big deal.

"What about your dad?"

Carmen shrugged. "He's away on business. I guess he'll find out when he comes back in a couple of days."

Drew frowned. "You don't seem that upset. Are you?"

Carmen leaned back against the leather booth. Thinking about it made her tired. "I don't know," she said. "I mean, maybe it's time for me to get my own place. I'm an adult, after all."

"Barely," Drew said, and Carmen swatted him on the arm. "Ow," he yelped.

Carmen laughed. "You look so big and tough, but actually you're a total baby."

"You look so small and nice, but you're actually a total brute," he countered. "But hey—where are you staying then?"

"Luke's place," Carmen said, taking a sip of her drink. "It's nice. It's this cute little cottage in Venice."

Drew looked concerned. "Does Kate know?"

"It doesn't matter—Luke and I are 'broken up,' remember? We're just friends." But even as she said it, she knew it wasn't entirely true. There was something different between them lately. Something strange—and almost electric. In the mornings she woke up and walked into the kitchen and he'd already be there, drinking coffee and reading *Variety*. He'd smile all sweet and sexy and ask if she wanted him to make her toast.

He seemed more than happy to have her staying with him. But he also seemed a bit jealous when he found out that Kate and Drew were hanging out. So what, really, was going on in his head and heart? Well, she didn't know.

"Have you told her?" Drew asked again.

"Why do you care?" Carmen asked. "It's not a big deal. If you had picked up your phone the night I called I'd be staying with you."

"I just don't want Kate to get hurt," Drew said.

Something about the way he said it confirmed her

suspicion: Drew liked Kate.

She took a moment to let this sink in. It was not a pleasant feeling.

She thought about their high school years, when Drew would drop anything he was doing to be at her beck and call. She suddenly decided she needed a Slushee at midnight? He'd bring it to her. Her car broke down on the side of the 101? He'd be there before any tow truck. He had doted on her utterly and completely. And she'd counted on that.

She gazed off into the dimness of the bar. It was getting louder every second. What was going on with her life? Suddenly everything was different, and not in a good way. Someone close to her was leaking private information to the tabloids. Her mother had kicked her out of the house. And Drew—her best friend, her rock, for a decade—was now focused on someone new. Professionally, Carmen was getting everything she dreamed about, but personally . . . well, it felt like everything was being taken away.

28

SO MANY SECRETS

Ryan drove them along PCH as the sun began its descent. It was one of the last perfect fall days of the year, and Madison felt happy, for the first time in a long time. It was all because of that kiss they'd shared—and the lovely things that had come after it. The hike in Topanga. The picnic in Malibu. The night spent watching Judd Apatow movies. The coffee on Ryan's deck in the morning.

It was too bad that he wouldn't let any of their time together be filmed, but by now, Madison had come to terms with it. She was working hard to get other screen opportunities, but she was also learning how to relax a little. She was staring at the ocean, feeling almost blissful, when Ryan interrupted her reverie.

"I think you should come clean," he said.

For a moment she had no idea what he was talking about. "What?"

"Living with a lie is a horrible thing," he said. "You've told me how anxious it made you before your sister outed you on *L.A. Candy*. Why would you want to do that to yourself again if you don't have to?"

Madison shook her head. "Ryan, what's done is done. I lied under oath. I don't really have a choice. I made my bed, and now I'm lying in it."

"I have to admit something," Ryan said suddenly.

Well, that's a sentence that never leads to anywhere pleasant, Madison thought. She watched his profile as he grimaced slightly. "What?" she asked. She felt a sudden chill from the open window.

"I told your sister."

"You—what?" Madison didn't understand. She'd never even told Sophie about Ryan—what in the world was he doing talking to her?

Ryan looked sheepish. "She called the other day while you were in the shower and I picked up. Maybe it was overstepping my bounds, and I'm sorry. But she's your sister! You should see her more often. She should be more of a support. I mean, that's what families are for."

"Yeah, nice families, maybe," Madison muttered. She felt a surge of annoyance. What business was it of his? Her relationship with Sophie was between her and Sophie.

"Well, she sounded concerned about you. I was only trying to get you guys together, but then it just came out," Ryan said. "I told her that it was your dad who took the necklace."

Madison burst out laughing.

Ryan frowned. "What?"

"Oh, Ryan, you think she doesn't know that?"

He turned to her, a look of astonishment on his face. "She knows? And she's letting you take the fall for a guy who abandoned you, a guy she doesn't even really remember?"

Madison shrugged. "She respects my decision."

Ryan laughed. "I'm sure she does. And I'm sure you realize that your selflessness in taking the fall for your dad has helped her career. She's all over *The Fame Game* these days."

"What, you still watch?" Madison asked teasingly. "I thought you had no respect for my little corner of the entertainment industry."

"Your sister is taking your place," Ryan said. "Don't you care?"

"Of course I care. But I can't exactly do anything about it, can I? The most important thing is that no one goes after my dad. And if everyone keeps thinking I'm the thief, then he's safe."

She hadn't heard from Charlie since that single post-card (*I will make it right, okay? Just give me a little time*). She tried not to think of him anymore, because when she did, she felt wild with anger. Didn't he know what she was going through to keep his sorry ass out of jail? In a way, it was almost stupid that she didn't turn him in. But at this point it was a matter less of love than it was of principle. She hadn't been aware that she had principles, but apparently she did.

"I don't want you to think you can't change your mind," Ryan said. He reached across the seat and put his hand over hers. "You could show a lot of people a different side of you that way."

"I made a career out of being a bitch. Why would I want to stop now?"

Ryan didn't answer. He turned off the highway and followed a road that wound through the canyon. In the trees, the air was cooler and smelled like eucalyptus and wild dill.

"By the way, you didn't tell her about us, did you?" Madison asked.

"What do you mean?"

"Does she know we're dating?"

Ryan shook his head. "I'm not the kiss-and-tell type," he said. "I told her I was your boss."

Good, Madison thought. Because if there was one thing she knew about Sophie, it was that you couldn't trust her to keep anything a secret. Unless, of course, doing so served her purposes, such as letting Madison suffer alone for their father's crimes.

"I'm starving," Madison said, wanting to change the subject. "Are we there yet?"

"As a matter of fact, we are." He pulled into the parking lot of a small café nestled in a grove of madrona trees. "This is one of my favorite places. They make the best meatballs and their orecchiette with broccoli rabe is off the hook."

"Off the hook?" Madison repeated. "You sound like some twelve-year-old Venice Beach rat."

Ryan opened the door for her and ushered her into the cozy room, which was lit by dozens of candles. "More like my sisters. They just discovered Snoop Dogg."

"They're so cute," Madison said fondly. They'd talked her into staging a fashion show in the Tucker living room the morning after Ryan's birthday, and they'd been adorable in their boas and leg warmers and long, beaded necklaces. They were so sweet—no wonder Ryan had no idea how crazy sisters could be.

She sat down on the chair Ryan had pulled out for her and opened her menu. "Do you want to split a salad?"

"I want my own damn salad," Ryan said, grinning and grabbing her hands. "And the biggest plate of pasta the world has ever seen."

"Sounds good to me," Madison laughed.

Then Ryan leaned across the table, still holding her hands, and she tipped toward him, heart fluttering in anticipation. When had a simple kiss ever felt so perfect? Right as their lips met, there was a flash in the corner of Madison's eyes. When she broke away and turned toward it, she saw the middle-aged woman who'd walked in after them hurrying back out of the restaurant.

"Hey," Ryan called after her. "Hey!" He pounded his fist on the table. He seemed on the verge of getting up and going after her, but Madison put out her hand to stop him.

"It's no big deal," she said soothingly. "She was probably

just getting a souvenir picture of me for her daughter."

Ryan did not look comforted. "Of two people who are trying to have a nice, private dinner? I came here because no one knows about Rosa's. That's why I like it. You could be Elvis risen from the dead and no one would snap your picture."

"Seriously, it's harmless."

Ryan shook his head. "How do you know that picture was just for her? As if the paparazzi aren't bad enough, now everyone with a smartphone and a Twitter account thinks they're a reporter."

Madison gave him an odd look. What was he talking about? The chances of that picture showing up anywhere public were slim, because sadly, she wasn't the tabloid fodder she used to be. Carmen had definitely replaced her on that front. But what did he care, anyway? She knew he didn't want to be filmed, but what was so horrible about a little snapshot? She was going to ask him, but he looked so peeved that she decided to change the subject. "Wine," she said brightly. "Red or white?"

In the morning, her phone woke her with its endless buzzing. (She'd put it on Vibrate, and now it was humming and dancing across the bedside table.) She rolled over and saw Ryan, still sleeping, his lashes dark against his tan cheek. She watched his chest rise and fall, and she wanted to nuzzle into his shoulder and fall back asleep. For a moment, she almost did. But then another text came in. It was so rare that her phone rang anymore; of course she was curious.

Yawning, she entered her password and checked her text messages. The first one she saw was from Gaby. It was a single word: "D-Lish."

Madison gazed at the screen, still feeling sleepy. What could Gaby be talking about? Was her roommate featured in a *Caption This* post? Had Carmen started fake-dating someone new? Or was there a picture of Kate getting a key to the city in central Ohio? Whatever the story was, Madison was quite sure it had nothing to do with her.

Sleepily she clicked over to *D-Lish*, the website run by Jane Roberts's old pal Diego. Her first thought, when she saw the photograph, was: *Playboy bunny Holly Madison has a dress just like mine!*

But then she realized that the picture was of her. And of Ryan. And they were kissing.

"Oh," she cried suddenly, and Ryan rolled over, only half-awake, and planted a kiss on her arm. Samson jumped on the bed and wedged himself between them, his favorite place to be.

"Morning," he said, his voice still thick with sleep. "What are you doing?"

"Looking online," Madison said.

"Why? It's not even nine a.m."

She bit her lip. "Well, it seems like you were right about that woman from the restaurant."

"What?" Ryan sat up and grabbed the phone from her hands. All of his warm grogginess vanished.

"She gave our picture to *D-Lish*," Madison said, in case

that wasn't perfectly clear to him by now.

"Oh no," he said.

The look on his face frightened her. But then she bristled: Was it really so bad that they were caught kissing? She scooted away from him. "What, are you that embarrassed to be seen with me?" she asked.

"No," Ryan said, still staring at the screen. "That's not it at all."

"Then why are you freaking out?"

Ryan sighed and gave her back her phone. "Here. You can read all about it if you want."

Confused, she scrolled down to the story below the picture. EX-PARTY BOY BACK ON THE SCENE WITH CONVICT PARTY GIRL, said the headline.

"Party boy?" Madison asked, looking up at him.

"Yes. But there's more."

"The real question is why you're the star of the headline and not me," Madison teased. "Also, I'm not a party girl. I like to have a good time, but moderation is key. When you get drunk, you do stupid things, and your makeup smudges." She thought maybe she should keep talking, as if it would distract Ryan from whatever was bothering him so much.

"Just read it," he said.

She scooted closer to him and said, "I don't want to read the story. Those things are always wrong. Tell me what it says. Or if it's really off base, tell me the truth behind it."

Ryan sighed and was silent for a moment. Then,

without looking at her, he began to speak. "I used to drink a lot. When my parents were away I'd throw huge parties, and when they were in town I went to other people's parties."

"That doesn't sound so bad," Madison offered.

But Ryan ignored her. "One night, when I was driving my best friend home, I lost control of my car. We crashed. I only broke my wrist, but Stephen . . ." He paused. "Stephen was thrown from the car and killed."

"Oh—" Madison gasped.

"I wasn't tested for my blood-alcohol level that night, because my parents have powerful friends. I wasn't charged with manslaughter. I didn't have to face any consequences, Madison. Any consequences, that is, besides waking up every morning knowing that I killed my best friend." He ran his hands through his hair. "Funny, isn't it? You got punished for something you didn't do, while I didn't get punished for something I did."

"That's so awful," Madison whispered.

"The press had a field day with it. 'Tucker gets off free.'" He got up and walked over to the window, wearing only his boxer shorts. His broad shoulders hunched. "That's why I'm at Lost Paws," he went on. "Stephen's aunt helped found that shelter, and he was the most dedicated volunteer they'd ever had. If I couldn't bring him back, I could at least do the work he believed in doing."

"I can't believe you never told me this," Madison said. She went to join him at the window and slipped her arms around his waist.

"It's not really something I like to talk about."

"I'm so sorry," she said. *Why do we all have so many secrets?* she thought.

Ryan nodded. He gave her shoulders a squeeze and then he turned toward her. "I think we should give this a rest."

Madison didn't know what he was talking about. "What?"

"I think . . . I just . . . Madison, I can't do this again. I can't be in the spotlight, and it seems like, with the two of us together, that's exactly where we'd be. I've spent the last two years trying to make up for my mistake so that someday I can move on. But now I feel like I'm reliving it all. I've embarrassed my family enough. I've hurt Stephen's family, all of our friends . . . I can't put any of them through this again."

Madison let her arm fall to her side. "Don't do this," she said. "Please."

"I'm sorry," he said. "I like you, Madison. I really do."

"Then be with me," she said.

Ryan smiled sadly and he bent down to kiss her cheek. "I can't."

Madison wanted to beg him to think about what he was saying, to reconsider, but she could tell his mind was made up. And even the new Madison Parker didn't like to beg.

She quickly got dressed, gathered up Samson, and let herself out.

29

A SATISFYING AMOUNT OF COMMOTION

Kate knew she ought to unpack, but instead she was bouncing around her apartment in a pair of cut-off jeans (it had been puffy-coat weather back in Ohio!) and singing along to the radio. She was so glad to be back in L.A.! As complicated and crazy as life here was, she'd missed it terribly. The traffic on Sunset was so familiar. The billboards looming above the streets, advertising everything from tanning salons to *The Fame Game*, were like signs pointing her back to Park Towers. Her apartment, with its sleek, uncomfortable furniture and shockingly messy rooms, felt like home. She had even missed the stupid fake palm tree by the elevators, the one that Gaby always stuck her gum on.

"Baby, take a chance or you'll never ever know / I got money in my hands that I'd really like to blow," Kate sang as she took a break from dancing around and searched for a decent dress to wear. She was supposed to do a quick on-camera pop-in at Madison and Gaby's to talk about her trip, and she thought she ought to look a little nicer.

Plus, she'd already had a Fashion Don't that morning. PopTV had filmed her arriving at LAX, sleepy and rumpled and wearing a sloppy sweatshirt and some old Uggs. (A week in Ohio and her fashion sense went straight back to zero—she needed Natalie, stat.) As if the TV camera weren't enough, Trevor had alerted a few paparazzi so that his airport scene would have a satisfying amount of commotion and flashbulbs.

No, Kate was definitely not going to look at the gossip blogs for a day or two, and she was going to throw away those Uggs. (At least she'd managed to hold on to a pair of big black sunglasses, which she'd worn as she hurried toward baggage claim.)

She yawned as she plucked up various dresses and then threw them back down again. She was going to have a hard time staying awake for the Madison-Gaby dinner-table confab. But, more importantly, Kate was going to be beat by the time Drew arrived. She'd called him the minute she got off the plane and asked if he'd come over. He was heading to her place as soon as he finished at Rock It! for the day—but that was still a couple of hours away.

It had taken Kate a while to understand her feelings for Drew, but now that she did, she couldn't contain them. She was dying to see him. And he'd sounded pretty excited to see her, too. Tonight, something was going to happen between them. She was sure of it.

And when that thing did happen? It was going to complicate things with Carmen, without a doubt. But after what Carmen had pulled with Luke, she really didn't have much say in the matter. Carmen would simply have to accept it, because Drew was definitely going to kiss her. Tonight. Or she was going to kiss him.

Of course, she needed to be awake for that to happen, which meant that she needed coffee. She glanced at the clock. She had just enough time to run around the corner to the Coffee Bean if she hurried. She didn't want to be late for the shoot; she was done with causing problems.

Inside the coffee shop, her song was playing on the radio, as if the very chain she used to work for was welcoming her home.

"Oh my God, you're Kate Hayes," the barista said as he steamed the milk for her latte. "I'm seeing you while I'm listening to you. That is so trippy."

She grinned happily—"I know, right?"—and left a generous tip.

As she hustled back to her apartment building, she ran through the things she'd say to Madison and Gaby. Her old hometown did look smaller. The show at Lloyd's Coffee Shop and Comics Store . . . well, it wasn't her best performance, but it wasn't her worst, either.

She wished she could end the wrap-up there, but she'd have to talk about Ethan, too. Their unpleasant on-camera conversation had led to a later, more polite one, in which Ethan had apologized repeatedly for his behavior. He said it was all because of nerves—he hadn't expected such a big crew, so many cameras—and Kate was ready to believe him. So it was odd, then, that he kept begging to film with her again. "Come on," he'd said. "I was close with our old choir teacher, too. Bring me along to your coffee date!" Of course he'd come to her show and sat in the front row. He'd tried to invite himself to every single shoot.

He was selfish and he was an underminer; Kate saw that now. He was mad that she'd left, and even more mad that she'd succeeded.

She sighed. It was almost funny: First she'd had a boyfriend who'd tried to subtly sabotage her, and then she'd found one who'd tried to pretend she didn't exist. *You can really pick 'em, Kate Hayes,* she thought. But Drew, of course, was different. *Third time's a charm,* she thought, and wondered if that could be part of a chorus to a new song.

As she turned into the parking lot of her apartment building, Kate saw the PopTV van nosing into a spot. The sliding door opened and Bret hopped out; a moment later, Laurel slid out of the passenger side. She waved at Kate. She, too, looked tired but happy to be back. She raised her own Starbucks cup: a toast from one jet-lagged person to another.

As she approached them, Kate's phone buzzed. There was a text from Madison.

DON'T LET THE CAMERAS UP. GABY'S IN TROUBLE.

Kate stopped in her tracks. What did that mean? What should she do?

"Hey," Laurel called. "Look at you! Coffee after six p.m.! I must be rubbing off on you."

Kate just stared at her.

"You coming over?" Laurel said. "We can mike you out here instead of inside."

Mute, Kate shook her head. She placed her coffee cup on the ground, gripped her phone, and started running.

"Hey, where are you going?"

"Suddenly I have to pee so bad!" Kate yelled, not turning around. She raced into the lobby and pressed the button for the elevator. The doors seemed to take forever to open, but finally did, and she flung herself inside and hit the button for their floor.

She didn't knock on Madison's door. She just dashed in and locked it behind her, calling, "Where are you? What happened?"

"Back here," Madison yelled.

Kate threaded her way past shopping bags and piles of magazines, following the sound of Madison's voice. Samson, Madison's ugly little dog, looked up at her and whined.

Madison sat on the edge of Gaby's bed. "It's going to be okay," she was saying. "It's going to be okay."

Gaby was lying on her bed, still as death. Her skin was so pale it seemed almost blue.

"I don't know what she took," Madison said. Her hand encircled Gaby's wrist.

"Is she—"

"She's barely breathing. She's unconscious. I called 911."

"Oh my God," Kate whispered. "Oh my God, what can I do?"

"The ambulance will be here any minute. Just sit with me," Madison said. "With us." Her voice was soft. As Kate watched, a tiny, shimmering tear slid down her perfectly powdered cheek.

Kate sank into a chair and took Madison's other hand. "It's going to be okay. Just like you said." But who was she kidding? She didn't know that!

She and Madison sat in frightened silence, staring at their friend. Then came the pounding at the door.

"Hey," Laurel called. "What's going on in there? Someone let me in!"

Kate looked at Madison with panic in her eyes. "Shit! What are we going to do?"

And in the distance they heard the ambulance's siren wail.

30

THE STARS CAME OUT

The hospital waiting room felt as cold as ice. Madison shivered and wrapped her arms around herself as she paced.

"Please stop moving so much," Laurel hissed. "We only have one camera. We need you guys in the same shot."

Madison ignored her. She didn't think Laurel ought to be there, or at least not with a PopTV camera turned on. What sort of power did Trevor have that he'd managed to get clearance for them to shoot in this wing of the hospital? They had limited them to a handful of crew members and one camera, but still. Bret stood in the corner of the room, trying—and failing—to be unobtrusive. Madison felt like kicking him.

Kate and Carmen sat together on the couch, their faces pinched with worry. Once the ambulance arrived, Madison had raced after it with Kate, with the PopTV van racing after them. She'd texted Sophie on the way.

GABY OD. COME TO CEDARS-SINAI.

She shook her head. She should have seen this coming.

"I didn't take good care of her," Madison said fiercely. "I could have stopped this."

Kate looked up. "Didn't you take her pills away?" she asked.

"Yes, but how hard was it for her to get more?" Madison gestured down the hall toward the room where Gaby lay. The doctors had pumped her stomach, but she hadn't woken up yet. They didn't know when she would. "Clearly not very hard. Especially with that moron Jay around. I should have been watching her more carefully."

"She's an adult," Carmen said softly. "It's not like you can babysit her twenty-four-seven. Or should have to."

Madison turned to face her. "But I should have talked to her about getting treatment. She was really upset after that night you all went out, the night she saw Jay with that girl. And of course he was a total dick about it—he convinced her she was jumping to conclusions. I'm sure he told her to take something to calm herself down—it wouldn't be the first time."

Kate bit her fingernails. "I just can't believe it," she was saying. "I've never known anyone this happened to. She's going to be okay, though? Right?"

Madison sighed and ran her fingers through her hair. Carmen put her hand on Kate's shoulder. But no one answered Kate's question, because no one knew how to.

Madison wished she could call Ryan. Just hearing his voice would calm and reassure her. She doubted he'd even pick up. Space. He needed space. But damn it, she needed him! She sat down and put her head in her hands. She wished the hospital allowed dogs—how could Samson possibly be more disruptive than a TV crew?

A moment later, Madison smelled the familiar scent of patchouli and spice that announced the arrival of her sister. She looked up and smiled sadly. It had been a long time since she'd seen Sophie, and she was ready to forgive and forget. Nothing like a little life-and-death situation to make a person rethink her anger.

"How is she?" Sophie asked, sinking into a chair next to her.

"We don't know yet."

"What happened?"

"She took a bunch of pain meds and basically went into respiratory arrest."

Sophie clutched at the crystal suspended from her necklace. "Oh God," she whispered.

Then Carmen, who had momentarily disappeared, came back into the room. "They're saying they're cautiously optimistic." She sat down. "Cautiously optimistic," she repeated, as if to herself.

"Is she awake yet?"

Carmen shook her head. "No. But when she wakes up—assuming she wakes up—they're going to do a psych evaluation."

Kate frowned. "Why?"

"I guess they want to make sure the overdose wasn't intentional."

"It wasn't," Madison said firmly. "It couldn't be."

She believed she was right—but the tiny voice in her head said, *How would you know? You never spend time with her anymore.*

Kate got up. "I need to do a little stress-eating. I'm getting something from the vending machine. Anyone?"

"Get me a Milky Way," Carmen said. "Please."

"Anyone else?"

"No thanks." Even though it was past dinnertime, Madison would never eat something from a vending machine.

The girls sat in silence for a while. They weren't doing any good there—Gaby was out cold, and they wouldn't be allowed to see her even if she woke—but they couldn't bring themselves to leave.

Carmen picked up a *Time* magazine that was at least six months old and idly flipped through the pages. When Kate returned with her candy, she brought out her phone and started playing Angry Birds. Probably any minute Laurel was going to text one of them to say:

NEED MORE TALKING. SHARE MEMORIES OF GABY?

Madison, at that moment, couldn't think of any. How could that be? Was she so focused on her own problems that she couldn't even remember having a nice time with her roommate? No wonder Madison had felt alone so often—she really had been.

Those few weeks that she'd had Ryan in her life? Those were the only good ones lately. But all that was over now, thanks to a woman with an iPhone.

Madison had been going over it in her mind, and she found it pretty strange. Most people who took pictures with their phones didn't go running to a gossip site with them. It was almost as if the woman had known what she was doing. Almost as if she had been sent there.

But who had known about Ryan? No one.

Then Madison looked over at her sister, who was sipping at the tea she'd brought; it smelled like wet hay.

No one except Sophie—Sophie had talked to Ryan the day he answered Madison's phone.

Madison realized that she needed to know more. "So . . ." she said casually. "I heard you talked to my boss."

Sophie flashed her sly, beautiful smile. "Is that what he is?"

"Um, yes."

Sophie crossed one long, lean leg over the other. For once she wasn't wearing a maxidress, and she looked almost polished in a short, haute hippie shirt and loose-weave sweater. "I got the distinct impression that there was something else going on between you two."

"Oh you did, did you?" Madison tapped her fingers on the arm of the chair. What was it that she'd said about forgiving and forgetting? Give her ten minutes in the same room with her sister and already she was doubting such a thing was possible.

"I'm very sensitive to people's energies, Madison. Plus, I mean, he did tell me he was taking you out to dinner at Rosa's. Of course, he claimed it was just to mark the final weeks of your community service."

Madison's gaze was icy. It was all becoming clear now. "You did it, didn't you?"

"Pardon?" Sophie said, blinking. "Did what?"

"You knew where we were, and you tipped someone off. That wasn't just a random woman who took our picture, was it? Because it showed up on *D-Lish.*"

Sophie stiffened. "First of all, I have no idea what you're talking about. *D-Lish?* I don't look at that stupid site. Second of all, I've never known you to balk at an opportunity for publicity, sister, so I can't see what the problem is," Sophie said. She took a sip of tea and sighed thoughtfully. Then she turned her blue eyes on Madison. "And third of all, if you think I'd bother to ask someone to take your picture, you're crazy. In case you haven't noticed, people don't care that much about what you're doing these days."

Madison gritted her teeth. She could feel the camera focusing in on them. "But you told someone," she pressed.

At this, Sophie shrugged. "I might have mentioned something to Trevor when he called . . ."

"You what?"

"I mean, he was wondering what was up with you, and he thought I might have some insight. He said you seemed happier lately." She paused. "He only wants the best for you, you know."

Madison was seething. "That's a load of crap, *Sophia,* and you know it." She walked to the window and stared down at the hospital parking lot. She understood what had happened; she could see perfectly the chain of events. Sophie had told Trevor about Ryan, and Trevor had quickly done his research. When he uncovered Ryan's past, he'd decided to use it. Of course. Maybe Madison Parker wasn't news anymore, but Madison and an upper-crust former playboy with blood on his hands . . . well, that was news.

Madison felt like screaming. Did Trevor ever consider, for one minute, that he might destroy the first real relationship Madison had ever had? And if he did, did he care? Or had he already decided that it couldn't work? Because as he always said, *If it didn't happen on TV, it didn't happen.* Which meant that a boyfriend who wouldn't film was worse than no boyfriend at all.

"I hate you both so much right now," Madison said quietly.

Sophie held up a hand; bangled, bell-strung bracelets jingled down her golden wrist. "Peace, sister," she said. "Peace."

"Oh for God's sake!" Madison whirled around, shouting. "You act like you're so full of love, but you're the same manipulative bitch you've always been. You can't just leave me be. When are you going to realize that everything you have now came from me, and that you should be grateful? That you should stop messing around with my life?"

Sophie blinked, affronted. But then she drew herself up and her eyes narrowed. "Everything I have came from you? That's a laugh. You'd be nothing at all if you hadn't spent thousands of dollars on surgery, trying to make yourself look like me in the first place. Do you think PopTV would have looked at you twice in your real body? Do you think the world wants to see a fat brunette with crooked teeth trying to make it in Hollywood? Because I don't fucking think so."

Sophie glared at her, her blue eyes cold. Triumphant.

She'd managed to rat out her sister again. On-camera.

And in that moment, Madison realized that she had had enough. Of her bat-shit crazy sister. Of her criminal father. Of manipulative, scheming Trevor Lord. Of *The Fame Game* itself. She stood up, nearly five foot ten in her beautiful gold heels. "That's it," she said. Her voice was calm and cold. "You're all fucking crazy, and I can't deal with any of you anymore. I'm out of here. And this time I'm not coming back. I quit."

She grabbed her purse, handed her mike pack to Laurel, and then headed for the door. Kate and Carmen stared at her in shock. "Wait—" Laurel shouted, but Madison kept going.

Outside, alone on the street, Madison was struck by the enormity of what she'd done. She had just severed ties to everything that had kept her grounded. Everything that had brought her success and happiness.

It was a good thing she had her principles, she thought, because right now she had absolutely nothing else.

She began walking faster. Where to, she didn't know. The sky above her was dark and clear, and one by one, the stars came out, twinkling.

ACKNOWLEDGMENTS

A special thanks to all the amazing people who made this book possible . . .

Farrin Jacobs for sticking with me this long and being so damn good at her job.

Emily Chenoweth whose contribution to this novel was invaluable. We couldn't have done it without you.

Max Stubblefield, Nicole Perez, Kristin Puttkamer, PJ Shapiro, Dave Del Sesto, Matthew Elblonk, Maggie Marr, Sasha Illingworth, and Howard Huang as well as the team at Harper Collins: Melinda Weigel, Christina Colangelo, Sandee Roston, Catherine Wallace, Gwen Morton, Josh Weiss, Cara Petrus, Sarah Nichole Kaufman, Kara Levy, and Stephanie Stein.

William Tell for his musical expertise.

And, as always, a big thank-you to my friends and family. I love you all dearly, and you mean the world to me.

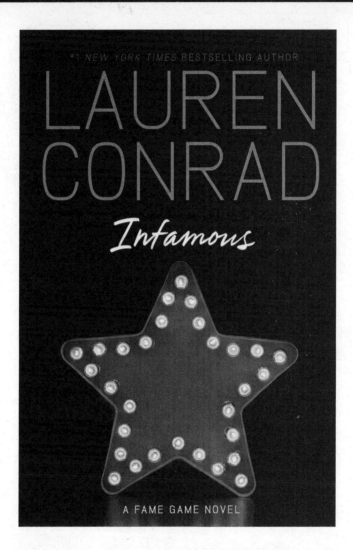

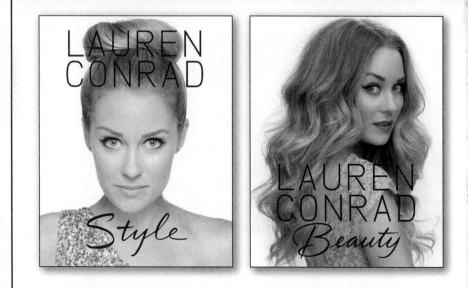